D0436339

# BEHOLD THE BONES

Also by Natalie C. Parker

*Beware the Wild*

# BEHOLD THE BONES

31652002945351

## NATALIE C. PARKER

HARPER TEEN

An Imprint of HarperCollins Publishers

HarperTeen is an imprint of HarperCollins Publishers.

Behold the Bones

Library of Congress Control Number: 2015938993
ISBN 978-0-06-224155-9

Typography by Kate Engbring
16 17 18 19 20   CG/RRDH   10 9 8 7 6 5 4 3 2 1
❖
First Edition

*For Joane,*
*who blazed her own trail*
*so girls like Candy could, too*

# PART ONE

*Hear this the tale of Mad Mary Sweet,*
*Who crawled through the swamp*
  *on her hands and her feet,*
*In the wild lost her way,*
*Her voice it did fray,*
*And now she's got none but her teeth.*

GRANDPA CRAVEN KICKED IT THE day I was born.

It's a family tradition: Once in every Craven's memory, a child will be born on the day some other Craven dies. In the infinite loop of cosmic justice, that child will grow up to be killed by the birth of another. We call it the Craven Curse and every year on the anniversary of Grandpa's death, we visit the family graveyard and listen to Uncle Jack recite the list of all those who have carried this fine tradition of death by birth forward.

That's why every year, before they wish me happy birthday, my family hauls me to a backwoods graveyard to remind me that I, Candace Craven Pickens, killed my own grandpa.

The family plot is on the forested piece of Nanny Craven's land. August is a brutal time to be tromping anywhere in Sticks, Louisiana, but a braided cover of pines makes it bearable. Nanny Craven is set up in a deluxe camping chair right next to Grandpa's headstone; one of her bejeweled hands caresses the cold stone, the other grips a jar of Clary hooch. As Uncle Jack continues through the line of our cursed ancestors, Nanny alternately sips and pours a bit on Grandpa's grave.

Nearly all of my living relations are here, crammed inside the low, wrought-iron fence that separates holy ground from regular old ground: twenty-three cousins—second cousins, double cousins, and cousins some-number-removed—two sets of aunts and uncles, my parents, and the bones of who knows how many ancestors. Everyone is dressed in their Sunday best but for footwear—only a fool would cut through the summer wood in anything less than a full boot. We're an odd collection of Sunday hats and cowboy boots, button-up shirts and sweat stains.

We've been standing in this sticky heat for exactly thirty minutes and though we were a jubilant parade on our way here I can see tolerance draining from the faces of my near and distant kin. I can't hardly blame them. The older ones keep their eyes glued to Jack, willing him to lose the spirit of telling this familiar tale, the younger ones slouch against gravestones and fiddle with the cell phones in their pockets, and the very youngest get away with playing a quiet game of hide-and-seek. The pervasive feeling is that we'll be here until we're ready for the very graves on which we stand. This is the sort of thing we do because we always have.

Jack lords over Grandpa's grave like a pulpit. He abandoned his jacket first thing and now his sleeves are rolled to the elbow, his forearms are tanned and muscled, his hands broad and calloused. He speaks with the authority of someone who was there to witness the passing of each Craven.

"Louis Paul inherited the curse from his father and passed it on to his daughter. He was injured in a fishing accident and took ill from his wounds. On the day little Annemarie Craven was born, in the winter of 1788, our great-great-great-great grandfather passed away in his bed, God rest his soul," he says with immense sympathy. "And as most of us well know, Annemarie did not have an easy life. Married at the young age of eleven, she was ill-treated by her husband. The poor girl ran away into the swamp one night and was never heard from again. Only when the death of her cousin Lettie-Rae coincided with the birth of Johnny Jacob Tatum did we understand that Annemarie had passed away when Lettie-Rae was born. She is the only soul not resting here in this very yard."

In between each story, Aunt Daisy rattles a tambourine,

and Nanny Craven solemnly tips a little hooch for Grandpa. It's a waste of good hooch if you ask me, but nobody ever has or ever will.

The stories and sweat stains continue to grow. Finally, Jack reaches the tale of Solomon Craven, who fought in World War II as a young Army man, prized working with his hands, hunted gators and ducks and deer, and was tough as nails. His death took everyone by surprise, as did my birth, for which I was one month early.

"Dad was not a quiet man," Jack says, frowning at the sudden quiver in his voice. He clears his throat. "And even in the face of death, he was a mean old coot. What did he say as that heart attack squeezed his innards?"

Then comes the roar of my collective family, "Come at me, you bastard!"

Daisy's tambourine is ecstatic. My aunts and uncles hoot and holler, once again caught up in the spirit of the day. We're nearly done with this oppressive tradition. The anticipation is palpable.

Jack's voice cuts above the cheer. "And on that very day our Candace Pickens was born! What day was that?"

"This day!" Cousin Red calls from across the yard with a wink for me. He's no taller than me and never will be, but he makes up for it with biceps and soul.

"That's right. Happy birthday, Candace!" Uncle Jack cries. "May you carry this curse for a great many years!"

That, too, gets a rousing chorus of cheers as though there's nothing at all wrong with wishing a girl happy birthday by reminding her she's expected to die. The cheering quickly morphs into a discordant round of "Happy Birthday," and at the end, Nanny Craven lifts her jar of moonshine.

"Candace," she calls, bidding me to approach.

This is also a tradition. A strange communion some-how meant to demonstrate my willing participation in this family superstition. All my life, I've joined Nanny Craven at Grandpa's headstone and sipped from a small jam jar of white grape juice to bring this ceremony to a close. This year, she makes no move to swap the jar. I weave through the crowd of living and dead to reach Nanny's side. She presses her mason jar to my open palm with a dare in her eye. The nerves ruffling my stomach are senseless; this will not be my first sip of liquor, it will not even be the first sip I've taken around my family, but Clary hooch is the holy grail of moonshine and I've waited all my life for a taste.

*Don't cough*, I warn myself. *Don't you dare cough, Candace Pickens.*

I take the jar. Nanny Craven's face spreads into a danger-ous grin. Her lipstick stains one side of the rim. I choose the other and confidently bring the jar to my lips.

I am too confident. Warm liquor splashes against my mouth and nose. The sip I meant to take is more like a gulp. It's all I can do not to sputter at the sharp taste. My eyes water and I hear all my kin holler and laugh.

"Y'ain't a fish, girl," Nanny Craven chides. "Save some for Sol."

Even she is amused by my novice performance. Tears, made from pure alcohol, I'm sure, crowd my eyes. I barely see Grandpa's grave when I tip the jar and make my offering.

Jack has one more point to make. He begins it by clapping a hand to my shoulder. "We call it a curse, but this cycle is how we know Craven blood is thick. Whether we're Cravens or Pickenses or Tatums or even Lirettes, we are bound together, to this place and each other."

Smiles travel through the crowd like a virus. For a moment, all past hurts and slights, no matter how extreme, are forgotten. Second cousin Bart even reaches over to give second cousin once removed Joshua's hand a shake. Never mind the fact that Josh sold Bart's truck so he could buy an engagement ring for the fiancée he'd stolen two weeks prior. Even I feel a tiny swell of pride at having such a committed family. Everyone has been seduced by Uncle Jack's tale. This is manipulation at its finest.

Then it's time to eat.

The aunts file out of the graveyard first and down the small hill to where our feast awaits in foil trays and foam coolers. The menfolk brought folding tables and chairs out earlier in the day. They even saw fit to plant a generator where it could power a few Crock-Pots and strings of lights, haphazardly draped along the low branches of magnolia trees. My cake'll be a two-tiered tray of Twinkies and Snowballs, and we'll sit here in the shadow of our graveyard until the sun's down and the food's gone because this is how we party in the Craven family.

Nanny grips my arm in her bony hand, claiming me as her aid, and we begin our shuffling descent down the slope.

"Your mother says you're waiting on some bad news," Nanny says, prying. One of her favorite pastimes is mashing my buttons. It's my opinion that Nanny guards a secret hatred of me for killing her husband.

"Just news. We have no idea if it'll be bad." One of my favorite pastimes is denying Nanny anything.

Nanny laughs like a crow. "Not as she tells it."

I spy my mother at the tables. She stands in the crowd of women arranging store-bought rolls on a plastic tray. Her smile is the tightest thing about her and I've got no sympathy for her misery. She's not the one waiting to find out what's wrong with her.

"She shouldn't be telling it at all." Too late, I realize I've given Nanny an inch.

She pats my arm. "Don't you fret. Lots of girls have these sorts of problems. I'm sure she doesn't blame you."

Her needles are so practiced. She's stitched me into a corner with barbs masquerading as kindness. My options are to take it with a smile or be bullheaded.

I smile. She wins. I've made her day with this sticky silence. It's a small comfort, but if it means she'll leave the topic alone for the rest of the night, then in some way, I've won, too.

Nanny settles into her chair and sends me off with a command to bring her something to chew on. There's a line at the buffet, but Uncle Jack makes a hole for me at the head. I pile Nanny's plate with barbecue, fried okra, and creamed corn. I skip Aunt Sarah's loathsome green bean casserole because I'd like to keep what little of Nanny's good graces I still have.

Mom stands at the end of the table, fussing with aluminum foil and condiments we're all capable of opening ourselves. She hands me the hot sauce without a word. A small sigh escapes when I thank her.

Today is my seventeenth birthday and my mother won't meet my eyes. I am more dead to her than the generations of kin rotting beneath our feet.

I started to die earlier this summer when Doc Payola updated his concern over my lack of a womanly cycle. When I was thirteen, it wasn't an issue at all. When I was fourteen, I was simply a "late bloomer." But when I was fifteen and sixteen it went from "peculiar" to "problematic." This summer, it finally became something that warranted a visit to New Orleans Children's Hospital, where the doctors ran a few tests and listed possible causes as carelessly as they might a grocery list: late onset menstruation, amenorrhea, cancer. Now we wait for the results. And my mom seems to think I'm already dead.

I am alive. I am a ghost.

Just after delivering Nanny her plate, Cousin Red catches me around the neck and pulls me into a sweaty armpit hug. It's worth it for the cold beer he sneaks into my hand. I swivel and let his broad shoulders block me from view while I take a long pull. Half the bottle in one go. He's only two years older than me, but the Cravens believe in the eighteen-year-old adult—if you're old enough to vote and die for your country, you're more than old enough to drink. I, on the other hand, still have to employ stealth.

"Thought that was your 'save me' face," Red says with a satisfied laugh. He's compact as a tank. Every bit of him means business, from his tanned skin to his blunt nose.

I scoff. "I've never had a 'save me' face in all my life. You must be thinking of my 'I'll raze this village to the ground' face."

"Things that bad?" He steals the bottle and swigs. "I heard something about doctors . . ."

"I don't want to talk about it," I say.

Red opens his mouth to protest, but Leo appears at his shoulder. He stands a head taller than his little brother, which allows the Craven family girth to sit more comfortably on his sturdy frame. He's less a tank and more a semi. His brown eyes shine beneath the worn and curved bill of a baseball cap, and he gives his brother a meaningful shove.

"Respect," he says, and Red begrudgingly shuts his hole.

The food is exactly as it always is: salty and spicy and damn good. As expected, my "cake" is a mountain of cream Twinkies and pink Snowballs sporting seventeen wilting candles. And the darker it gets, the easier it is for me to slip my own bottle of beer so I can stop siphoning off Red and Leo.

When the sun's quit the sky, the party begins to wind down. Nanny Craven leaves first, propped in the Gator with Jack at the wheel and the majority of the folding chairs and leftover food in the flatbed. He'll be back for a second run, but their departure is the beginning of a slow bleed as folk decide it's time to pack it in for the night. Soon, there's only a small crowd left to shut down the generator and collect the trash.

The lights go out and the generator whinnies as it shivers to a stop. The night air is dense with the heat of the day; it gathers on my skin like a comfort. At the top of the hill, the graveyard is formless and dark but for the small figures of the Tatum girls racing between headstones. Behind it, skinny pines stripe the dim blue glow of the fading summer sky.

Every year this tradition grows in absurdity. This is not

how birthdays are celebrated; this is a charade designed to give everyone an inflated and unfounded sense of importance. I'm forced to be party to it but only for one more year. After my eighteenth birthday, I'll never spend another standing on the bones of my kin. Because I won't be in Sticks to do it. The Cravens, Pickenses, Tatums, and Lirettes will just have to find someone else to carry their curse.

A shrill scream knifes the air. Every one of us squares up to the noise as my little cousins Irene and Carol come racing down the hill. They run straight to their mama's legs. The men become a row of hunched shoulders and smoldering aggression, all searching for the offense.

Aunt Dee is coaxing sense from her eldest, Irene. She holds the seven-year-old's face in her hands, catching tears with her thumbs.

In a trembling voice, Irene says, "A haint, Mama. There's a girl ghost in the graves."

In the dark, it's hard to decipher all the faces, but there's a brief hesitation, a telling hush that surrounds us before Aunt Dee says, "Shush that nonsense. There ain't no such thing as haints." A few months ago, Aunt Dee would have done that with conviction. Now, after a summer of spirit sightings throughout Sticks, her words bear the hollow ring of falsehood.

Mom lifts little Carol into her arms. "Why don't we all head back to Nanny's? Brice, you have that flashlight?"

But before we can move toward the trail, Red drawls a long, "Ho. Lee. Shit."

"Redford Craven," Aunt Dee bites.

Red points. Following his index finger, I see dark brush, dark earth, and dark pines. Nothing at all of note. Except for Leo, who stands next to me with an expression of fierce perplexity on his long face.

Mom and Dee quickly move the girls toward the trail. Dad, taller than everyone here, raises the flashlight, training it on a spot between the graveyard and us. Red curses again. Leo joins him. The girls whimper.

"What do you see?" I ask Leo.

His eyes refuse to leave their prey. "A girl," he says, voice thick. "A ghost."

It isn't true, of course. There's nothing in the unsteady beam of Dad's flashlight but trampled pine needles. This is an extension of the strange new madness that's swept across Sticks since the night a small group of people walked out of the swamp after being lost for days or weeks or months. All the folk who used to swear from one Sunday to the next there wasn't anything more peculiar in Sticks than Featherhead Fred became superstitious overnight. Ghost sighting has slowly become the thing to do on a Saturday night. Yet another reason to leave this town behind.

The scene around me has come to a complete halt. My

family's eyes are wide and fixed to the same point of air. How is it possible they all see something I don't? My family may be nuttier than a pecan orchard, but they're not gullible. Not *this* kind of gullible. What if they're actually seeing something I can't? What if there's really a ghost standing a few feet in front of me? In spite of myself, a bracing wave of fear washes over me. Then it's gone and I take a step away from my family into the light.

"Brice!" Mom pleads with my dad at the same moment I hear Leo hiss, "Candace!" But too late.

I walk straight into the beam of Dad's light. My shadow is long and dark, my outline traced in hazy light. Behind me, my family holds their breath.

"There's nothing here," I say.

"What's she saying?" Mom asks.

"I said—"

But Uncle Trent cuts me off. "Not you, Candace. Her!"

Again, a cold feeling rushes down my spine as I realize they're all listening to something I can't hear. The only sounds that reach my ears are the quiet chirp of a few crickets and my family trying not to breathe.

"There is *nothing* here," I say, turning to face them. The light blinds me momentarily, but then figures shuffle forward, gradually becoming identifiable: Leo, Red, Uncle Trent, and Dad lowering the light, each of them looking around with cautious expressions of relief.

Red is the first to speak. "What the hell was that?" He spits at the ground.

"Does no one listen to me?" I say. "There was nothing there!"

"The hell there wasn't." He paces away to collect himself. Red's not great with this sort of intensity.

Dad holds the light so we're all lit from below with shadows streaking up our faces.

Dad says, "You all right, Possum?"

"Better than the rest of y'all."

Uncle Trent clears his throat and gives Dad an uncomfortable side-eye. His patience is thin on a good day, and it's clear that he's done with tonight. Leo has become solemn. He stands solid, studying me as though I've recently transformed. I'm lucky Uncle Jack isn't here. He's so full of the wrath of God, this entire affair would surely end in hellfire. As is, Dad merely nods.

He says, "Must've been the light," and holds Trent with a firm stare until he nods agreement. They won't be sharing this with anyone outside the family

We join the others at the trailhead. Everyone is anxious to get gone five minutes ago. Mom doesn't meet my eyes, and we pass through the woods in near silence.

THE RHYTHM OF STICKS, LOUISIANA, has always been a steady one, like the endless *punch-punch-punch* of a nutcracking machine. The school year may come with structure, but it's summertime that's usually predictable, with days swinging back and forth between babysitting and spontaneous parties, between painting houses and nights at our crumbling racetrack, between church and trespassing on Mr. Calhoun's creek. I've lived that rhythm for seventeen long years. I rely on it the way New Orleans relies on Mardi Gras. I may not be able to predict the weather, but I can sure predict who will and won't be a virgin by the time school starts again.

Not this summer.

This summer started with a shot that inspired a superstitious stampede through the fine folk of Sticks. One day, we were an unremarkable small town with a collection of sinister stories about our little swamp. The next, the swamp burped up a dozen people who'd been missing for days or weeks or years.

Overnight, our tales about the swamp swung from complete fantasy to an infectious reality. Folks are just as likely to talk about the ghosts that their sister/cousin/uncle saw as they are anything else. As much as I'd like to disavow all of it, there are still some things I can't explain. And far be it from me to discount a thing because I don't understand it. I wasn't blessed with a staggering intellect for nothing.

Mudding the day after my birthday is the good kind of predictable. I should be able to predict that my two best friends will salvage my birthday for me, but they're also in the camp of folk who see things I don't, so all bets are off.

I pick them up not-so-bright-and-early the next morning, because my dear Sterling doesn't appreciate the day until it's well under way.

"How was the graveyard extravaganza?" Sterling asks around a yawn, squeezing her dark blue eyes shut. She's been tired all summer, staying up late in the hopes that her newish boyfriend, Heath, will call from his forced internment in military camp. According to her, he keeps a prepaid cell in his shoe for the sole purpose of making illegal phone calls to her. It's riskier than I'd typically give him credit for.

"Same as always," I answer. "Except for the end when everyone thought they saw a ghost."

Abigail sucks in a breath. "Another one? How many does that make?" Her face was made to carry warnings—wide eyes, expressive forehead, defined cheekbones beneath a brown complexion.

"An even dozen since May. But I'm telling you, I was there for this one and I didn't see anything."

Sterling and Abigail share a look. It's a look that excludes me, a look that says they know more about these things than I do, a look I thoroughly dislike.

They agree that there's something very different about our swamp. It's filled with a kind of magic called the Wasting Shine. No matter how many times they've described the way it threads through the trees and mud and vines like glittering Christmas tinsel, I see nothing. In fact, apparently whenever I dare to draw near it, the Shine moves away as though it finds me repulsive. I'm glad to say the feeling's mutual.

"It could have something to do with the Shine," Sterling says. "That might explain why you didn't see it."

"Or it wasn't there," I challenge.

Again, Sterling and Abigail cut me out of their visual communication.

I've accepted that Shine exists. What else am I supposed to do when my two best friends agree so completely?

I say, "And that's all we'll have to say about that. Today is my *fun* birthday day and those are the rules." I crank the radio. After a summer spent listening to these two discuss things I can't see, and worrying about things that might be wrong with me, I've had enough. Today isn't going to be about the things I can't do.

We meet Leo and Red in the wide front yard of their parents' house. Two pickups with utility trailers bearing five all-terrain vehicles are parked on the grass. Uncle Jack is helping Leo secure the straps and imparting some final wisdom as though he hasn't done this a hundred times before. Red greets us with a hearty, "Y'all ready to get filthy with me?!"

This is how my *fun* birthday actually begins. With the best friends I've ever known, the cousins who may as well be my brothers, and the promise of mud and mayhem. We've all dressed for disaster: old T-shirts, old shorts, and boots. Sterling and I have our hair in short ponytails; Abigail has bound her collection of tiny box braids into a single one that ends at her waist.

Red's a walking grin in a camouflaged T-shirt and matching pants. He saunters over to us with a special leer for Abigail. Relations aside, his brain isn't big enough to account for girls who don't want him for his body. He sees Abigail as a perfect challenge.

Abigail says, "I'm riding with Leo."

"I love it when you play hard to get." Red is too proud to be affected, and Abigail is too assured. Their stories are the sort that will never intersect.

"I'll take Red," I say.

"And I'll switch on the way home," offers Sterling.

Leo signals that it's time to mount up with a short whistle. He and his faded red ball cap disappear inside his navy blue truck and the rest of us heed his command and follow suit.

We make a lingering stop at the Flying J gas station to fill all seven tanks and grab Cokes for the road. As we caravan away, Red cries through his open window, "Cooterville, here we come!" revs his engine, and sets the radio to stun.

Sterling sits in the narrow seat behind me and we spend the two-hour drive shouting to be heard above the summer wind. We know we're close when a sign for DEER PROCESSING appears at the side of a narrow gravel road. We arrive at Cooterville Mud Rides just in time for an early lunch at the Cooter Shak—we have to eat while we're clean enough to touch our food—then it's time for business.

While Leo and I unhitch the ATVs and Red backs them down the ramp, Sterling and Abigail take care of our passes and waivers. August is high season for mudding. Here in the dusty parking lot is a family of eight and a group of boys all suiting up for action. The sun is blazing in a cloudless sky, the air is thick with humidity and exhaust, and sweat is cooling on my skin.

"Ready?" I ask my girls.

Abigail doesn't even try to hide her grin. There's nothing about life in the Beale house that allows for this sort of freedom.

Sterling's excitement is a little less eager. She nods with an emphatic "Let's do this," but she does this because she likes to know that she can, not because she loves it.

We spend the day slipping, sliding, and sinking in mud pools. We take turns racing into hip-deep water, rocking the ATVs back and forth to keep them from getting stuck, and whipping down tracks at reckless speeds. Red goes first, I go second with Sterling and Abigail close behind, and Leo pulls up the rear. While Red and I are given to racing, no one else is in it to win.

I wait for a straightaway and overtake Red, accelerating until my wheels gain and lose traction, becoming unpredictably slick, and the mud pelts my skin. Red doesn't let me keep the lead for long, forcing my nose into a deep rut. This is how we proceed, laughing and cursing and sweating in the hot sun.

We pause at the edge of what will be our final conquest. My arms shiver with exhaustion. Here now, even Sterling is laughing.

The boys are deep in conversation—deciding how best

to attack this hole when what we really need to do is barrel forward. I spy one clean patch on Red's back. It's a clear target. I scoop up a handful of mud and lob it full force.

He spins, spots my grin, and returns it. "I'm so glad you did that."

He retaliates by darting behind me and locking my arms in his while Leo slops mud through my hair.

"Beale! Saucier!" I cry, but my friends are much too wise for this.

"Whatcha gonna do now, killer?" Red teases.

He should know. He and Leo are the ones who taught me to fight dirty, but Red's shock is immaculate when I slip his grip and spin to knock my knee into his tenderest jewel. Leo's long smile is approving.

These are the best parts of my life all thrown into one moment, the things I'll actually miss when I finally leave all this behind.

One day, this will be an interesting footnote in the life of Candace Pickens. I'll have traveled so far and done so much that when people discover I once got muddy for fun they'll raise an eyebrow and remark on the surprising depth of my character. People don't think much of southern intelligence. I can't change that, but I plan to use it to my advantage. I'll be the girl who performs in spite of her roots and therein lies my chance at winning a scholarship to a school where studying abroad isn't a sex joke.

I'll never breathe another word about the swamp as though it's anything other than a mud pit. There's a fine line between charming-country and eccentric-country, and I intend to stay well on the charming side of things. Shouldn't be hard. I'm charming as hell.

By the time we clear all twenty-five miles of trails we're all as mud-greased as we are sunburned. We hose the worst of the mud off ourselves and our machines then head back to the Cooter Shak for sodas. My treat. I even promise Red a bag of nuts since he's so in need of them.

That wins me a rare laugh from Leo.

Little yellow-green cooter turtles adorn everything from plastic glasses to neon T-shirts. The air stinks of mud, sweat, exhaust, and hot, hot summer. I thread through the filthy press of mudders to place my order. In the dingy mirror behind the bar I see myself as I so rarely am—blond hair caked in mud, skin splotched red and brown, and an easy smile that makes me look wild and careless—a girl out of control, in a state of blissful chaos. That girl doesn't care about ghosts or Shine or medical issues. To her, all of that is noise she'll soon leave behind.

Sodas and snacks in hand, I spot my friends and cousins sitting at a mud-stained picnic table in the full sun. Leo has his hat pulled low over his eyes, Red has fixed pure black sunglasses to his face, and Sterling and Abigail sit with their backs to the sun. As I approach, they all stop talking abruptly.

"What?" I ask. "Y'all talking about me?"

"Naw," Red answers. "The ghost from last night."

Leo punches him in the biceps. Predictably, he returns fire. But it's the way Sterling and Abigail look away that hits me. Guilty. Untrusting. Aware. My one rule for the day— no ghost talk—and they broke it.

The drive back to town is much too short. I sit next to Red with the wind in my face and mud in my hair. He's already fussing about how early he and Leo have to get up in the morning to report for work at Mr. Tilly's farm, but I only half listen. Sterling is in Leo's truck with Abigail, and all I can think about is how they're probably discussing things I can't see. It makes my teeth grind.

Before returning to Uncle Jack's, we pull into the Flying J to replenish the now very empty gas tanks of the ATVs. There's an unusual number of people loitering across the street on the porch of Clary General Store for seven p.m. on a Thursday night. It can't be a good sign. It happens in the wake of things like hurricanes and successful boar hunts and Monday-night Bingo. None of which happened tonight.

Red and Leo get the pumps going while the rest of us stretch our legs and scrape dried mud from our boots and jeans. The evening is sticky and warm, the sky a burning blue where the sun has recently been. I keep an eye on the crowd. Their chatter sounds like the thrum of cicadas, constant and pitchy. Before long, one little bug breaks away and jogs across the street.

It's none other than hater Hallie Rhodes, who's made a career of getting detention for chewing gum and both loathes and adores me. She hops up to us with a startled gleam in her wide brown eyes.

"Y'all been gone all day, huh?" she asks, snapping her gum. "You hear what happened?"

"Obviously, we didn't," I say, knocking my boots against the ground. It's best not to encourage her too much.

She grins, bouncing her curls and boobs simultaneously. "There was a ghost. Right here where we're standing. 'Bout ten o'clock this morning. One second there weren't nothing here, the next, *bam*. Ghost at the pumps."

"Must've been right after we gassed up," Sterling supplies with a special frown for Abigail.

Hallie nods. "And it just stood here, well, it was a he, so he just stood here, turning his head this way and that. Mrs. Trish saw the whole thing from inside the shop. So did Mr. Tilly and Featherhead Fred. They were up at Clary's."

The crowd on the Clary porch is thick. Among them, I spot Old Lady Clary herself, standing at the edge with her arms crossed over her ample chest. She's listening to her guests, but her eyes are trained on us.

"How did they know it was a ghost?" I challenge.

"Oh, they didn't. It was Quentin Stokes." Hallie brightens at the mention of one of Sticks High's most willing and committed bachelors. "He came for gas and saw the man just standing there, blocking the pump, so he parked and went over to ask him to move and when he reached out to touch the guy's arm . . ." She pauses, snapping her gum double-time. "Would you believe, his hand passed *right through* the guy!"

"Then what happened?" Sterling presses.

"Quentin says the ghost looked real bad. Ratty clothes, long hair, and a bunch of children's toys hanging from his belt. Creep-fest, right? And he just kept looking past Quentin, leering at nothing, until he finally turned and walked off toward the swamp."

"Makes a good story," I say. "In fact, it's a Clary tale we've all heard or told called 'Jack of the Trade,' which only goes to show how unlikely it is these are actual ghosts."

All three of them look at me like I've completely missed the point.

"People have been talking about it all day," Hallie continues. "Old Lady Clary says something's wrong with the swamp. She says all the ghosts folk have been spotting are coming from there. You oughta see the fence behind Clary General. It's lit up like Mr. Calhoun!"

Old Lady Clary's store is an exercise in vertical integration. She not only sells the booklets of the Clary Tales, ghostly swamp stories we all grew up on, but the candles and beads meant to keep those ghosts firmly on the swamp side of the fence. People buy superstitions and solutions all at the same time, leaving candles along the split-rail fence behind her shop. She's small-town brilliant.

"She's probably right," Sterling says with another frown for Abigail.

She doesn't say it, but I know what this look means. It means she's afraid she's to blame, that something went wrong when she freed her brother and Abigail from the swamp. That night is the reason I've been forced to believe any of this business about the swamp, but ghosts are still a stretch.

"It's kinda cool to live in a haunted town, don't you think? Have any of you seen one yet?" Hallie asks, strangely hopeful.

"I saw the one at Calhoun Creek," Sterling confesses. It's news to me. I was there five days ago when half the volleyball team decided a swim in the creek was worth trespassing on Mr. Calhoun's land. I let surprise blanket my face and Sterling admits, "It was after you left."

Abigail reveals nothing, but she also doesn't seem surprised by Sterling's confession. They both knew? They both knew. And neither of them thought to share it with me. My frustration with this entire situation starts to darken like the sky above us. Of course, I haven't said one word about the fact that I'm anticipating my own bad news, so I guess we're all guilty.

Hallie leans in, conspiratorial. "Kelly Thames and I are going to hold a ghost vigil tonight behind Clary General. Just a few girls. You want in?"

I can imagine nothing worse than spending the remainder of my fun birthday day in the presence of Hallie and Kelly hunting for ghosts behind Old Lady Clary's moonshine shack. Except once again Sterling and Abigail are sharing a look.

That's it. I'm not losing my friends to anything, least of all hater Hallie Rhodes. I loop my arms through Sterling's and Abigail's and change the course of the night. "We have plans. Thanks anyway."

Hallie shrugs and begins to back away. "Keep your eyes peeled for ghosts!" she calls, then turns and jogs across the street to Clary General, where Old Lady Clary hasn't moved an inch and still watches us.

"We have plans?" Abigail asks.

"Now we do," I say. I'm done being on the outside of this—whatever "this" is—and what better way to manage a complaint than by going straight to the source? "Beale, tell your mom you're sleeping over. We have a date with the swamp."

THE SWAMP IS EXTRA THICK tonight. The storm that blew
through early last week left everything good and flooded.
So flooded, in fact, that Mr. Tilly's old dinghy took a trip
down the drainage ditch and ended up parked at Miss Bon-
nie's full of stolen Wawheece & Sons tools. That led to a
storm all its own because it was Mr. Wawheece that found
the boat first and decided to hold it hostage on account of
it being full of his things. Anyone with sense would write
off a boat that old as collateral damage, but Mr. Tilly'll be
planning some sort of retribution, that's for certain.

My flashlight charts a bobbing path through dense
clusters of plants and skink-brown water. The last time I

voluntarily entered the swamp was the same night all those people reappeared. Then it was soggy and disgusting, but more or less walkable. Now it's bloated with so much summer rain we almost need a boat.

Ahead, Sterling walks without a light of her own, confident and capable. She bends around trees and makes steady progress, never wavering even when the water climbs to her thighs.

I waver. Gators don't like the high heat of summer, but evening temperatures like these make them very happy. I sweep my light at the level of the water, ready to pee if I spot the flash of eyeshine.

Behind me, Abigail sighs repeatedly in her efforts to remain calm. Abigail is a far cry from being a fan of the swamp and she detests doing anything she has to lie about, but she put on her big-girl britches and told her mom she was sleeping over at my house tonight. Which isn't a lie. It's just not all of the truth.

No one says anything as we continue our weaving path. Every so often, Sterling casts a glance over her shoulder to see that we follow and I think she looks excited to be trudging through rot water in the dark. Just as I've begun to suspect we've gone astray, we emerge in the clearing of the everblooming cherry tree, still a riot of pink blossoms when all other flowers have wilted in the blistering heat of summer. It might be the one and only cherry tree I've seen in my seventeen years of life, but I'm smart enough to know most fruit-bearing trees flower in the spring, not the tail end of summer.

According to Sterling, this is the tree from which all of the Wasting Shine is spun. We're pretty certain it's not the geographical center of the swamp, but it's the center of its magic.

Of course, all I see is a tree.

Sterling heads straight for it and settles herself between the roots. Her hand falls on a small chunk of metal protruding from a knot where two roots collide. She gives it a fond little caress.

You wouldn't know it to look at it, but that bit of silver only recently punctured those roots. It used to be a bracelet filled with the magic of the swamp and I watched Sterling stab it straight into the flesh of the tree earlier this summer as she fought to free her brother. The tree has healed around it so completely that anyone looking for the first time might assume it had been there for decades. I guess if the tree itself is made of magic, it ought to have magical healing abilities.

"So why are we here?" Abigail sits across from Sterling on the damp ground and flicks bits of muck and dead leaves from her legs.

"Because I'm really tired of being the one who doesn't see things." I peer at the tree, looking for any hint of the Shine the two of them so clearly see. But other than the fact of its seasonless blossoms, I see nothing unusual about it.

"And how do you plan to change that?" Abigail prods.

How *do* I plan to change that? It's not as if the Clary Tales offer any helpful advice on dealing with the swamp. All I know is that whenever I'm near the Shine, Sterling and Abigail say it moves away from me. It physically moves to avoid my touch. And when something avoids me that hard, there's really only one way to approach it.

I reach up and grip a low branch of the everblooming cherry tree with both hands.

Sterling gasps and draws to her feet.

Do I imagine it, or do I actually feel a vibration against my palms? The bark is rough and damp but also charged. I flatten my hands against the tree. There is a very slight, very constant buzzing sensation on my skin.

"Candy," Sterling says, moving back, her eyes taking in all of the tree. "You just—I don't know—you touched it and all the Shine shifted."

Abigail, too, has stepped to where she can see the whole tree. She nods to confirm Sterling's words and adds, "It's more concentrated now. More in the center of the tree and brighter."

"You mean I made it better?" I tease. I feel this. I actually feel this.

I try to imagine I see the Shine as they've described it: twisted strands of yellow and gold and brown all bound together in a press of light. But it's unsatisfying.

The vibration against my palms remains steady. It no longer feels like a thing happening *to* me. It feels alive and real and ecstatic. It feels like a solid, tangible thing I could push if I tried. So I try to do just that. Imagining it as a wall, I move my hands together and slide them along the branch, closer to the trunk. I feel the pressure receding as I go, the vibration intensifies.

"What did you just do?" Sterling asks.

"Tell me what you see," I say.

Abigail complies, disbelief heavy in her voice. "It's just a single column now. Like a spear down the center of the tree. Tidy. And calm."

So I can affect it with only a touch, but I can't see it? How is that just? My friends eat swamp berries and gain access to Shine. But I eat nothing and it avoids me?

An idea strikes. I release the tree and turn to my friends.

"You look like you have a plan," Sterling says.

"I might. You both see Shine because you ate swamp berries, right?"

"Technically, I saw it first because I was, ya know, wasting away, but yes," Sterling agrees. "We're connected because we both ate something that grew with Shine."

"Maybe I have to do something similar. I can't see it; it can't touch me, so what if all I need to do is establish a connection?"

They share yet another look, but at the end of this one, Sterling shrugs.

"I don't see what harm it could do to try."

"Beale?" I ask. I don't need her approval, but I'd like it just the same.

"I don't know why you'd *want* this kind of connection, but it's your life," she says with a disbelieving shake of her head. "You do what you want."

"I usually do," I say.

They watch as I select a single perfect cherry blossom from the tree and pluck it. I've never eaten a flower before, but it can't be any worse than undercooked turnip greens. I pop the collection of bright pink petals into my mouth and chew. Other than being slightly bitter, it doesn't have much taste.

"Do you feel anything?" Sterling asks, investigating my eyes.

"Nope," I say, having swallowed my swamp treat.

"Hmm." Sterling turns her confused face to Abigail and I actually feel my very invisible hackles rise from my neck.

"I say you're lucky," Abigail declares.

"I'm not done. Part two. Anyone have a knife?" They both reach into their boots and produce knives. A worn switchblade for Sterling, and a particularly vicious fixed blade for Abigail. I grin at my friends and produce my own: a folding buck knife with a camo handle, compliments of

Red on my thirteenth birthday. "Now it's a party."

"Why do we *all* need knives?" asks Abigail. "This is about you. Right? *You*."

"I just wanted to see that you had them. Congratulations, you're smart enough to live in the South."

That makes Sterling chuckle and Abigail frown. As always, entertaining one means disappointing the other; such is the dance of our friendship.

Sterling moves to my side, facing the tree with her little nose held high. "Blood?"

"Blood," I confirm. "Unless you have a better idea."

"Nope. Okay." Her blade opens with a click. Deep breath in, deep breath out.

"You don't have to do this with me."

She scoffs and holds her own hand out against her blade. "Won't be the first time I've bled beneath this tree. How much do you suppose is enough?"

"Better more than less." I have no way of knowing if this is true, but it sounds good. I unfold my own blade and press the tip to the meat of my left palm.

"Wait, wait, wait." Abigail holds up a hand. "Eating a blossom is one thing, but do you really think it's a good idea for you to go feeding your blood to this tree? I mean, you can't take this back. Blood given is blood taken."

I pause with the blade resting lightly in my palm. "I know, but I don't want to be the one who doesn't see anymore. I don't like being on the outside of something you, my family, and the entire town is part of. I want to see Shine and this is the only way we know how to make that happen. I'm willing to take the risk."

Abigail shrugs. "I still don't think it's a good idea. But I'm not going to let either of you do it without me."

With a sigh, Abigail comes to stand by my side, placing me firmly between her and Sterling. She lifts her eyebrows along with her blade. "Fools do it on three?"

"One," I say.

"Two," Abigail adds.

"Three," Sterling finishes.

It doesn't take much pressure to break the skin. I press and slash in one quick motion. The sting is sharp as the blade. Goosebumps crawl up my arms and down my legs as blood wells in my palm. Beside me, Sterling hisses. Abigail comes as close to taking the Lord's name in vain as I've ever heard.

We pump our fists and I squeeze until my fingers tingle. Our blood paints the top of the roots a dark color, blending in with the mud and bark. I can't see where the swamp begins and my blood ends, and for a moment I imagine my veins, the veins of every soul in our little town, pump with muddy, brackish waters instead of blood. I imagine my heart beats in time with Sterling's and Abigail's, that it *tha-dump-tha-dump-tha-dump*s in the rhythm set by the swamp because everything in this damned town is connected.

Then comes a single word, spoken into my mind in a thin, tortured voice: *bones.* It ghosts through my head, revolving like the barrel of a gun. *Bones, bones, bones.*

I shiver and after what feels like several long moments, we move away from the tree.

The air is close and warm, the swamp slipping into the calm of night, and in the dark everything is both obscure and so clear. There is Abigail, towering with her many long braids bound and spilling down her back. There is Sterling, cupping her hands, eyes wide with pain. There is the tree, stretching its gnarled arms around them both. I gave my blood, but I see no Shine.

I shouldn't be affronted, but I am. "This is really going to suck when we have to go hit volleyballs next week," I mutter, pinching the broken skin of my palm together. The blood has gotten gummy and thick. Pain is not far from this moment.

"No, it won't." Sterling stoops and collects thin air— Shine, I reckon—into her hands. She speaks over it and patty-cakes it into her wound. When she removes her hand, the wound is nothing but a pale, pink line. She smiles.

"Swamp witch," I tease.

"You try, Abigail," Sterling urges, but Abigail won't hunt. "We talked about this; it's not evil, Shine simply *is*.

It's what we do with it that matters, and healing is inherently a good thing, right?"

I don't think Sterling's going to win this one, but she can't help herself from trying. One of her beautiful flaws is her desire to convince people her way of thinking is the right way. I think it's why she loves Abigail and me. Neither of us is easily convinced.

Abigail is the most steady thing in this swamp. "This isn't natural. Giving blood to a tree is one thing, but taking that kind of power in my own hands is another."

"It's not—" Sterling stops herself. Wisely. There's no winning Abigail at this point and we're all too tired to really struggle. "At least let me do it, then?"

Begrudgingly, Abigail releases her wounded hand to Sterling. Just as before, it takes a moment and a whisper to repair the cut that marred the smooth light-brown surface of Abigail's palm. Abigail doesn't resist, but she looks up, fixing her eyes on a single star in the cold sky so she doesn't see her skin knit itself back together.

The more I think about it, the more it makes sense to me that Abigail is good at turning a blind eye to things that make her uncomfortable. As long as her parents—or God, for that matter—don't see her doing anything questionable, she can pretend it wasn't her fault if it was done *to* her.

What a horrible way to live.

When it's my turn, Sterling takes my hand and goes through the same motions. I hold my breath, keep my eyes trained on the cut, and wait for the moment it dares to vanish before my very eyes. Only it doesn't.

"What's wrong?" Exhaustion is winning the race against my desire to be here one minute longer.

"I'll try again." Sterling closes her eyes this time as she whispers over her invisible Shine and presses it against the wound on my palm. Again, nothing happens except the same stinging sensation. "I—I don't think it will work on her," she says to Abigail.

Whatever that means to Abigail, it makes her look at me with a mixture of confusion and wonder that bothers my skin. Sterling has the decency to look perturbed. I don't know why any of us is surprised. This swamp mistrusts me as hard as I mistrust it. I just never expected to care as much as I do in this moment. It doesn't matter what I do, I'm a dead end. In every aspect of my life it seems.

It didn't work. There is no new connection between me and the Wasting Shine.

I feel tears threatening like a storm.

"I know how to work a bottle of hydrogen peroxide and a Band-Aid," I say more harshly than I intend. "Let's just go home."

Band-Aids don't cut it. The blood in my hand pumps as hard as my heart, keeping me up half the night fetching new ice from the kitchen. In the morning, the wound is crusted and sticky, the skin around it shiny and red, and every time I move my fingers my hand burns.

Abigail likes to sleep in when she stays the night. Her parents aren't fans of anything that can be construed as lazy. Even on the weekends, their entire house is up with the sun solving global crises or composing the next great musical sensation or making pancakes. I'm a natural early riser, but letting Abigail sleep gives me an excuse to avoid my parents. I don't roll out of bed until I hear Mom's car pulling away.

It's hard to linger in the shower with a busted hand. No matter how I shift, keeping it out of the water is awkward and irritating. When I'm clean enough, I give up. Clearly, slicing into my own sweet flesh on some stupid supernatural hunch wasn't one of my best ideas. The only thing that's changed is my ability to pull up my own damn underwear.

Abigail's awake when I return, waiting for her turn in the bathroom. While she washes, I head to the kitchen and start lining up boxes of cereal on the counter. I set the milk next to our bowl of bananas, but break out the frozen blueberries for Abigail since she hates yellow fruit.

The doorbell rings and I open the door to find a FedEx guy sweating on my porch. With a smile, he offers me his handheld tablet and stylus. "Special delivery for Miss Darlene Pickens," he says.

In one hand, he holds a stiff, white envelope with the word CONFIDENTIAL posted across its front in blocky red letters.

I sign on the slippery screen and trade the tablet for the envelope. In the upper left corner, the return address is printed like formal letterhead: NEW ORLEANS CHILDREN'S HOSPITAL.

It's very possible that I shut the door in his face. I don't remember as I walk back to the kitchen in a twisted stupor.

My mother's name is on the front. But the letter inside is for me.

Then the letter is open. The envelope dropped on the counter and my eyes move across the paper too fast to comprehend the words printed there.

I slow down and start again.

It begins with a gentle greeting and a recitation of what tests they ran when we visited. The letter recounts all the things I tested negative for, which includes precancerous or cancerous cells. I feel my chest move again as I draw my next breath.

Then I read, "Diagnosis: amenorrhea."

The letter falls from my fingers.

Years of wondering have been reduced to a single word. One that means my body is dysfunctional and I am sterile at the ripe old age of seventeen.

I don't know how to think about this. It's an answer. I like answers. I like the certainty of them. But this one provides me with no certainty.

I'm not dying. That's certain. But what do I do about this?

It's then that I realize Abigail is standing next to me. She's collected the letter from the floor and is holding it.

She's holding it. She's looking at it. Reading it.

"Shit!" I snatch the letter from her hands.

I wasn't paying attention. I dropped it and now Abigail's looking at me with her insightful, patient eyes and she knows. She knows. She knows.

"Damn it!"

But Abigail says nothing. She stands there with her eyes trained on me, her back to the kitchen window so sunlight gilds her shoulders and laces through her long box braids. But she doesn't speak and I really need to know what she's thinking right now.

"Abigail?"

"Candy."

"Say something."

"It's not my place to say anything." Here she adds a graceful shrug of her shoulders as casually as if she happened upon a flyer for a party. "If you don't want to talk, we won't."

My heart begins to thump in a less frenzied way and I feel my left hand unclench, allowing a fresh wave of pain to wash in. It's biting enough to bring me back to my senses. Of course Abigail won't force the issue.

I take a steadying breath and carefully replace the letter in the envelope. "It's not a big deal. I don't want to talk."

Her nod isn't meant to assure me, but she does it anyway saying, "Okay. No talk." She crosses to the kitchen bar and selects a cereal. Then she adds, "I thought we'd have a pool day. Just the three of us. Mom's taking the boys shopping for school stuff and Valerie won't bother us, so we'd have the pool all to ourselves. Think about it."

We've spent a good third of our summer in and around

the Beale pool. Having it to ourselves is a rare occasion. But my head spins and my hand hurts and the thought of lying out in the sun leaves me nauseated.

"Um, maybe," I say, and she doesn't press.

After breakfast, Abigail heads off, leaving the promise of hours of unfettered girl time with her and Sterling on the table. I leave it there, too.

Instead, I spend the day reading the last cheerful book on our AP English summer reading list, *The Bell Jar* by Sylvia Plath. It's terrible, I decide. Not because it's bad, but it's as painful as the gash in my palm to read. It's the story of a girl not much older than me who moves to New York and is constantly told that in order to be someone you must allow yourself to be reduced and defined by others.

Too many of Esther's words worm their way inside my mind as though I've thought them before. And when reading them becomes more uncomfortable than my palm, I stop and send a picture of my wound to Cousin Leo along with *fix it.*

His response is immediate: *ffs come over.*

It's only a few blocks away, but I justify driving because my palm turns into a pulsing volcano when I let it hang by my side for more than thirty seconds. I wait until I'm sure they're in their active hours and head over. I turn down the narrow path they call a driveway just as my clock reads five o'clock.

I smell the boys before I see them. The second I open my car door, the sweet stench of rotting meat hits me. Only, it's not rotting meat, exactly. It's the smell of deerskin and blood and guts all heated to their evaporation point. Who but a bunch of Craven boys would have a skull boil at five p.m. on a Friday evening?

The path around their rusted trailer is littered with all the things they think they might use and probably never will: old chairs, mismatched tires, an ancient tractor's steering column. They've all been where they are for so long, I could walk through them in my sleep.

Firelight glows at the end of the path. I find the boys exactly where I expect to—lounging with beers in hand next to a giant noxious cauldron of boiling animal parts. They keep this area clear for the sole purpose of fires, barbecues, and going rounds on the heavy bag strung up in a young oak. The surrounding woods are thick with underbrush, making the whole area feel close and isolated.

"Hey, coz," Leo drawls. His shirt's already come off his tan shoulders and his eyes are glazed as doughnuts. "Beer's in the cooler. You'll need one."

He tips his own beer toward the neon orange cooler that's been in the same spot so long it's wedged into the earth. Five feet from their back door, beyond which lives a brand-new refrigerator, and they can't be bothered to travel that far for a drink.

I snatch an ice-cold can, pop the top, and take a long pull.

Red chuckles. "Shit, C, did you get dumped or what?"

In response, I rip the three Band-Aids from my hand. Fresh blood smears across my palm.

Red leaps to his feet. "Who did it?" His teeth clench as tightly as his fists.

"Christ, any excuse for a fight. *I* did it. To myself. It was an accident. I was sharpening my switchblade and it slipped. That's all. Want to fight me about it?"

He takes a deep breath, floundering now that I've challenged his testosterone rush. "Well. Yeah," he says.

Leo pushes Red aside to take my hand. His brows knit as he prods the swollen skin. "Red," he commands, "go get the kit. It's worse than it looked in the picture. You slipped?"

Leo's intelligence isn't wide, but it's also not shallow. He knows as much as there is to know about a few things, blades being one of them.

I choose not to perjure myself or insult his specific wisdom. "Sorta not."

No questions follow my admission, only a single nod. I love my cousin.

Red returns with a kit slung over one shoulder and a jug of water clutched to his chest. I sink into a rusting metal chair and let the boys fold me into their practiced rhythm of tending to their hunt. Leo keeps my hand held firmly but gently between his as Red opens their jug of sterile water to flush the cut. They follow that bath with a cotton ball bursting with hydrogen peroxide, and I curse to high heavens as the sting courses through my blood like a snake.

There's no one in the world I'd trust to stitch up my hand like Leo. He's got nerves of steel and a heart of soft spun gold. No part of his ego relies on how many deer or boar he kills, and though he keeps a coin of antler from the first buck he shot, he doesn't keep trophies.

The same can't be said for Red, who I wouldn't trust to stitch me up as long as Leo was an option. If Leo wasn't a voice of reason, Red would have antlers strapped to the grille of their truck.

Leo threads the needle with ease, then looks up to meet my eyes. "Ready?"

"Ready," I confirm.

I keep my eyes on the needle as Leo pushes it through my skin. It pinches, actually it stings like a bee, but I grit my teeth and bear it. If Red thinks I'm suffering, he'll suffer and that will make this harder on everyone. Mostly me.

Leo's hand moves quickly. Each stitch is clean and precise. He never hesitates or pauses, and at the end of five minutes, I have a line of tiny green x's down my palm.

"Keep it clean," Leo commands.

"You want the superglue?" Red offers a small tube, but Leo shakes his head.

"Too deep. Just put a bandage on it and change it every day. Keep it dry." He pauses, glancing away briefly, then keeps his voice too low for Red to hear and says, "You sure you won't say how it happened?"

A warm feeling makes my breath momentarily tight. For whatever reason, my parents stopped with one child—a fact Nanny Craven is quick to use to guilt her daughter into doing whatever it is she wants done. I think they probably tried. There's more than enough room in our house for a proper brood, but around the time I entered third grade, Mom and Dad took up the "we only ever wanted one child" party line. I've always envied Leo and Red, and Carol and Irene, their close connections. I'd be a stellar sister. Leo makes me feel like I am.

"It's nothing to worry about," I promise. I give my fist a testing squeeze. The skin feels tight, hot as a sunburn, but somehow better. "Thanks."

While Leo and Red pack the kit away I finish my shitty beer. In the cauldron, the skulls burble and roll their hollow eyes skyward. Bits of flesh still cling to one of the snouts and they wave in the rush of water. The smell is stronger than the taste of my beer, thick and savory. Later, it'll make a nice stock for their mother.

49

The sky glows blue and orange through the trees, the final rays of sunset casting the bones and bubbles in demonic orange. The fire hisses and pops. My eyes slip to the glowing embers. I watch the lights in them surge and fade like ripples on water. The heat starts in my knees and fingertips, then spreads up to my nose and cheeks.

My body warms until I'm certain my fingers are as hot as the embers, my skin absorbing and creating heat like the thick underbelly of the swamp.

The flames inside fill my lungs with an airless smoke. My head feels light, my feet fluid, and in my mind, a voice sings, *Her skin will shiver, shiver, shiver, when she sleeps in the river, river, river.*

"Candy!"

My shoulders shake. Red's face appears before mine. His meaty hands on my shoulders. He's shaking me. Saying something else.

*She's mad, mad, mad*, rings in my head.

Breathing takes effort. Too much effort. I gasp, destroying my lungs to get them to cooperate and fill with air.

The voice fades and I push unsteadily to my feet.

"The shit," Red says, ushering in reality and staring into my eyes. "The shit was that?!"

"Nothing." I pull out of Red's grip, all too aware of the concern masquerading as anger on his face.

"Nothing? Bullshit. You were singing like a creepy-ass zombie and then wheezing. What. The. Fuck."

"Never mind," I say. But I have the same question and it's spinning up into something like panic. I was singing? "It was nothing. I have to go."

Leo steps into my path, imposing. Sometimes, being the center of attention is the worst thing in the world.

"I'm fine. Swear it. Thanks for the stitches." I step around him. Mercifully, he lets me go.

I escape to the sounds of Leo barring Red from pursuit. It's full dark now. Outside the ring of firelight, the path is difficult to see. *How long was I here?* My phone says it's nearly seven. Two hours? How did two hours pass?

The cold sensation slithering down my spine is probably called dread. I hate it. I dismiss it and climb into my car, where I blast my most aggressively cheerful playlist reserved for breakups and bad grades—Katy Perry and One Direction and Disney music.

It's not until I'm on the road that I remember I had a beer. How long ago? I have no idea. The absolute last thing I need in my life is to do something butt-stupid like drive drunk, so I pull over and do a pirouette on the side of the freaking road. Katy's voice filters through my open car door and I do another pirouette for good measure. I spin in the grit on the side of the road for no one to see, my balance perfection, like a ballerina trapped in a jewelry box. It doesn't make me dizzy and after a few deep breaths of cool night air, my heart starts to settle. Not drunk.

Whatever it was that happened to me just now, it wasn't caused by my cousins' shitty beer, which isn't as comforting as it should be.

BETWEEN THE NEWS OF MY biological impairment and the freakish voice that took my head for a spin last night, I'm surprised I sleep. But I do and not only do I sleep, but I sleep late. I wake just in time to rush over to the Tatums' for my standing Saturday-afternoon babysitting job.

At least it's diverting and helps me avoid talking to my mother for a few more hours.

My little cousins Carol and Irene chase each other back and forth across the backyard in a game called "Hunt the Boar." They've donned their camouflage overalls for the occasion and take great care when firing their finger guns.

It's a testament to Aunt Daisy that they practice gun safety on an imaginary hunt.

My phone buzzes in my pocket. Since it's just after noon, I assume Sterling has graced the world with her presence and climbed out of bed for her dreadful coffee. I answer without looking.

"Yes?"

"Are you babysitting today?" Sterling asks.

I glance up. The girls are creeping to the far end of the yard, arm-rifles held to provide accurate sight lines. One day, they'll realize boar hunting requires less guile and more all-terrain vehicles.

"As I do every Saturday afternoon," I answer.

"Have you . . . ? I mean, any changes with your vision?" she asks. I hear the hope in her voice. Even she is anxious for me to see Shine.

Today, the weight of that inability feels at once heavier and less significant. "No, no changes," I say.

"Well, maybe it'll just take time," she offers. "We missed you yesterday."

For a fraction of a second I panic that Abigail said something to her and she's fishing. But I remember that Abigail's life is built on secrets. It wouldn't even occur to her to share mine with Sterling.

I should tell her. Not just about my useless ovaries, but about my weird spell last night. That's what friends do.

But as I sit here watching Carol and Irene take down their imaginary boar, I feel so heavy. To tell Sterling anything, I'd have to feel something, and right now, my emotions are comfortably distant. It's as if I'm at the bottom of a deep, dark well; the sky above is where my heart burns, but it's a long way up.

"Yeah, I just wasn't up to it."

"By the way," she adds, "I heard that Hallie's little ghost vigil turned up nothing, but she and Kelly are pretending they saw something."

I roll my eyes. "I'm sure they're not alone. I'd be willing to bet half the stories we hear are fabricated."

"It's harmless, I guess."

"Stupid is rarely harmless," I counter.

Sterling laughs and we hang up just as the girls present me with the head of their imaginary boar. This, at least, makes me smile.

It's late when I finally make it home.

"Candace?" My mother's voice finds me like a sonar, bouncing back to a sensor in her head in the shape of me. "Candace, would you come here, please?"

I consider pretending I didn't hear her. After all, it's been nearly a week since we spoke; it's plausible I don't recognize her voice anymore. But this is one of those situations where Mom Law rules supreme. She can ignore me for as long as she wants, but the second she's done, I'm expected to snap to.

I find her seated at the kitchen table behind several short stacks of paper. She straightens one of them, nervously tapping at the edges, then braids her acrylic-tipped fingers in front of her. "I know you read the letter," she states.

I turn to stone.

"I wish I'd been here when you did. I'm sorry you had to read that alone, I really am."

I bite the inside of my cheek. I don't want to talk about this.

"You must be so disappointed." Sympathy, heartbreak, and anguish all pool in her eyes. "I—I've been doing some research about . . . your condition and I think we should discuss a few options."

Research? She jumped straight from my disappointment to finding ways to fix me? I don't even know if I *am* disappointed, but she sure seems to be.

"You know it wasn't all bad news, right?" I ask. "Remember that cancer was a possible outcome? Cancer! And I don't have it. All things considered, I'm miles away from disappointed."

I don't think I realized how true that bullet was until I fired it at my mom. Saying it, I do feel relief. I'm not dying. *I'm not dying.*

Mom blinks. "Oh, honey, that was such a remote

possibility. You didn't think you might actually have cancer, did you?"

"I—" But there aren't any words there. While I've been preparing for the worst, she's been denying it existed. What a luxury.

"Of course I'm happy, relieved, you aren't sick," she continues. "And I've been reading up on how many girls with problems like yours are able to fix them."

"Not interested," I say.

Her hands flatten against her research. "You think that now, but one day you will be interested, and the sooner we attack this the better."

Now she knows better than I possibly can? Her presumptions are the only thing I'd like to attack.

"Not. Interested."

"Please, try to be rational about this, Candy." Her gaze hardens for battle. I feel every bit of my body go contrary in response. "All of these doctors say there's hope that this . . . condition isn't permanent, but it requires treatment. Early and often."

And suddenly anger rockets through my limbs.

"Oh really? If I take their snake oil, I'll stand a chance at fulfilling my one true purpose in life as a child-bearing woman? Let me be superduper clear about this: I'm. Not. Interested."

"Candace, please. At least read these." She pushes one of

her stacks toward me. "You're dealing with a lot and there's no harm in reading."

Coming from the woman who still hides her romance novels beneath the bed and thinks I don't know, this assertion is laughable.

It would be easy to take the stack and leave. It would make her feel better, but it isn't going to change anything. This is the reality we've been working toward for a solid year. The past three months have involved several secret trips to New Orleans for X-rays, CT scans, blood work, and more, all because I'm a seventeen-year-old girl who doesn't have her period.

I feel dangerously close to the surface of my deep well, so I take a breath and sink back down. "I just don't think you understand that it doesn't bother me."

"Well, it *should*." Her voice falters and her eyes cut away. "It's such a disappointment."

She says "it's," but I hear "you're."

I want to say something caustic in response. I want words so corrosive they melt the acrylic on her nails. But what I have is this pinching feeling in between my lungs.

I spin on my heel and leave the way I came. Instead of my car, I grab my bike from the garage and hit the road. Fresh air is a cure-all for mother-daughter confrontations. I pedal faster and faster until my body has no choice but to breathe hard, until biology overrides emotion and I exist apart from my thoughts. Matter over mind. I refuse to shed a tear over my mother's baggage. Instead, I focus on the things I can control: my breath, my pace, my path.

Dusk is thick on the road. The song of the evening has traded crickets for cicadas. When sweat begins to run from my temples, I slow my furious pace. Wind lifts my shirt over my back, cooling my fever, and I choose a meandering course through the streets I know so well.

In the space of a few days I've gone from regular old Candy to "Candy, the barren" and "Candy, the permanently Shine-less." These might be secrets now, but it won't be long before every story ever told about me starts with one of those two phrases. And around here, the story is all that matters. That's the trick of living in a place like Sticks—knowing that the capital $T$ Truth isn't what happened, it's what people *say* happened.

Resentment flares hot in my cheeks.

Before I know it, I've taken the side road past Sterling's light blue house and turned at the old bridge. On one side, the Mississippi River glides along in ribbons of moonlight; on the other, the vast architecture of oak trees rises like a wall. I barely spot the driveway of the historic Lillard House, which sits beneath them. It was probably gorgeous in its day, but now it's just as tired and forgotten as the rest of Sticks.

As soon as I've left the main road, the night changes.

Here, beneath the canopy of oak and Spanish moss, it's hard to distinguish branches from sky. Every sound is amplified in this dark cave; the language of trees is spoken in snaps and groans and voiceless whispers. It's like listening to the elderly, and in spite of myself goose bumps raise along my forearms.

This would be a perfect place for something to appear.

If I were a ghost, I think I'd hide up in one of these old trees, releasing snot-freezing wails when someone is about to die like the Banshee Hale. I like the idea of being prescient in that way. And terrifying.

I study the branches as they pass overhead, searching for any sign of something unearthly. They're twisted and gnarled exactly as they should be, unadorned by ethereal shrieking maidens or raving madmen.

For a flash of a second, I'm disappointed. My life is quickly being defined by the things I can't do. I'm not used to feeling inadequate at anything except singing, and I accepted that shortcoming a long time ago, so why is it that two things completely beyond my control feel like personal failures? I pedal faster, anxious to leave these feelings behind.

The Lillard House stands in all its decrepit glory at the end of the long tunnel. Fog hides some of its more embarrassing age spots, but its dusty walls can't hide the fact that they, like Nanny's hands, long for younger days. It's beautiful in the way only destroyed southern relics can be.

When I leave the shelter of the oaks, I drop my bike and walk slowly. This close, the house looks different than I remember, especially the lower levels, where the siding looks sturdy and the paint pale. It makes an unsettling contrast to the weary upper floor.

On the third level a perfect black circle of a window sits in the peak of the attic. It's just large enough to remind the person on the other side that the sun exists. If I were telling this story, now is the moment a hand would appear there, insubstantial and pale, fingers splayed with distress, suggesting some unseen horror in the darkness beyond. This is the moment the spirits inside this dying house would do the worst thing they possibly could . . . they'd notice me.

But this isn't a story, and I shouldn't waste my time with such ensnaring flights of fancy. If I keep my wits about me I'll escape this town without too much superstitious country attached. In less than two years I'll be on my way to a place like Harvard or Yale or UCLA—somewhere far from here where no one gives credence to talk of ghosts and magic, and no one cares about my uterus except old white congressmen. To a place with a post office that's open more than twice a week. With any luck, I'll have a volleyball scholarship. Without luck, I may have a regular, intelligence-based scholarship.

I'm smack dab in the middle of an ego boost when I

spot them: three figures climbing the hill behind the Lillard House. Fog parts for them, swirling around their ankles and legs, turning them into dark silhouettes against a white background. One is so small it could be a shape made from night and fog, but the other two are tall enough to distinguish. A boy and a girl, for sure. The third, I realize, is a child. With no good reason for being way out here by the house Sticks forgot.

Ghosts.

I think it before I can reject the idea. There's no such thing. It's impossible. It should be impossible. I should *want* it to be impossible.

Except part of me wants it to be true, too.

I look away. I close my eyes, blink them several times, and count my fingers to ten. If I'm going to join the ranks of those who've seen a ghost, I'm going to be damn sure. Once a story's been told, it becomes true.

But I need mine to be true *before* I tell it.

Convinced that my vision is clear, I raise my eyes again.

The figures have stopped at the crest of the hill, thin and indistinct in the moonlight. Together, they turn their heads as if listening to some distant call. The boy reaches for the child's hand and pulls him closer, but they don't move from that spot. I watch, transfixed, wondering if I should get closer, fearing that they will get closer. My heartbeat pounds in my ears. I need to see their faces, and it's this thought that finally convinces my feet to move forward two inches.

Then, all at once, they look right at me. They *notice* me.

The yelp I utter is involuntary, but that was eerie as shit and I'm not ashamed. I run for my bike and leap on, pedaling halfway down the drive before I dare to look again. There's no sign of them, but I don't slow down. I go home as fast as I can. Not 'cause I'm scared, but because I'm immensely satisfied that I, Candace Craven Pickens, once again exceeded expectation by sighting not one, but *three* ghosts at once.

THERE'S NO MERCY IN A hot summer day spent inside a church.

Though the air conditioner's taking a vacation, Father O'Connor's got no interest in compassion and keeps us trapped inside this cumulative cloud of B.O. as long as possible. I don't like people telling me what to think, so I try not to pay too much attention to his homilies.

Father O'Connor aside, I like sitting in church. Usually, I like the smells—incense and wax and wood polish. I like the way the light blinks through the high windows of stained glass. I like how the tall ceilings give me room to think. But this morning my mind is a dangerous place to be. The corners are all full of thoughts with knives, images and sounds from that night with Leo and Red, my mother's disappointment, ghosts and trees and blood. I bounce so quickly between them, I trick myself into thinking I'm spinning.

Finally, the service ends and we leave the chapel a bouquet of wilted flowers.

Sterling's unusually chipper when we meet in the parking lot. She dances on her toes, looking more awake than someone ought to after sitting in a spiritual sauna for sixty minutes.

"Guess what?" she sings, climbing into my car and snapping her seat belt.

"Please, just tell me."

"Heath's home." She claps her hands in her lap and I swear the girl's trying not to bounce in her seat. "He got home late last night."

"So what were you doing in church?" I tease, smiling as my plans for the day, the week, and all eight days before school starts up again, crumble.

"Sweating. I need a shower, but I told him I'd meet him at the Lillard House in"—she checks her phone—"fifteen minutes! Curse Father O'Connor and the horse he rode in on!"

"Don't panic," I say, pulling out of the parking lot and speeding down the road. "It's not like he'll give up on you."

I didn't say it to be sweet, but Sterling presses a hand over her smile and fades into some romantic thought. I'd like to say I'm not jealous of what she and Heath have, but I'm not dead inside. Just not so lucky. The last guy I dated thought it was a good idea to give me camouflage underwear for my birthday and ask for a fashion show. And boy did I give him a show. Though not the sort he expected. It involved the panties. It just also involved a lighter and a megaphone.

No one's ever accused me of being too subtle.

When we get to the blue house, we race upstairs and Sterling sheds her Sunday clothes on her way to the bathroom. I pick through her closet to find a new outfit—white shorts and a navy blue tank—and sit on the bathroom counter while she scrubs off the sweat.

"I need to tell you something," I say to the red-and-tan shower curtain.

"That sounds ominous."

"It might be. It's definitely strange. I'm not sure how I feel about it, actually."

Sterling's face appears around the edge of the curtain. "Tell me you're not talking about sex."

"Why does everyone always think I'm talking about sex?"

"One," she says, disappearing, "I don't always think you're talking about sex. Two, you are frequently talking

66

about sex. And three, when we do talk about it, promise me it'll be face-to-face."

"Lord a'mighty, Saucier, I promise. Face-to-face."

Floral-scented steam clouds the ceiling, wisping this way and that like fog from the river. I concentrate on the word, *amenorrhea*, and the explanation, *absence of menstruation*. She should know. There's no reason not to tell her. Compared to everything we've dealt with lately, this, at least, isn't in any way supernatural.

"I saw ghosts." The words are out of my mouth before I know it—one confession replacing another. "At the Lillard House last night. Three of them."

The water cuts off and Sterling's hand snakes out for the fluffy towel in mine. Two seconds later, the curtain snaps open and her stone-blue eyes fix me in place.

"Candace Pickens, say that again."

I slide off the counter and try to recall the victory I felt as I fled the scene. "I saw three ghosts on the hill. A boy, a girl, and a kid. Plain as day."

"Candy!" She steps out of the tub. "Why didn't you tell me right away?"

"Because it's still crazy," I say, turning my back so she can get dressed without showing me all her naked glory. "Besides, I wanted to sleep on it and make sure saying it out loud still sounded like a good idea."

She rustles behind me, quickly climbing into the outfit I chose, and nudges my shoulder when it's okay to turn around. Her expression is nothing shy of joyful.

"I have to admit, even having said it, it still doesn't seem like the best idea."

"Candy!" She rises on her toes. "You saw a ghost! This is great!"

"Sometimes, I think you're not playing with a full deck of cards."

"Oh, come on, this *is* great. It means what we did at the tree worked; it just took a little longer on you. Doesn't this make you feel better?"

"Maybe," I say, smiling in spite of myself. It's strange to recognize that some part of me wished for this. Now that I've admitted it, my brain resumes its normal functions. "But the issue remains: Why are we seeing them at all?"

As Sterling squeezes water from her hair, her face falls into a winsome expression I've come to recognize. She's pondering the events of earlier this summer, when her brother, Phineas, was taken by a tortured swamp spirit and replaced with a girl, Lenora May, who became the sister Sterling never had. It cost Lenora May her life to free Phin.

I was there. I was essential for my Shine-repelling qualities. I hadn't seen things the way others did. I saw the swamp as the dull mud pit it is, and I saw a dozen confused people wander out of the mire. The strangest thing I remember was that one minute I didn't remember who Phin was and the next I did.

I pluck at the ugly leather band Sterling forced me to wear before we knew Shine had no effect on me. Supposedly, it bears a Shine spell that protects the wearer's mind from being altered by the swamp. Except mine, of course, but I've gotten used to the band.

"At the beginning of the summer, the Shine couldn't cross the fence," she says, "but now it can and does. It doesn't go far and it's not dangerous, I don't think, but the Shine is definitely different. Maybe the ghosts are, too?"

"That's an assuring thought," I say.

She watches me in the mirror as she layers a little powder over her skin and dabs her lips with gloss. "Time?"

I gladly swap talk of ghosts and magic for talk of Heath. "We're out of it. Ready?"

When we turn down the side road, Heath's sad excuse for a truck is parked in the long grass by the river. He leans against it, staring at the water in that stoic way of his. The sun glints off his short hair and hangs on his shoulders as if he's a painting in dusty strokes: *Study of a Truck and Its Boy.* Beside me, Sterling holds her breath.

I stop several feet behind the truck. Sterling's running before I've put the car in park. A better person might leave them to whatever reunion they're planning, but I'm nobody's chauffeur. I'll have a greeting and a thank-you-very-much before I go.

I delay my approach by changing out of my delicate Sunday sandals and sliding into my cowboy boots. Calm, faded brown with exquisite rows of tan and teal stitching, they complement my amber cotton skirt. I spend an extra minute fussing with my phone before slamming the door.

Heath's eyes shift to me ever so briefly. He gives me the courtesy of a slight nod before falling into Sterling's gaze once again. Moving closer, I notice how different he looks. His hair's been shorn into a standard buzz cut, his face is thinner, his shoulders more broad, and he's actually standing up straight for once. As far as punishments go, he wears this one well. In just a few short months, Heath has gone from distant and guarded to someone who actually lives inside his own face.

"You look like a proper meathead," I say. "Can you throw a decent punch yet?"

"Nice to see you, too, Candy," he answers. You can always tell a decent boy from a dangerous one by the trail their eyes cut during conversation. Heath's eyes are unwavering; they promise stability and honesty and roses on Valentine's.

"I thought you were supposed to call everyone 'ma'am' now. Don't they do that sort of thing at military camp? Change your vocabulary? Lord, was it horrible?"

"Some parts," he says with a meaningful glance at Sterling.

He's my height, which makes him the preferred four inches taller than her. I'd forgotten what a neat set they make. Or maybe I never knew. They've both changed since the start of the summer. They both beefed up in all the right ways and adopted healthier practices in general. Without the weight of drugs, or swamp magic, or starvation, they glow, and his golden tones are just the right contrast to her winter hues.

"How long do we have?" Sterling asks, already anxious.

During the last week of school, Heath made the crucial mistake of aggressively telling his parents that he quit taking his antidepressants because of Sterling's influence. Not long after Sterling's stepfather gave Heath a speeding ticket, and still not long after that Heath snuck out to help Sterling save her brother. All of that became Sterling's fault, and Heath's parents promptly sent him to military camp for the summer with strict instructions to clean up his act. Essentially, Mr. and Mrs. Durham turned Sterling and Heath's relationship into the quintessential forbidden fruit. Now, my two little lovebirds will stop at nothing to have each other.

"My parents think I'm out visiting Blake and the boys at the field." Heath holds up his cell phone. "I'm sure they'll call me in for dinner."

She tugs at his hand. "Want to go up to the house?"

"Ah, that's my cue," I say, and start to leave, but Heath's next words stop me in my tracks.

"I don't think we're allowed. Looks like someone's moving in."

"How?" Sterling sounds offended. "It's a state historic site. You can't just move into that sort of thing."

Heath shrugs. "There's a slew of trucks up there and I'd have sworn at least one was a moving van. That's why I met you down here."

He's still talking as we start moving toward the driveway. We're halfway to the house when a large white van rumbles past. The driver waves. Casually, because we all know him. It's Mr. Napoleon. He's the school plumber, which means he's also the town plumber. He's smiling like it's totally normal for him to be out at the Lillard House, which hasn't seen a piece of plumbing in a century.

It's possible that the town council has suddenly taken an interest in the house. But not likely. The Lillard House is as far from the town's attention as Sticks is from getting a mall. At least that used to be the case.

At the end of the oak tunnel, there's a flurry of activity. People pass constantly in and out of the front door. Hammers bang, buzz saws whine, and men shout. Long strips of white paint lay scattered across the grass like dandruff. Most of the trucks parked on the lawn are marked as part of the Wawheece & Sons Construction fleet. The rest must've come from outside of Sticks.

On one side, there's a crew of boys on ladders, sanding off the old paint and replacing rotten boards. I recognize the beautiful blond head of Quentin Stokes and the bald one of Riley Wawheece among them. It's likely there are a dozen other boys from our grade scattered around the site.

Everything is in motion, but we three become more rooted than the trees lining the road. At least this explains why the house looked mismatched last night. They must've started work yesterday.

Sterling breaks our silence. "But they can't." There's real panic in her voice. This is where she and Phin used to hide when their jackass of a dad was on a bender. It means something to her. "How can this be happening?"

"Let's find out," I say, striding ahead.

The closer I get the more dramatic the changes appear. The walls are barely white for all the sanding, the windows are all flung open, the front porch is in a state of transformation, and the roof's been skinned and prepped for new shingles. There's no part of it that hasn't been touched. I can only imagine what's happening on the inside. And how many people it's taken to make this happen in the day since I was here.

Sterling trots along beside me muttering half sentences I don't fully hear.

"Cut that out before we get up there, Saucier," I chide. "You sound cracked."

We follow the trail of sawdust to the front porch and step carefully around discarded tools and stacks of wood to get to the open front door. Heath urges caution, saying, "Maybe we shouldn't," but I wave him off. Girls can get away with more rudeness than boys. So long as I remember to use wide eyes if I get stopped, we won't catch much trouble.

Plastic coats the floor in all directions, and there's so much dust in the air I could chew it. Two men carrying long planks of wood pass us to climb the winding stairs, another zips up after them, and not one of them looks at us like we shouldn't be here. Encouraged, I lead my timid troops down the main hallway to the back of the house. The room we congregated in to prepare our final foray into the swamp for Phin has been stripped of its infested wallpaper and prepped for something new. It's a marvel, really. Uncle Jack's been remodeling his spare bedroom for the better part of a decade. The day he and Dad peeled off the wallpaper some eight years ago was the last day it looked good. These guys must've started working early to make so much progress. And on a Sunday. Around here, that takes money. Whoever is doing this, they're serious.

Heath releases a low whistle. "Looks like new neighbors."

"It can't be," Sterling says, panic rising. "It isn't. Maybe it's just a restoration effort to keep it from dying altogether.

Maybe it's just for tourism or history."

"Hate to burst your bubble," I say, peering through another arching doorway, "but there's a dishwasher in there, which is the epitome of an anachronism." Sterling looks like she's going to vomit, so I add, "But maybe they're just sprucing it up for some sort of—"

A child in a hard hat swoops through the room with a shriek. He dives around the corner into the kitchen and then is quiet. I know a game of hide-and-seek when I see one.

"Time to get," I say, ushering Sterling and Heath to the door. Not fast enough. I usher them right into a girl with bangs as heavy as her eyeliner.

"Oh!" She stops short of Heath's chest. "So sorry, I wasn't watching and I— Wait." Suspicion streaks across her face as she realizes we certainly, definitely don't belong. "Can I help you?"

I'm not one to notice hair, but hers stands out as decidedly not Sticks: a short bob with sharp pieces framing her face, all of it a silky dark brown. The pale brown feather hanging by her ear is the only part that moves when she does.

"We were just passing by and noticed all the commotion. Sorry to intrude," Heath says, smooth as butter.

"Everyone around here is so polite," the girl says with a smile.

"Who did you say you were?" I ask, stepping in front of Heath.

"Nova!" The whine comes from behind. "You promised."

The child in the hard hat slumps around the corner with arms crossed. Half his head is lost beneath the helmet. He has to tilt his head all the way back to see Nova.

"I'm not breaking my promise, Thad," she says gently. "But we have guests. Can you introduce yourself?"

Without shifting his glower, Thad extends a hand. "Thaddeus Roosevelt King," he pronounces carefully. "I'm four."

Taking his hand, I say, "Nice to meet you, Thaddeus. Big name for such a small kid. I'm Candace, but call me Candy."

His eyes brighten, but the scowl remains. Maybe his brow's just too heavy for his face. Some kids get stuck with awkward faces for a while. Nanny says strange-faced babies make beautiful adults, but that's hard to imagine.

"Thad," he says, pumping my hand twice. "This is my house."

I can practically hear Sterling's back stiffen. Time to get as many details as possible.

"This is Sterling Saucier—she lives just down the road from here—this is Heath Durham, and I'm Candy Pickens.

We're all juniors this year." The last is for Nova and she takes the bait.

"Me, too. Oh, I'm so glad to have met you. I hate awkward first days at school." She looks eagerly between us.

"Sorry, but, what's going on here?" Sterling asks, bringing us back to our original point.

"Renovation," Thad says carefully, rubbing his hard hat back and forth on his head.

"Yeah," Nova confirms. "We're moving into the nineteenth century because central air is so bad for your health."

"But the Lillard House is a historic site. You can't just move in. It's protected." Sterling's starting to sound slightly hysterical. She doesn't always deal well with change. "I mean, just who are you?"

To her credit, Nova shrugs right past Sterling's tone. "My dad made some deal with the town council, I guess. In exchange for letting us live here, he agreed to update it to ninety percent of its original glory."

"Ninety percent?" Heath asks, ever the nonconfrontational element.

"We can't be expected to live without modern appliances." She leads us into the kitchen where, in addition to a dishwasher, a refrigerator has been pushed into a corner. "You guys want a Coke or something?"

Nova hands out cans of Coke, shoves an extra into the

surprisingly accommodating back pocket of her shorts, then leads us outside and down a side path I've never noticed before. Going by Sterling's expression, neither has she. It branches off from the main drive and immediately cuts away through the oaks.

Thad trots out ahead, doing his best to lead, though he has to stop every few feet to tilt his hard hat and relocate the path. I walk next to Nova with Sterling and Heath following just behind. On the way to wherever we're going, we learn that though the Kings travel a lot for their dad's work, they consider Washington State home, specifically a little town called Seal Harbor on the Olympic peninsula. Sticks High will be Nova's third high school in as many years. She doesn't play sports but has nothing against them. She's more into things like debate and Model U.N. She shares these bits of herself with ease and confidence as though extracurriculars are the most important representations of a person. I suppose moving so often would help a person get over all the awkwardness inherent in first meetings, but it makes me wonder what she's hiding.

The path ends at a little shack so far from the house I can barely hear the buzz saw anymore. It's ragged but looks like a sturdy log cabin. The door leans against the wall, its hinges long rusted, leaving the entryway shadowed and empty. On either side of it are windows with broken panes of glass. The whole thing bleeds dead kudzu. I think this is how the history dies; one choking vine at a time.

"Isn't it wild?" Nova asks. "It's like an old witch's hut."

"Is it an old slave quarter?" Heath looks endearingly horrified at the thought.

"No," says Nova. "According to the old plans, the slave quarters would've been much larger and closer to the swamp. It was torn down when the Lillards renovated in the early nineteen hundreds. This was just some sort of storage shed, but everyone thought it'd been torn down, too."

"My brother found it," announced Thad with a proud grin. "I was with him and I'll bet there's ghosts in there."

"Aren't there always?" Nova mutters wryly, tugging the Coke from her pocket. "Hey, Gage! You in there? Gage!"

"What?" The shout comes from behind the house.

"I'll get him!" Thad shouts, running already.

While we wait, we sip at our Cokes and poke our noses inside the old shack. It's practically cool inside and the air smells sharp and musty. It's packed with all sorts of rusted junk: ancient bicycles, some sort of plow, an anvil, and several somethings that look like dangerous farm implements. Nova explains that the plan is to clean it up and turn it into a fort for Thad. That's what older brother Gage is out here working on.

"That is, of course, assuming it's not haunted," she adds.

"Why would it be haunted?" Sterling asks, tugging at a bit of withered kudzu.

Nova's answer stuns each of us. She says, "Haven't you heard? This whole town is haunted and my dad's here to find the cause."

Sterling and Heath go rigid. Not a game face between the two of them. They might as well come right out and admit the Wasting Shine is real and they know how to find it. There's no question Nova sees their alarm. Sees it and maybe understands it, but lucky for everyone, Thad chooses that moment to career around the side of the shack.

"Found him!" he cries.

The boy I assume is named Gage King is two steps behind. And I see that brow that sits so heavily on Thad's little face has a bright and beautiful future. Like tectonic plates, the King features have found the shape they were meant for on Gage's face. Sweat and dirt make tracks down from his temples. His loose jeans are distressed here and there and one wrist is wrapped in bands of leather. He wipes a hand down the front of his jeans then reaches out. I take his hand on instinct before realizing Nova was making introductions and he was reaching to shake Heath's hand. Not mine.

Shit.

"Candace," I say, rushing to cover. "Pickens."

His smile is less revealing than his tank. "Gage King. It's a pleasure."

I know I'm with a group of classy people when no one

points out my mistake and guys say things like *It's a pleasure*. I spend the rest of the intros convincing my cheeks that pink is a tacky color and nobody cares anyway. Least of all me. It was a dick move to reach for the only other boy's hand first anyway. I was closest. He's the one with cause for embarrassment.

It's not until Gage, Nova, and Thaddeus stand together that I see it: a boy, a girl, and a child.

I catch Sterling's eyes. She sees it, too. Now my cheeks are pink for an entirely different reason. I didn't see ghosts last night.

I saw these three Kings.

THE THREE OF US ARE strangely in sync as we extricate ourselves from the Kings and run to our cars at the end of the driveway. There's no question Sterling and Heath have already sacrificed their reunion on the altar of finding out what the hell is going on.

"Clary General?" I ask as the two of them swing around opposite sides of Heath's tragic green truck.

"We'll follow you," Heath confirms.

And with that, we're off.

If you want to get to the bottom of a mystery in Sticks, the place to start is always Clary General. It's also the place to avoid if you want to keep a secret. A fact I learned hard and fast from Red's brief tenure as a high school pot dealer. He'll be haunted by that poor choice until he himself is a ghost.

Sunday afternoons are always a popular time to hit Clary General for a quick cup of coffee and a bit of town gossip to start the week off right, but today the crowd is especially large. The rocking porch is crowded with kids younger than us sipping Cokes and licking rainbow-colored ice pops. They're all old enough to know something's up, but young enough not to care. The useful part of the crowd must be inside.

The three of us hop up the stairs and ease through the front door. Apart from a few folks standing nearby, no one notices the chime of the bell. They're all too busy chattering. We meander through, catching snippets of conversations as we pass. Mr. Tilly, a real scarecrow of a man, is fussing at Mr. Calhoun about "those money-grubbing Wawheeces" pushing aside lifelong customers for fresh deep pockets. Mrs. Gwaltney towers over a group of women near the back of the store, each of them shaking their heads in mirrored dismay.

We keep going until we've found a spot up by the counter where Old Lady Clary is conversing loudly with none other than Sterling's stepfather, Deputy Darold Gatwood.

"It's all perfectly legal, Ida, I promise you that," he's saying loudly enough for everyone to hear. "They went through all the proper channels. No one's rights are being trampled here."

"Easy for you to say, Gatty," she counters. "There's plenty this town wants to keep to itself. We don't need a television crew in here hunting down all our secrets."

Television crew? We came looking for information on the Kings, but it seems there's more going on than we bargained for.

Deputy Gatwood continues. "Everybody just needs to calm down a doggone minute. Yes, Mr. King is here to film his show, but no one will be filmed without giving their express and *legal* permission."

"He's already been in here asking questions." Mrs. Clary's voice rises, bringing other conversations to a hush. "He wants to know who knows what about our swamp. People like him have a way of getting what they're after, you mark my words. He'll take our quiet riches and leave us with nothing!"

At that the crowd stirs. Deputy Gatwood raises his hands and hollers, "Simmer down, now!" losing all the final consonants to his accent. "I've met the Kings and they are good people. They've as much right to be here as anybody, and they're doing a very fine job on that old river house. Do yourselves a favor and give them a chance."

That's all for the deputy. He nods ever so briefly in Sterling's direction and threads his way to the door. The second he's gone, the shop fills with chatter again. We hover just long enough to catch the fuller picture: Mr. King is the producer and star of a ghost-hunter show we've all seen called *Local Haunts* and he's here in town on account of hearing our swamp was full of ghosts.

There are conflicting stories about how he heard. Some say he has spies who sift through every ghost-inhabited corner the internet has to offer. Others say someone from town must have contacted him directly. And some say it doesn't matter because he's loaded and a rising tide lifts all ships.

Whatever the cause, the Kings are here to stay and Sticks is about to fall into an uncomfortable spotlight.

Sunday dinner calls all of us home earlier than we'd like. By the time I stepped through the door, the conversation was in full swing. Everyone's heard the news and our table is packed with extra chairs to speculate about the Kings. Nanny's here, of course. Leo and Red, having stopped by to return Dad's power washer, were invited to stay, which means Aunt Sarah also had to come. Uncle Jack was invited but failed to show up, and by the end of dinner Sarah confesses it's because he lost his teeth on Highway 15 somewhere between Sticks and New Orleans.

Now that his mom's spilled the beans, Red tells the story with tears in his eyes, about how he was on the phone with his dad when he started cussing up a storm and hung up. When Jack called back, he admitted to dropping his dentures—hard won by the age of forty—out the open window. He says he was shaking out a napkin to kill a spider on the dash, but Red's opinion is that he was littering and forgot his teeth were chilling in a crumpled napkin.

"How does the man survive?" Red asks, still laughing at his father's incompetence. "I swear, you gotta be some kind of special to lose your teeth on the highway."

"If anyone could do it, it's my brother, God bless him," Mom adds, having paused kitchen cleanup to hear the full tale.

"Keep that boy away from my teeth," Nanny says, shaking her head.

"You don't even want to know what happened the time the dog got ahold of them." Red's primed to tell us, though, belying his words with a devious grin.

Leo uses the group distraction to whisper in my ear, "You okay?"

I stare at him. He stares at me. He always looks a little vulnerable without his ball cap. I can see the faint depression of the band around his hair, forcing the ends to curl at his ears. And after a long minute he drops his gaze to the bandage on my hand.

"Oh," I say. "Um, yeah."

Truth be told, I haven't noticed the cut since he stitched it up Friday night. Which, now that he's looking at me with his brows knit together, I realize is weird.

"Can I see it?" he asks.

I lift the edge of my bandage and barely manage not to curse. Beneath the line of immaculate green stitches, my palm is 100 percent healed. There's a pale pink scar where there should be a gash still crusted with blood.

Leo grabs my elbow and tugs me in the direction of the back porch. I follow and when we're safely outside, he rips the Band-Aids from my skin and pulls out his pocketknife. I hold my hand steady as he chooses the scissors and begins snipping at his stitches. They slip out one at a time until all that remains are their tiny depressions on either side of the scar.

"What did you do to it?" he asks with a shake of his head. "Didn't we just put those in?"

"I'm as surprised as you are," I admit. "Maybe it wasn't as deep as we thought."

Leo drops my hand and folds his knife away. "No, it was deep."

I blame the swamp. I don't know how or why, but I do. Maybe eating that blossom did do something, just not the something we expected it to. Whatever it was, the most likely source of superhuman healing in Sticks, Louisiana, is the swamp. But I can't say that to Leo. Not out loud.

"Well, I've always said my genes were superior. Now you have proof."

He drapes an arm around my shoulders, turning us toward the house again. And just before we move through the door, he mumbles, "I've never needed proof."

I prod him in the ribs for daring to be so sweet. "You'll rot your teeth with that sugar," I warn as the feeling of being loved squeezes my heart like it's a lemon.

We return to the dining room in time to catch the result of some appetite-killing story Red has told. There's not a single straight face around the table and Red's looking mighty pleased with himself. At the sight of us, he lights up, ready to go at it again, but a knock on the front door saves us from a detailed retelling. Mom goes to answer, returning with a guest in tow.

"Everyone, look who stopped by." Mom's heels on the hardwood *tick-tick-tick* like a bomb. "This is Mr. Roosevelt King; his family's just moved into the old Lillard House by the river," she says as if we weren't discussing him all through dinner.

"Good evening," he says with a modest nod of his head. "I don't mean to interrupt your supper."

"Oh, you haven't," Mom assures him. "We're done. Just visiting now. Can I offer you a cup of coffee? It's decaf."

"That's very kind, but I won't take up too much of your time. I just wanted to come around and introduce myself personally. I know how quick rumors can travel and I wanted to make sure you knew who I was in case you have any questions."

The man, this Mr. King, wields a lasso of a smile beneath a spotless white cowboy hat. He's neatly dressed in slacks and a blazer, and while his features are more rugged than his son's, it's in a way that makes him middle-aged handsome.

It seems too obvious to me that all of this is designed to keep us calm and agreeable, but I know better than to trust a man who wears a hat indoors. At night.

"Well, we're glad you've stopped by." Mom's voice is intentionally cheerful as she introduces us one by one.

Mr. King moves gracefully between us, offering everyone firm smiles and handshakes. When it's my turn, I make sure my smile is polite-reserved instead of friendly.

"Miss Candace," he says, "I understand you've met my children already—Gage, Nova, and Thaddeus quite enjoyed your visit."

"Really? Well, that's wonderful." Mom's smile says she can't believe I failed to share this bit of news. "Candace goes out of her way to make people feel welcome."

Red snorts. I can't blame him. I go out of my way for friends and roadkill and not much else.

Mr. King continues as if he didn't hear. "It's a wonderful thing. Moving can be tough on the kids and I'm grateful for people like Candace."

Mom's hand falls on my shoulder with an approving squeeze. It's more contact than we've shared in days. How is it possible that this man, this complete and total stranger, has walked into my house and inspired my mom to love me again? I'm so intensely resentful I have to look away or risk eating his face.

But no one notices because Mr. King has more to bestow on his loving public.

From the inside pocket of his blazer, he produces three black envelopes, passing one to Mom, one to Aunt Sarah, and one to Nanny. "One final thing and then I promise I'll be out of your hair. My son's eighteenth birthday is coming up, and as a way of saying thank you to all the good people of Sticks, we'd like to invite you to join us for a celebration and see all we've done to restore the old Lillard House. My only regret is that I'm giving you such short notice. The gala will be this coming Friday night."

"Oh!" My mother sounds dazzled. "That *is* soon, but of course we'd love to come."

"All I ask is that you come ready to dance and eat your share of birthday cake. I'm afraid the one I've ordered will be quite large and if you don't help us reduce its size considerably by the end of the night, I'll have to charge it rent."

My parents eat it up. Nanny eats it up. The cousins eat it up. If the invitations were edible, they'd eat them, too. Their words of thanks and awe blur together after a while.

I tug the invitation from Mom's hand and slip my finger beneath the flap, easily popping it open. The interior of the envelope is lined in shiny gold foil, and just like the envelope, the card inside it is black and heavy. Pulling it out, I find curly white font that reads:

*Mr. and Mrs. Roosevelt and Ruth King*
*Request the honor of your presence*
*At the eighteenth birthday celebration*
*In honor of their son*
*GAGE ROOSEVELT KING*

The sight of Gage's name pulls him to mind: standing dirt-streaked and gallant as he shook my hand. I wouldn't mind seeing him again and I certainly wouldn't mind dancing with him.

The rest of the invitation includes the address and date all spelled out as though using numbers is déclassé. The very last line on the card reads, "Formal Attire Requested." Anyone seeking to fulfill that request won't do it by shopping in Sticks, where our options are Kristy's Kountry Stitchin' or nothing.

There's definitely nothing in my closet that would satisfy this sort of request. No, this is going to require an out-of-Sticks trip if I want to do it right. And that'll be tricky with our preseason volleyball camp starting up tomorrow. But a gala held at an old plantation house? Even I can admit it sounds romantic, and I'd look damn good in a corseted dress with a sweeping, layered skirt.

Red clears his throat dramatically and I look up to find all eyes on me.

"What?"

"Possum, didn't you hear Mr. King's offer?" Dad has no sense of when pet names are and aren't appropriate. He stands at Mom's back, towering even above Mr. King.

"Nope," I say. "Wasn't listening."

Mom sighs, but Mr. King is once again smooth.

"I was telling your parents that I'd like to shoot an episode focused on the stories all the local kids tell about the swamp. I hear that you're the girl to see about that and I was hoping you'd consent to sitting down with me sometime. Informally, if you prefer."

The promise of fame has Mom's face all lit up. She's already planning my walk down the red carpet. Looking at me with renewed interest because of Mr. King.

It infuriates me.

"Sorry," I say, pointedly not looking at my mother. "Not interested."

Mom protests, but Mr. King's smile is practiced.

He says, "Fair enough. I can see you're determined and far be it from me to force anyone into show business if they don't want it."

With that, he begins to say his good-byes. I hear the cousins thank him more than necessary and tune in long enough to learn he's offered them jobs on the film crew. Everyone smiles. Thoroughly, thoroughly charmed. And I guess maybe I have been, too, because I can't stop imagining what it will be like to dance around those tall, white columns in a gown that swirls around my feet like a river.

THERE ARE THREE THINGS WE leave Sticks to buy: cars, clothes, and contraceptives. The upcoming gala requires at least one of those.

It's been two days since Mr. King made his missionary tour of Sticks and stirred the town into a frenzy. Since Sunday night, I've heard more talk about *Local Haunts* the show than local haunts the problem. Between daily stops at Clary General, the usual stream of gossip I enjoy on my phone, and my own research, I can say that the show is to be called *Local Haunts: Shining in the Bayou*, that Mr. King's wife has yet to be seen by anyone, and that the town is ready to serve up all our stories on a silver platter.

The only ghost sighting I've heard of since his arrival happened at the end of day two of our preseason volleyball training. I was just leaving the locker room when all of a sudden Kelly Thames started shrieking that there was a crying girl in one of the shower stalls. Though it couldn't have been a full minute from when I heard her scream to when I arrived at the shower, I saw nothing. And based on what Sterling reported about Kelly and Hallie fabricating a ghost story, it's just as likely this was a fabrication, too.

This is just the kind of drama the scent of fame inspires.

Wednesday after volleyball, Sterling, Abigail, and I drive south to New Orleans to shop. It's a long trip—a necessary one if we don't want to end up in the same dress as three other girls—and we had to promise hourly check-ins to all three of our mothers to avoid a chaperone. Even then we were allowed to go only because Sterling's brother, Phin, goes to Tulane and is close enough to be male in case of emergencies. But the true testament to how excited our mothers are lies in the credit cards we each carry in our wallets.

This dance is serious Sticks business.

I drive because unlike Sterling, I have a car, and unlike Abigail, I don't have to share it with a twin sister. This part of Louisiana is all long rows of pines with pockets of swamp and small towns and plenty of underworked cops looking to make a buck. I set my cruise control at the limit because

I like my driving record spotless.

"Do you want to know what I found out about the Kings?" I ask when yet another radio station crashes into static.

"How is there possibly something you haven't told us yet?" Sterling leans up from the backseat.

"Are you not buckled in?" Abigail snaps. "Sterling Saucier, don't make me come back there."

"I only found it last night on some ghost-hunter forum," I continue.

"How do you even know how to look for this stuff?" Sterling asks, clicking herself into the center seat belt.

"She's part bloodhound," Abigail explains, which is close enough to the truth. I've always been good at tracking down stories.

"According to this site, Mr. King got into ghosts because of a near-death experience he had as a kid. He was driving home from visiting his grandparents with his dad. It was late and they were near some marsh in Washington State when it started to rain. They were taking a back road and were in the middle of nowhere when Grand Mr. King swerved off the road and drove straight into the water. Somehow, Little Mr. King got free, but his dad drowned."

"Oh my God." Sterling shrinks in my rearview mirror. "That's horrible."

"It is, but this is where the story gets crazy. He was, like, nine years old or something and all alone in the middle of a rainstorm, swimming through the bog. But he didn't give up. He swam to shore, followed the road until he saw lights in the woods, and headed for them."

"I don't want to hear this," says Abigail. "This isn't going anywhere good."

I ignore her because she definitely wants to hear this, she just doesn't know it yet. "Little Mr. King struggled through the forest toward the lights, which turned out to be a little cabin. What choice did he have? He knocked on the door and a beautiful woman answered. 'Oh my!' she cried. 'What's a little boy like you doing in a storm like this? Come in, come in.' And she swept him into her house and warmed him by the fire."

Abigail's eyebrows keep climbing and Sterling's shoulders have rolled in on themselves. But they're still listening.

"Well, Little Mr. King told her what had happened to him and his papa, and she soothed his little tears and told him that the storm had knocked the power out, but she'd call the police first thing in the morning. Poor Little Mr. King cried until she sang him to sleep, and he slept all through the rest of that terrible storm.

"He woke the next morning to the birds chirping and the sun on his face and in the full light of day, he could see that the roof that sheltered him all night was full of holes and animal nests. There was no sign of the fire that warmed his skin or the woman who sang him to sleep. He made his way to the road where the police were searching for him high and low.

"The amazing thing is, the sheriff said that Grand Mr. King's car was so far submerged in the bog that they never would've thought to look for Little Mr. King if they hadn't received a call from a woman who refused to leave her name. She told them exactly where to look." The look of gentle horror on their faces gives me a grin. "Supposedly, the house is still there and the police report corroborates everything."

"No wonder he hunts ghosts," Sterling says, exhaling heavily. "I just wish he didn't have to do it in the Lillard House."

"I wish he didn't have to do it in Sticks," I add, but Sterling shrugs.

"If you ask me, it's about time we started talking openly about the swamp. Nothing good comes from pretending it isn't unusual."

"Nothing good comes from *reality TV*," I all but spit.

"At least he's asking questions," she counters.

Sometimes, I think Sterling is tragically simple. She thinks people are what they seem and that exposing the truth is uniformly better than hiding it. But sometimes the truth is a secret because it's personal and no one's business but your own.

"Just because he's asking questions doesn't mean we have to answer them," I say.

"Someone should." Sterling keeps her voice light, her eyes averted in her version of determination. Which looks a lot like avoidance to me.

"Nothing good comes from giving another person power over you," Abigail says. "Trust me."

Traffic thickens as we approach the city and I hush everyone so I can concentrate on not killing us. It's an eternity before Abigail announces the exit I want and I steer us off the interstate to the rougher roads below.

Almost immediately I regret wishing away the rushing chaos of the interstate. The roads of the city are tight, twisting things that branch off in unexpected directions, crossing traffic that doesn't look friendly, depositing you onto even smaller one-way roads with unreliable street signs. By the time we find a metered parking lot, I'm sweating and my heart is racing.

"Good job," Abigail says with an encouraging pat-pat-pat on my shoulder.

"I have no idea where we are," I return, looking around at the brightly colored buildings. It's not my first time in the city, but somehow the rows of fuchsia, lime, coral, and gold—colors that should not look as good pressed together as they do—look strange and new.

"Magazine Street," Sterling says cheerfully as though I

haven't just been through an ordeal. "Or, off of it, actually. It's right there."

We step onto the blistering pavement and head in the direction Sterling points. I take a deep breath of air that's coated in grease, sugar, and something decidedly not sweet.

"What is that smell?" Abigail asks before I've recovered.

Sterling takes a deep breath. Having been in these parts of the city twice in as many months, she's our resident expert. "That's the city," she says. "Three parts grease, two parts Hurricane slushy, with a splash of piss."

I take another breath. The second taste isn't so bad, and by the third breath it's very nearly pleasant. "Better than the swamp."

"Okay," Sterling says, studying her phone. "The shop we want should be just down this way. Also, I was wondering if, uh, well . . ." She pauses abruptly, looking between me and Abigail as if she expects us to read her mind.

"We're actually aging before your eyes," I say, impatient.

Sterling frowns but carries on. "I was wondering if we could stop at a drugstore before we go home."

"Sure? Why are you being weird?"

"It's just in case. I mean, I want to be prepared in case Heath and I . . ." She raises her eyebrows.

"Oh! Right. Yes. Of course. Obviously." I might've kept going except Abigail gives me a shove.

"Thanks. I just can't imagine buying anything like that

from Old Lady Clary or the gas station."

"Nor should you," Abigail says, genuinely shocked. "The things they carry are so old, you might as well make your own."

We laugh both from horror and hysteria.

The shop on Sterling's map turns out to be a two-tiered creaking building with several cats and an attendant with makeup that doesn't look real. She can't be much older than us, but she welcomes us with a sort of disinterest that makes her seem out of our league. Or maybe it's that we're out of hers. Far, far below her league. But I'm not intimidated. I give her a cool smile of my own and breeze past racks of airy pastel tops and skirts to the second floor as if I know where I'm going. I don't, but since I didn't spot a single dress on the ground floor, the only way to go is up.

The top floor opens like a little ballroom. The ceiling is strung with paper lanterns and Mardi Gras beads. Mirrors line one entire wall, reflecting rows of gowns all gleaming like jewels in the sunlight. Silk, satin, chiffon, and more fabrics I'm not cultured enough to name. This place smells expensive.

We stop in a clump at the top of the stairs. Unmoving, but moved nonetheless by the scene before us.

"I don't think I can pick," says Sterling.

"I wish I didn't have to pick," says Abigail.

"We're going to have to pick for each other," I say.

And that's exactly how it goes. For Abigail, Sterling and I find dresses that look like the sun—in shades of daffodil and amber and smoke. For Sterling, we go for the drama of jewel tones—indigo and ruby and plum. And for me, they pick the aggressive colors of spring—peach and lilac and moss green. We know one another better than we know ourselves because even as I turn my nose up at the sight of a peach-colored gown, I see how perfectly it complements my skin.

It works to our advantage that we have no time to agonize over our choices. Sterling goes for the indigo, Abigail for the amber, and I pick the moss. Together, we'll be balanced and beautiful.

We spend what remains of Wednesday shopping hours tromping up and down Magazine Street, dodging tourists and street merchants, gasping or vomiting at price tags, and, finally, purchasing the rest of what we need: accessories, shoes, and new underthings.

Our final stop is the drugstore. We choose the huge one on Canal Street even though it requires a short drive deeper into the city. Size, in this case, matters because the larger the store, the less anyone will care about three seventeen-year-olds perusing the contraceptives.

Canal Street takes us temporarily away from the press of multicolored houses and storefronts to a wide street separated by trolley tracks and two rows of towering, corporate buildings. Here, the crowd is different from the lazy tide of Magazine Street. Here, the people look bored and alive and hungry in a way that manages to be enticing. I decide this city is an intoxicating wilderness and I must have it one day.

I press myself into Abigail's side, gripping her hand in my own. "Look at this place! Isn't it amazing? I can't wait to leave Sticks for a place like this."

She leans into me. "It's all right."

"All right? Beale, this place is freedom personified! You can't tell me you wouldn't love it here."

"Maybe," she answers thoughtfully. "But I don't know if I want to leave home."

That stops me in my tracks. She stops a step ahead of me and turns. Sterling stops ahead of both of us, the neon lights of the drugstore flashing around us like rain.

"But you have to leave," I say. "How will you ever be yourself, the real Abigail Beale, in Sticks?"

She frowns at me like I'm stupid. "I *am* the real Abigail Beale."

"No, you're not."

At that, her shoulders pull back and she folds her arms across her chest. "What are you getting at, Candace Pickens?"

"Really? I'm getting at you're gay, Beale. You like the ladies and you're terrified to say it at home."

Sterling steps to Abigail's side looking around nervously. But the city doesn't care if we have this discussion because the city doesn't care if Abigail's gay: her parents do.

"You don't know what I'm afraid of," Abigail answers.

I can't believe what I'm hearing. Abigail should want to leave our town just as much if not more than I do, and here she is saying she might not leave at all?

"Y'all, not to derail this touching conversation, but I'm a little afraid of getting home late, so can we save this for the drive?" Sterling tugs on each of our arms, a literal return to reality.

We have to skirt past a woman dressed like a Las Vegas showgirl and a man performing both sides of Romeo and Juliet's balcony scene to get inside the drugstore.

I can't believe Abigail doesn't see this place and dream of a different, freer life. I can't believe she doesn't feel the same stubborn pull I do and hate the thought of spending two more years in a town no one can place on a map. She's either lying to me or herself, and I think I know which it is.

The drugstore is probably as big as our high school with high ceilings dripping fluorescent lights and yet more Mardi Gras beads. The place is hopping for seven p.m. on a Wednesday and it takes us a solid five minutes to find what we're after, sandwiched thematically between "Women's Hygiene" and "Diapers & Baby Formula."

"Okay, Sterling, the world is your oyster," I say, stopping in front of a wall of condoms.

Sterling is a special shade of pink. On the spectrum, it probably falls somewhere between "I didn't know he was my cousin when I kissed him" and "1985 fashion." She blinks rapidly, eyes skating away from the display to make sure no one's watching us.

"What kind are you getting?" she asks me.

"I—" I stop. I was going to say, *I don't need them.* Which is sort of true and sort of not. "I wasn't going to get any," I finish.

Abigail meets my eyes and doesn't look away. Confirming, sympathizing, but not revealing. Guilt pinches my thoughtless heart.

"What?" Sterling's hand flies to her chest. "There's that party this Friday! School is starting! There's no way you aren't making plans for this year, and who knows when we'll have this chance again!"

She's right of course, but something inside me shrinks and slides down the wall of that deep well. I wasn't expecting to confront my limitations in a drugstore of all places. But standing here before a wall of condoms, I see how even these rules are different when applied to me: I'll only ever need them to prevent STDs, not pregnancy.

Sterling misreads my hesitation. "You have to get some. I can't buy these things by myself!"

"These things?" I ask, climbing out of my stupor. "If you can't say the word, Saucier, you can't have them."

"For Pete's sake, Candy, of course I can say it: *condom*." She says that last at a whisper. "I just don't want to be the only one buying them."

Again, I hesitate.

Abigail snatches a pack from the wall. "C'mon, I'll buy them."

With a pointed look at Sterling, I say, "Really? The one of us who needs them least of all is going to buy them?"

Sterling stares at the package in Abigail's hand, clearly searching her guts for the courage she grew this summer. "Oh God, okay, fine," she says at last, retrieving the box.

"Good girl," I say, reaching for my own box.

On our way to the counter, Sterling stops for a bottle of Coke, a pack of gum, and a notebook covered in superheroes. She places it all on the counter in front of a cashier old enough to be our mom with the condoms on the very bottom, as if that will make this moment any less awkward. Luckily, we are far from the most outrageous thing this woman has seen today, maybe in the last hour, and all she does is smile approvingly.

When we're done and back in the car for the return trip home, Sterling says, "Abigail, I thought you hated bananas."

That's when I notice that in addition to a Coke and bag of chips, Abigail did indeed purchase a banana.

"I do," she confirms, "but I figured if you were that twisted up about buying condoms, you probably oughta practice putting one on before it comes time for the real thing."

For just a moment, we sit in silence. Then we shriek and laugh and collectively learn how to dress a banana.

ON THURSDAY, STORMS DESTROY THE sky. The rains are unrelenting and for a moment, there is a rumor—started by unreliable Rena, a sophomore with a flair for overreaching—that the King extravaganza would be canceled. But Friday morning, the sky clears and the humidity relaxes, leaving us with a much cooler summer day.

It's our last day of preseason volleyball training and Coach squeezes us for all we're worth. We start off by jogging a soggy mile around the football field, then it's up and down the bleachers until our thighs burn like coals, and then practice truly begins.

Sterling, Abigail, and I hold our own against the seniors,

and it feels like we've been working toward this kind of choreographed ruthlessness for years. No matter what comes over the net, I'm there to dig and pass neatly to Sterling, who sets up beautiful hits for Abigail. It doesn't matter that we're exhausted by the end; it feels like we could take on an army.

Coach lets us out a full thirty minutes early to do whatever it is people do to prepare for wearing more money than is decent. How people could need more than thirty minutes to comb their hair and pull on a dress is so far beyond me it may as well be in Florida. I shower, shave my legs, and blow my hair into obedience. In all of ten minutes I do my standard formal dance makeup, then slide into the new silvery-green gown.

When I'm done, I face the full-length mirror in my bedroom and I have to admit, I'm a sight to be seen. My hair looks soft and bright, its blond strands set off by my tan and the moss-green damask of the dress. The gown brushes the floor but won't when I've strapped into my heels.

Dad comes to the door, looking smart in a three-piece suit and holding a red velvet box. He stops before opening it, eyes softening like butter.

"Oh, Possum, you look beautiful." His voice clouds and he clears his throat. "I mean, you *are* beautiful."

Engineers are notoriously bad with verbal expression and Dad's no exception, but at this an uncontrollable smile squishes up my face. "Thanks, Daddy."

"Ah, I thought you might like to wear these." He snaps the box open, revealing a string of tiny, misshapen pearls, every one of them silver as the ocean. "They were your gram's, and I think she'd want you to wear them tonight."

He latches them around my neck, then offers his arm and together we walk to the kitchen, where Mom waits in a conservative burgundy gown with enough sparkling opals dangling from her ears to do Nanny Craven proud.

The sun's a rainbow sherbet puddle on the horizon when we leave. We take Mom's SUV and join the line of cars streaming down the side road toward the Kings'. If there's one thing Sticks has in abundance, it's cars, and all the finest are out tonight. It takes ages to reach the river, then another year before we drive beneath the oaks.

Mom gasps. Dad's foot falters on the gas, and I lean between their seats to get a better view.

What I see is a house that's been transported from the lustrous, romanticized past and planted right here in Sticks.

The oak canopy has been tinseled with tiny lights and shimmering silver. The whole thing looks like a glittering night sky. Along either side of the drive are posts with hanging lanterns marking where we're meant to park. And running up and down the drive between parking cars and the house are two horse-drawn carriages. The house glows, white and grand, at the end of the tunnel.

"Oh my," Mom says. That doesn't even begin to cover it, but all the words I'd choose to share are too dirty for my dress.

"Ladies." Dad offers an arm to each of us and we walk on the freshly graveled ground to where people wait for the carriages.

An elderly white man with a glowing white coat, black pants, and gold cummerbund holds the reins of a jet-black stallion. I don't know which to look at first—the horse, the carriage, or the man who offers a gloved hand to Mrs. Gwaltney as she steps into the carriage. It's all I can do to make certain my mouth isn't a flytrap.

"Pet 'im, if you like, miss," a young black man calls from the driver's seat. He wears a top hat, a black coat with long tails, and a very warm smile. "He don't bite. Much."

Laughter breaks the tension building between my shoulder blades. "Same here," I say, resting my fingers on the horse's whiskery muzzle.

The driver gives a hearty chuckle, then checks to see that his carriage is full. I step back, and he snaps the reins over the horse's back. The carriage is surprisingly dexterous, making a tight turn before trundling toward the house. I've heard of these troops before. Groups of men and women who'll come add some vague historical flavor to any gala—within reason, of course. They have horses and carriages and costumes, and they don't come cheap.

It's our turn next. The footman assists Mom first, then me, but leaves Dad to balance on his own. I'd be nice and ticked about that if my gown didn't demand I use one of my hands for its flowing skirt. We've barely settled into the red leather seats of the carriage before we're *clomp-clomp-clomp*ing down the lane. Behind us, cars continue their slow stream into the lantern-lit parking spaces. I can just make out the river beyond, reaching for moonlight.

"Mom, Dad," I say, leaning back to watch the lights pass, "*this* is how you throw a birthday party. I hope you're taking notes."

Dad laughs, but Mom's response is a little more serious. She says, "Well, get moving on that celebrity career. All it takes is one moment on camera to be discovered."

I can't believe she's still upset I won't give President King an interview. Except that I can. "Never. Mind," I say.

We pull up to the house and are assisted to the ground by another white-frocked footman. Gold banners wrap the newly restored white columns, top to bottom, pooling elegantly around the base. The door is attended by yet another footman, who raps once sharply as we approach. It swings open to gowns and suits and laughter. Nearest the door, Mr. King stands with his eldest child at his elbow. He looks Kingly, indeed, with his auburn-and-ice hair slicked back from his temples and a gracious smile at his mouth. He's giving out more than a double-handed handshake, that's for sure.

Beside him, Gage echoes his father's smile gloriously. He's at ease in this stately atmosphere, all charm and open arms.

As I get closer, I see Gage's suit is anything but typical. Three pieces and black, and the vest is pale yellow with gold embroidery around the edges. Long jacket tails fall to the backs of his knees, and peeking out from beneath his sleeve I spot a red leather band. He may wear his suit well, but here is a hint of rebellion in the little prince.

Looking up, I find he's caught me staring. I drop the smirk from my lips, but not before he's mirrored the look. Between this and our first meeting, he's going to think I'm always this awkward.

Mr. King greets my parents like old friends, patting my mom's hand and my dad's shoulder. He turns to me last, offering his hand.

"Good evening, Mr. King," I say.

"Please, call me Roz," he returns, looking from me to my parents. "I insist. 'Mr. King' makes me feel like we're negotiating contracts."

I wish I could roll my eyes at how he simultaneously lowered himself to our level while reminding us he's a big shot who has to think about contracts.

"The house is a marvel," my dad says, eyes roving the foyer with admiration.

"All credit for this renovation goes to Mr. Wawheece

here," Mr. King says, gesturing to the man standing on the other side of Gage. "He and his crew have worked 'round the clock to transform this house, and I swear the craftsmanship is some of the finest I've seen."

The last thing I expected to find here was the sight of Mr. Wawheece in a suit, which is probably why I failed to recognize him immediately. He stands with his hands folded before him, his bulbous nose red from years in the sun, beaming in the light of Mr. King's affections.

And beside him is none other than his own son, Riley Wawheece, who picks at the sleeves of his suit like they're scabs.

The men are quickly falling into an endless circle of compliments, and Riley's gaze has fallen on me like a wet blanket, which means it's time to go. I move toward the crowd of perfume and puffed chests, but a hand catches my arm. I turn to see a hint of pink in Gage's cheeks, which he hurries to cover by bowing over my hand to say, "Thank you for coming."

It's so utterly unlike anything a boy's ever said to me that I can think of nothing to say in return except, "You're welcome."

But he's not finished. "I hope you'll save me a dance."

"It's not like they have a shelf life," I say, defensive and not entirely rational, but the crowd around us—the one that includes Mr. King, Mr. Wawheece, Riley, and my parents witnessing this awkward exchange—bursts into laughter.

Gage's fingers tighten on mine before he refreshes his smile and says, "Can I take that as a yes?"

"Yes," I say.

His thumb brushes my knuckles briefly before our hands fall apart like petals. He and his father turn their dazzling smiles on the next guests to enter and the charm repeats itself with amusement-park precision.

With my parents close behind, we make our way through the hallway to the back of the house. All the doors and windows have been flung open. People stand inside and out, mingling on the deck before an outdoor ballroom of sorts. Instead of using the rooms of the house, the Kings have covered a portion of the backyard with hardwood flooring, and surrounded the area with hanging lanterns and more sparkling lights.

It's with more than a small amount of relief that I spot Abigail standing in her layers of amber chiffon. With her dark brown skin and coils of smooth braids wrapped impossibly around her head, she looks like she should be surrounded by flocks of adoring fans. Beside her stands Valerie, her twin sister in structure alone. Everything about Valor is sharp. Her short hair, her short fuse, and—I'd bet—her teeth. Tonight's no exception. She's swathed in red that cuts in at the waist and dips low in the back. Though she's ten times the rebel Abigail is, she gets away with more for walking a suitable life path. It's not my business, but if I had a sister and she didn't stand up for me, I think I'd steal her allowance, buy a stuffed bear, and call it sis. At least then I could hug it without feeling shitty.

They greet me with smiles and we do the obligatory trading of compliments, engaging in small talk until some of Valor's friends arrive. The crowd slowly but steadily grows around us. Waiters pass by with silver trays loaded with flutes of sparkling champagne or appetizers so detailed they must've required an architect to build. By the dance floor, a traditional brass band sits on a raised platform, warming up. Pretty soon, I'm sure every single person I've ever seen in my life has passed before me.

I don't know how I feel about the Kings having every resident of Sticks here to ogle their home. And I don't know how I feel about the fact that all of Sticks can fit in their backyard.

"I didn't know we had so many people in town," Abigail muses, looking over the crowd as only she can.

"We're full of surprises," I say drily. "There's our gleaming couple."

Sterling and Heath, she in stunning blue and he in very traditional black, make their way toward us. In spite of both sets of parents being somewhere in the crowd, they let their hands swing between them. Joined with white-fingered desperation.

Sterling answers my unspoken question. "We're taking a stand," she says with a proud glance at Heath. "Mostly he is."

Heath ducks his head, the picture of modesty. "What're they gonna do to me in public?"

"Damn straight," I say. And then specifically for Abigail, I add, "It's always best when things are out in the open."

Abigail is unruffled. She ignores me, but I see her eyes slide across the crowd until they find Shannon Ryals, whom she's eye-stalked since last year. Shannon's as dressed up as punk rock gets: short-skirted black dress with classy fishnets and tall boots, dark eye makeup and strawberry blond hair styled in a doughnut bun. She's a very specific flavor of sex on a stick.

Their eyes meet and it's a terrible thing to watch— Shannon's kohl-rimmed eyes brightening with hope, Abigail's shoulders collapsing with defeat. I can already see how this will end.

The sad thing is I think Abigail can, too.

We mill with the rest of town, admiring all the very fine work the Kings have done to restore the landmark so dear to so few people. We try the artful hors d'oeuvres, spot Nova making the rounds with little Thad at her side, and generally wonder why we're all dressed up, until finally a bell calls our attention to the dance floor. Mr. King stands with Gage at his side, one arm draped across his son's shoulders. When everyone has gathered on the deck, on the steps, and in a semicircle around the floor, Mr. King steps away from his son and begins.

"First, please let me say it warms my heart to see all the fine people of Sticks here tonight. I regret that due to illness my wife couldn't join us, but she sends her gratitude as well. We are so very pleased to be here, among such generous people. I've traveled a lot in my years, and there's no doubt in my mind, the South is the most welcoming place on the planet."

Applause. People do love pandering statements about the South. The only good thing about the applause is the noise covers my snort.

He continues in this way, telling us all how good we are to have taken in his family and how much it means to him to be filming in a place like Sticks. Once he has the good will of nearly every person here, he mentions that the film crew will be here tonight filming and, yes, interviewing. At that, the crowd titters excitedly. And I have to admit, it's brilliant. Giving anyone who wants it a chance at five seconds of fame, and spotlighting the town in its only glorious moment since President Jefferson Davis of the Confederacy passed nearby and didn't stop. Finally, Mr. King reminds us why we're all here. Beaming, he turns to Gage and claps him on the back.

"But tonight is really about my eldest son, Gage." He pauses for applause. "It isn't every day your oldest turns eighteen. Gage, I remember when you were just a small boy, holding your baby sister in your arms like she was more precious to you than your own life. I asked you, 'Gage, what do you think of her?' And do you remember what you said to me? You said, 'How is she real?'" He pauses and this time the whole world of this backyard is silent as stone. "I've felt that way since the day you were born. It's an amazing thing, watching your children grow up, becoming more and more real every day. You amaze me, and I'm damn proud to call you son."

The silence shudders into more applause, and Mr. King folds Gage into a hug, one arm holding his head like a baby's. It's touching. I can't deny it's touching to see Gage close his eyes and listen to whatever private words his father whispers. Not to mention intrusive. Looking around, I see misty eyes and quivering smiles on every adult face.

Only Abigail seems to share my sense of intrusion. She's looking at the sky, willing her eyes to remain as dry as stone.

I take her hand. Without shifting her gaze, she threads her fingers through mine and closes her eyes.

The dancing starts a moment later. Gage and Nova take center stage and show us how it's done. They cut a pretty picture as they move together—Gage in sleek black with gold trim, and Nova in the reverse, a gold damask gown with dark shadows beneath the filigree pattern. Mr. King pulls Old Lady Clary—dressed in all the colors of the peacock—to the floor. She's the picture of delight, drinking up every minute of Mr. King's attention. More couples follow. I give Abigail's hand a tug and she lets me drag her into a dance neither of us knows how to do. It doesn't matter. We choose the steps we do know, two-stepping and spinning and waltzing until we're both laughing too hard to continue.

Abigail abruptly stops and spins me around. Gage has come to claim his dance and stands there with one arm behind his back. Then, just as he did at the door, he bows and offers his hand. I can't stop the sudden rush of blood to my ears. I don't think I imagine the abrupt rash of whispers that surrounds us as the crowd shares my internal reaction. For just a moment, all eyes are on me, wondering how I managed the first nonfamily dance with Gage, and admiring that I have. I only hope my hand isn't sweating when I place my fingers on his.

The band carries us across the floor with some old-timey jazz number. Gage settles one hand on my waist, keeps the other in my hand, and somehow we become highly competent waltzers. I'm gratified to find my feet know more than I'd given them credit for. So is Gage, I suspect.

"I don't really know what I'm doing," I admit.

"You know more than you think," he says.

I rarely have occasion to dance, but he's right. I'm guided

by the music and the gentle pressure of his hands, and soon my nerves relax. He lifts one arm and spins me in a tight circle. Dancers blur against the black sky.

I have a sudden need to fill the silence, so I say, "My dad used to dance with me when I was little. We danced our kitchen floor into submission."

"Mine, too."

I laugh. "Oh my Lord, you're not joking."

Gage shakes his head proudly. "A lot of times, Dad was all we had, so he had to do everything. Even the dancing."

"I don't believe you."

"My hand to God, it's true." Gage is all grins at the memory and my very unladylike, bald-faced gaping.

He spins me again. This time he pulls me closer. My shoulder presses his and I see the small nick on his jawline he must've gotten while shaving not so long ago. His hand tightens at my waist and he fixes those dark eyes on mine.

If I were brave, I would kiss him here and now. That's what I want to do. He wants it, too, and why wouldn't he? But counting now, we've been in each other's presence for all of a few hours and therefore kissing is out of the question.

Instead, I tip my head and study the sky.

"There's Aquarius," I say.

"And Sagittarius," he adds, nodding to the opposite edge of the sky.

I snap my eyes back to his. "You know constellations."

I've never met another person in Sticks—outside of my mom and dad, who read the night sky like a book—who could name any constellation other than Orion.

"No matter where we went, they stayed the same." Gage lifts his eyes. "Pegasus."

"Delphinus," I counter. The game is on.

"Sagitta."

"That's almost cheating. Sagittarius and now his arrow?"

"Technically a separate constellation."

"Dirty pool."

He grins.

"Capricornus."

I see the skin tighten around his mouth. We're approaching the limits of his considerable knowledge. "Aquila," he says, less certain now.

"Cygnus," I answer, and I'm sure I've won.

There's a long pause. His eyes skim the sky for victory and I've started to smirk. Then there's a low laugh, and when he looks at me, I know I've lost. "Cepheus," he says.

"I've never even heard of that one. You made it up."

He laughs. "It's definitely real."

"Who or what is it, then?"

The song ends. Neither of us lets go.

"He was Andromeda's father, Cassiopeia's husband, and," he says, bringing my hand to his lips, "a king."

I can't even begrudge him the victory.

A new song begins and around us the dancers shift their steps to match. Gage steps back, once again bowing over my hand.

"Thank you for the dance, Candace Pickens."

I surprise myself by responding with a short curtsy. "My pleasure," I say, thinking this is the first time I've ever said those words and meant them.

I return to my girls without feeling the ground beneath my feet, and the night wears on with more dancing and uniquely crafted hors d'oeuvres. As promised, the cameras roll out on broad platforms, each manned by two eager attendants including my damned cousins. Leo and Red are far from inconspicuous in their all-black outfits, with headsets and clipboards. Red's all grins, Leo's all business. The second they turn a camera on me, I flip them off.

Seemingly out of nowhere, Nova joins us having scored several flutes of actual champagne, not the sparkling grape juice on hand for all the teens.

"Please, save me from more socializing," she says. "You are the only people here I feel like I know."

"Who are we to turn away a lady bearing gifts?" I answer for all of us.

We drink the champagne quickly, with the exception of Sterling, who sees only her abusive, now absent father in alcohol. Heath, though, surprises me by tossing one back faster than the rest of us.

The dancing halts when a very tall, very chocolate cake is wheeled onto the deck, melting with gold candles and icing. We sing a dramatically tuneless round of "Happy Birthday" before Gage lifts Thad to help him extinguish the candles. All in all, it's a pretty spectacular party. Mr. King has played this round well; the town is his for the taking.

While all attention's on the cake, Nova and I sneak into the house and steal a few more flutes from the kitchen. Once they're in our hands, everyone assumes they're juice. Handy that they're the same color. And maybe a little dumb on the Kings' part. It would've been smarter for them to use red juice for the minors, but I'm not about to look a gift horse in the mouth.

Cake acquired and demolished, Sterling and Heath return to the dance floor for a romantic experience, while Abigail, Nova, and I continue our efforts to become a roving speakeasy. It makes a good game and it's not very long at all before my head starts spinning in that gentle way and I forget all about the pain in my pinky toes from my heels.

"You know, I think I like you, Nova King," I confess.

"This night is turning out so much better than I thought it would," Nova says after successfully nabbing another glass from a waiter. "I was afraid it would be all awkward and dull, but this is just . . . not."

Abigail laughs and pulls the half-empty flute from Nova's fingers. "Let me help you with that."

"You've said that an awful lot tonight, Abigail." Nova grins but doesn't protest as Abigail assists her with her drink.

"Do you think we could ride those ponies again?" I ask, suddenly bored and done with the dance floor. "What do you think they're doing right now?"

"Candy, you are brilliant!" Nova sets off and we follow a dimly lit and newly constructed marble path to the front of the house.

There the two carriages stand side by side, unattended and empty. The horses stomp their feet and jingle their harnesses, clearly bored and in need of entertainment.

"How hard do you reckon it is to drive a horse?" Nova asks with mischief in her mouth.

I am not a reckless person. Chaos is the enemy I stand vigilant against. Yet in this moment I'm ready to do something perfectly senseless simply because the thought occurred to me, and I like the way it makes me feel.

Beyond the carriages, the oak tunnel shimmers invitingly. I think complacency must be its own kind of chaos.

"Won't know until we try," I say.

It's possible that if we weren't several flutes in and ornery, we wouldn't be climbing into the driver's seat of a horse and carriage. It's possible we'd have elected to leave our shoes on instead of tossing them to the floor of the carriage. It's even possible I'd think better than to shout "Giddy-up!" before snapping the reins over the horse's strong back.

Possible. But I'll never know how likely.

We lurch forward with such enthusiasm that Nova rolls backward into the carriage with a shriek. I mean to aim for the oak river of lights, but when I twist to see that Nova's okay, the carriage twists with me. Beside me, Abigail grumbles my name like a curse and tries to pull the reins from my hands.

"I've got it!" I insist, struggling with her for control as the horse drags us along around the house.

No. No, no, no, not around the house.

I pull hard to the left, but it's not soon enough. The whirling, twirling dancers come into view and all heads start to swivel.

Abigail notices, too, and together we tug the reins straight back. In slow motion, the horse drops to a walk before stopping altogether. Right next to the dance floor, where all of our parents wait with scowls of varying severity.

Except for Mr. King.

He strides across the grass and he's . . . laughing.

"Nova!" he cries so that everyone can hear. "When I told you to take the girls on a carriage ride, I meant with one of the coachmen!"

"Am I drunk?" I murmur to Abigail. In response, she reaches over to pinch my thigh. "Ouch! Shit. What?"

"That hurt?"

"Yes!"

"Then you're not lit up."

Mr. King is assisting his daughter down from the carriage. His smile is unwavering, but I think I detect a flash of tired irritation pass between them. Nova holds her shoes in one hand, her father's hand in the other, and manages to look appropriately chastised as she apologizes for the misunderstanding we didn't have.

The crowd moves from whispers to bemused laughter. Searching for my parents and Abigail's, I discover they're laughing, too. They bought Mr. King's blatant lie hook, line, and sinker.

That's when I realize I've found the first important piece of the puzzle that is Mr. King: the appearance of control is more important to him than immediate reprisal. I choose to ignore how familiar that feels and file it away for future reference.

Beneath me, the carriage inches forward as the horse dances uneasily. Time to get down. Gathering the fabric of my skirt in one hand, I study the drop. It would be easiest to sit on the not-totally-clean floor and scoot off. I can just imagine the dirt my butt will collect in the process, but jumping seems similarly unwise.

I press my eyes closed and take a deep breath. When I open them, there's little Thad peering up with his hands clasped behind his back.

"I would like to assist you, Miss Candy," he says, so serious beneath that brow I can't bear to correct him. "But I cannot reach you."

Before I can assure him that I don't hold his height against him, he throws up a hand and says, "Stay there!"

There's no telling what he's gone off to find, but I'm reasonably sure I shouldn't wait. From the other side of the carriage, Abigail's accepting Mr. King's hand. No time to waste. I spot the vicious-looking metal hook that coachmen must use to get up and down. It's only a foot or so beneath the floor. Skirts still in hand, I twist to descend the carriage as I would a ladder. My bare toes find the hook easily enough, but it's the next step that kills me. Too busy trying to save my skirts from dirt, I lose my balance and slip, but instead of hitting the ground in a graceless heap, I'm caught by strong arms.

"Oh Jesus H.," I say, realizing my skirt is hiked treacherously high at the moment.

The hands around my waist loosen enough that I can lower my skirt and turn around.

"Just Gage, if you don't mind," he quips with a quick grin.

He's so close I can feel his chest rise with his breath.

The horse whinnies and hops behind me. Again, Gage's hands grip my elbows. He pulls me away and I hear more than see why. Something has spooked the horse and it struggles in its harness.

"Thad!" Gage barks, calling the boy to our side.

When we're several feet away, I can finally get a good look at the scene. Though one of the coachmen has arrived and stands before the horse with reins in hand, the horse hops and rears in panic, backing away as it does. We can hear the calming voice of the coachman between the horse's distressed noises. It isn't doing much good. The horse is inconsolable.

On the other side, the crowd has started to move away as we did. Then someone shrieks and attention shifts to the dark hill at the edge of the dance floor. The one that slopes away toward the swamp. The one that, until a minute ago, was clear but for tall summer grasses rejuvenated by rain. Now the whole of the hill is covered by a thick, creeping fog that shifts quietly in the night.

Gage draws a sharp breath. His fingers tighten on my elbow, pushing me toward the house. Instead of following his pressure, I follow his eyes to a point in the fog that billows ahead of the rest.

It's difficult to see through the lights of the dance floor. Did something dart forward just there? Yes. The sounds of shock from the crowd confirm it.

I push at Gage's hands, keeping my eyes on that shifting spot where I know something to be.

Again, it shifts and—there!—a hand reaches through the fog to claw the earth. It's followed by another, then the shape of a face, pale and nearly indistinguishable from the mist around it.

The grass is cool beneath my feet. Wet from the rain. It squishes between my toes as I move.

The hands appear again as the figure crawls up the hill. Closer and closer. I don't take my eyes from its—her?—face. I don't dare lose this sight. My world is this moment. Me and the girl climbing the hill with muddy fingertips.

She pushes through the fog, crawling hand to foot to hand, with stringy hair swaying before her face and uneven patches shorn clean off. Her mouth moves and her eyes slide from side to side as though untethered. Her dress is tattered, torn completely away from the knees so she can crawl without catching on it.

I move closer, leave the light and the party behind until I can hear that she's speaking, or whispering clips or nonsense phrases that spin around and around each other in meaningless circles.

"Take a stone, take a flower, flower, flower, these will only last an hour." Her lips are cracked and she slurs her letters as though she's missing teeth. "But take a bone or take some strife, these will last for all my life."

"Hello?" I ask, crouching down a few feet away.

Her eyes snap to mine and widen. "Mary, Mary, Mary,"

she sings. "She's so mad, mad, mad, she's so very bad!"

The poem is familiar to me. I've read it hundreds of times, recited it hundreds of times, but hearing it like this, falling in and out of order from a troubled mind, it sends a shiver down my spine. I know this girl. I know her story and her name.

Suddenly, she stands and with hunger in her eyes, she rushes me.

Without thinking, I jump to my feet and hold up my hands. "Mad Mary Sweet!" I cry. "Stop!"

But, of course, she doesn't stop. Shrieking, she rushes straight into my hands. She's cold, so cold against my skin, but then she vanishes like fog.

For a moment, I can't move. All I can hear is the thrashing of my heart in my head. My hands pass a shiver through the rest of my body. Finally, I stutter into a deep breath and turn to face the house. And I see three things that shock me equally.

My town stunned into silence.

A smile the size of California on Mr. King's face.

And cameras pointing their soulless eyes directly at me.

# PART TWO

They say she was born 'neath a sad pale
   moon,
And her grandfather died as she gave her first
   croon.
They knew what that meant,
Her path it was bent,
By the power from which she'd been hewn.

I SAW A GHOST.

This time there's no denying it. I saw her, everyone saw her, and then they saw her vanish at my touch.

This isn't how I wanted things to go. I wanted to see ghosts, sure, but I wanted to see them the way the rest of the town does, privately or as part of some small group. I wanted to share in the spectacle so I'd stop feeling so ousted by it. Instead, *I* became the spectacle—the girl caught on tape talking to a ghost.

Shuttered away in my bedroom, having run away from the party, forcing my parents to follow and us all to come home, my disappointments mount faster than mating rabbits. My phone won't quit buzzing beneath a pile of dirty clothes, where I buried it the third time it lit up with a message about that ghost. I turn my stereo up and climb out of this ridiculous dress. The hem is a darker shade of green now than it was at the beginning of the night, stained with water and mud. Doesn't matter. I don't plan to wear it again. Cousins Carol and Irene can benefit from my current siblingless, future childless state.

For now, I'll trap it deep inside my closet. I don't want to think about tonight any longer than necessary.

Mom is determined to make that difficult. I've barely shed Gram's pearls when my door opens. Without invitation, Mom turns my music down.

"Dad's making hot chocolate," she says, tugging at an earring.

"I just want to go to bed."

She doesn't move but studies me as though considering an exercise in matriarchal agitation.

"Okay," she says after a long minute. "Get some sleep. We'll talk in the morning."

"Can't wait," I mutter as she pulls the door shut.

I turn my music up again and plant my face in a pillow. I'm tired of looking at things. For that matter, I'm tired of thinking about things. That voice—Mary's voice—repeats in my mind on an endless loop: *take a stone, take a flower, these will only last an hour* and on and on and on until her final words dominate everything, *She's mad, mad, mad.*

Now that I'm alone, my mind is pulling threads together, weaving a story I want no part of. *She's mad, mad, mad.* But sometimes stories catch you off guard. Sometimes, a story catches you the way a hunter snares its prey. And suddenly, things you thought you could ignore become the burning center of your world.

*She's mad, mad, mad.*

I thought I could ignore it. But no matter how I try to convince myself otherwise, the truth is I recognize the words and the voice. They've been in my head once before, the night I went to Leo and Red's for stitches.

*Shut up,* I think, stern as can be. *Shut up, shut up, shut up.*

I wish I could be like Abigail and let music obliterate my mind until I'm asleep. But even focusing on sound, my thoughts are weedy. Instead of fading, they blend with the song. My panic over having banished a ghost in front of my entire town, my girlish and aimless concern about Gage's reaction. Beneath it all, the deep, thudding drumbeat of Mad Mary's song, and the dread of having seen a ghost . . .

And that she saw me.

She looked right at me. In all the stories I've heard so far, that's never happened. The ghosts are ambivalent creatures, unaware that there's a flesh–and–bone person standing anywhere near them. Even when Quentin Stokes touched the one at the Flying J, he did nothing but turn his hobo head and walk away.

This was different. In every way it was different.

Desperate for distraction, I go to my bookshelf and yank the books into a chaotic heap. Then I let my mind sink into the task of returning them to alphabetical order by subject and author. I let that task lead to another and another until my entire bedroom is in a controlled space. On any normal night, this would be enough to relax me. But this is not a normal night.

It's years before I get anywhere near sleep. Eventually, I do, and it's as smooth as hopscotch. I don't even dream. I just swing in and out of this mad, desperate swirl in my mind. When I wake, and shuffle down the hallway in my pajamas, my parents wait in the kitchen, as promised. Mom's working the toaster with none of the skill of a human. The air's already slightly burnt from at least one failed attempt. Dad's chicory is fresh and thick as sap in the pot. Its chocolate smell is heaven. He raises an eyebrow when I pour a mug.

"Possum," he starts, ever gentle on approach. "We want to talk about last night."

The sip I take is too much, too fast. It burns my tongue and brings me to my senses with an unpleasant aftertaste. Bless chicory for being at once so tempting and so foul.

"Milk," I croak, perching on one of the stools at the kitchen bar.

Dad lifts a pot from the stove. Knowing that I prefer

milk to tar, he transforms my cup into a decadent café au lait. He lifts his brows to communicate that he still wants to talk.

"I'd rather not." I reach for the sugar.

"That doesn't change much," he says, finding his backbone in my rebellion. "We're concerned about how this might affect you, so we're going to discuss it sooner or later."

I don't answer, but Mom fills the space, sliding a piece of singed toast under my nose.

"Listen, Candace, if you don't let us help you, you'll be harassed by everyone in this town, and wouldn't you rather talk to us? You want raspberry jam or fig preserves?"

I take the figs. "Harassment, I can handle. I go to high school, in case you've forgotten. I'm not worried and there's nothing to discuss."

It's the way Dad clears his throat. Unnecessarily loud and obvious. He looks away and I look to Mom.

"What?" I demand.

"There is something to discuss, actually. Something I think is really rather exciting." She presses her hands to the cabinet, a pleased smile twirling her lips. My stomach clenches. "You see, we've had a call from Mr. King this morning—"

"No." I push my toast away. "No way. I know what you're going to say and no way."

"Candy, just listen," Mom urges. "He's reviewed the

footage from last night and he says it's some of the best they've ever managed to capture. You in that dress with the light on your hair and that haint rolling out of the fog? Well, can't you just imagine how cinematic that must look? He says it's exceptionally rare for something to come across so clearly."

"No. Way."

"Well, I can. I think it must be stunning," she continues in the way of mothers, unwilling to concede a point until it's bruised and bloody. "And he wants to use it."

"In. Hell."

"Candace." Dad's chastisement is as sharp as it is dull, cutting and soothing all in one stroke. I've never been able to master the technique and it galls me to no end.

"Now, he has a good point about why you ought to consider letting him do so," says Mom. "He says when something like this happens in a small town like ours, you've got to get out in front of it. Show folks you're not ashamed of what happened by letting word get out that you've agreed to have it broadcast. The more open you are, the less they'll come knocking at your door to get answers."

"No. No. No, Mom. No." My feet slip from the rung of the stool, cold with sweat.

"I think—your father and I think it's a good idea. Not only will it dissuade folks from talk, but it might just have a few unintended consequences. Don't you remember that

story of the girl who was discovered because she was singing at a gas station, of all places?"

Her cheeks have gone rosy with the prospect. As if this
alone can compensate for my useless uterus. She's so busy
imagining some famous future for me that she can't see my
horror. Let Mr. King use footage of me in his show? I might
as well set fire to every college brochure I've ordered over
the summer. Even if I got out of Sticks, I'd *be* Sticks wherever I went.

"I'm not interested," I say, slow, steady, and without a
stutter.

"And he'll pay you. A few thousand up front and then
some percentage when it's aired. Just think how that would
help pay for college," Mom argues.

College money. So that's how he's going to play it. I have
to admit it's a good tactic. But I'd rather bet on myself than
easy money.

I hold a stony expression as I repeat, "Not interested. But
thanks for asking."

Mom's eyes flutter toward Dad and it plants a rotten feeling in my gut.

"What?" I demand.

"We gave him permission," Dad says.

"You *what*?" I don't know if I said it out loud. My ears
cloud and ring all at once.

"Don't overreact." Mom frowns and flaps a hand in my

direction. Like I'm nothing. Like I'm a child throwing a tantrum because I don't get ice cream for breakfast. "This'll be good for you. A line on the résumé at the very least."

"Mom. Have you ever written a résumé?" I spit, my mouth full of rage. "I'm not applying for small-minded hick of the year!"

"That was uncalled for, Candace Craven Pickens." Again, Dad both incites my anger and makes me regret it. I'm full of piss and vinegar. "Maybe you should go to your room and pound sand."

"That's your first great idea of the week!"

My stool scrapes the floor as I leave. Mom cringes, but I don't give a single damn about scratches on the hardwood. Let my parents apply their magnificent brains to something that isn't me for twenty seconds.

I slam my bedroom door so hard my junior high diploma falls off the wall. The frame doesn't shatter. It flops against the carpet with a dull and useless thud. I kneel to pick it up, brooding over the fact that my chances of getting a fresh start, free from the clinging hands of this small town, will be nonexistent if my parents make a public spectacle of me on *Local Haunts*. No one will think it was forced. They'll all assume that I was so anxious for a minute of prime-time glory that I'd debase myself by talking to ghosts in front of ten thousand strangers. Who gives a scholarship to *that*? Who takes *that* person seriously ever again in their lives?

And suddenly, my hand is through the glass frame. My knuckles against the paper. When I pull away, blood falls in fat drops, obscuring the curling script of my name. My hand, I realize. The blood falls from my hand. It should hurt. Shouldn't it hurt? There are pieces of me, my blood, falling away and I'm pretty sure that's supposed to hurt.

But I feel no pain. Only anger so loud it sings in my ears.

There's a knock at my door and I hear my father's voice calling, "Possum? Everything okay in there?"

Snatching a dirty T-shirt from the floor, I wrap my hand, and shove the broken diploma out of sight.

"Yeah," I call. "I'm fine. Go away."

He doesn't. Not right away. I can hear his stillness on the other side of the door and I can imagine his face, frowning, conflicted, wondering if he should press. But he doesn't. No surprise. I listen as his footsteps recede down the hallway.

AFTER QUIETLY CLEANING UP MY mess and bandaging my hand, I pull out my cherished collection of the homebound books Old Lady Clary sells to kids and tourists. They contain every swamp story I've ever told. I flip through each one, looking for some kind of clue.

It was an accident that I fell in love with these stories. It's impossible for anyone to remember how old they were or where they were the first time they heard one. This town all but bleeds swamp lore and I'd call anyone who claimed to remember hearing their first tale a stone-cold liar. But somewhere along the way, I do remember a sleepover where hater Hallie Rhodes told one so poorly I snored until she stopped.

"Aren't these supposed to be *scary*?" I'd asked.

"If you're such an expert, *you* tell one," she'd countered.

And since I'm incapable of backing down from a challenge, I did exactly as she asked and whipped those girls up into a satisfying frenzy of fear and delight.

After that, I very naturally became the queen of terror and have been responsible for recounting swamp stories on demand. I've never minded. I don't understand the thrill of being scared the way others do. I've been scared—really, truly scared—only once in my life, and there was nothing thrilling about it. When you're truly scared, something has gone horribly wrong and it's completely out of your control.

But that's not what these stories do. These stories give everyone a chance to be safe scared—they're imagining something horrifying from the safety of a sleeping bag, and in some strange way that's fun.

I've always seen the stories for what they are—tools of the very fine art of manipulation. I understand their parts in a way that lets me tell them again and again while keeping the thrill of fear very close. In some way, they're a skill of mine and I love that I'm good at it.

Right now, I feel like they're manipulating me and I don't love that much at all.

The image of Mad Mary Sweet lingers in my head. The events of last night play over and over in my mind until they feel as mythologized as any swamp story, until I could tell the tale of it as if it were any other piece of fiction.

Except it's not. It's a real thing that happened, and I'd like to know why.

It's hard to find clues in stories I can recite from memory. The tale of Mad Mary Sweet tells me what I already know: that she was a poor girl who went mad and roamed the swamp looking for her mother. I pass dozens of others that I know just as well: "The Hollow-Eyed Cur," "The Shine Child," "The Roving 52nd."

Then I land on an old favorite, a story called "Jack of the Trade," about a man who lures children into the swamp with the promise of toys. He's said to wander the streets with a long, ratted coat, a deadly grin, and his collection of toys hanging from his belt.

Exactly like the ghost Hallie Rhodes told us about that evening at the Flying J. Like Mad Mary Sweet, that ghost perfectly mirrored a swamp tale.

And reconsidering all the ghost sightings I've heard about thus far, I find that I can match half of them to various stories from these very books. Sticks isn't just being haunted, it's being haunted by its own ghosts.

The realization stuns me for a full minute. I should tell someone—Sterling, Abigail—but what good will it do?

I let my phone buzz all morning. It seems like the perfect kind of day to douse my mind in the rest of *The Bell Jar*, so that's exactly what I do. I curl up in my bed and read about someone else's madness for a while.

When I finally check my phone, there are text messages and calls from people who should really know better than to assume we're this friendly. I scroll through until I find the names that are after more than gossip. I have two missed calls and five texts from Sterling, one call and one text from Abigail, and two texts from Quentin Stokes letting me know there's a race at the track tonight and he'll be there. There's no love between me and Quentin, but he's pretty and uncomplicated and a good kisser. The kind you catch and throw back. One final Saturday night at the racetrack before school starts sounds like the sort of night I could use.

Opening a new message, I hit Abigail and Sterling at once: *racetrack? 8pm?*

Sterling responds first. *Yes. u ok?*

I return a picture of *The Bell Jar* along with, *i am, i am, i am.*

Abigail's response takes a few minutes. She says, *I'm in.*

I always assume that when she's home, she has to leave her phone where her parents can see it and they screen everything that comes in. Therefore, I don't send her a picture of my parents' liquor cabinet.

Lucky for me, the house is empty when I leave. Mom and Dad left a note on the fridge about hanging with Nanny tonight, which makes swiping a nearly full bottle of vodka from their stash less than sporting. They'll never miss it.

The way things have been going lately, chances are Mom'll assume she polished it off on one of her late-night "Why has my daughter forsaken me?" benders.

It takes some doing, but I convince Sterling to trade my practical yet unremarkable Ion for her brother's Chevelle. He left it in her care while he's away at college and she'd never move it if I didn't push. But sometimes I think Sterling likes to be pushed into doing things.

She's perfectly petite behind the oversized wheel of the old car, perched at the edge of the seat. This is one of the things I love most about my friend. She's as imposing as a spiderweb, but she's tough as bullets.

We rumble through town with the music up and the windows down. Together, we play the street like our own personal band: heads turn, boys whistle, and cars honk. I spot Quentin Stokes's blond crown and the rest of his sun-baked crew milling around their cars at the Flying J gas station, prepping for the race. I blow them a kiss and they reward me with a chorus of howls.

"You know, if my stepdad sees us, this night could get really short really fast," Sterling warns, but she's smiling, wishing she'd ever dare to throw a careless kiss to anyone.

We stop for Abigail first, who's dressed for school, not for fun, but her mother stands at the door with stern lips. I hop out, suddenly concerned that my short shorts could get

Abigail into trouble by proxy, then jump into the back. It wasn't fast enough. I see Mrs. Beale's eyes on me; I see her judgment. She'll probably go inside and light a candle for my soul.

Or not.

Abigail waits until we've left the driveway to shimmy out of her puritan shorts and into a skirt she'd stashed in her purse. The change transforms the top from vaguely frumpy to loose sexy.

"Much better," I say. "Shannon'll be there?"

In a display of uncharacteristic candidness, Abigail nods.

"Candy, are you going to volunteer to talk about last night or do we have to beat it out of you?" Sterling's foot has become far too light on the gas pedal. She means to have this out before we get Heath.

I lean back, stretching my arms to rest my fingertips against the sides of the car. "What do you want to know?"

"For starters, are you okay?"

"Why wouldn't I be?"

Sterling doesn't answer right away, and I see from the arch of Abigail's eyebrows that there's definitely something to be said.

"What is it?" I demand, leaning as far forward as the seat belt allows. Which isn't far. Old cars are selfish.

"People are talking." Abigail says *talking* the same way she might say *stupid*. "They're saying you exorcised the ghost."

I might have anticipated this. If I hadn't been so distracted by the fear of the entire known world learning my name from Mr. Roosevelt King, I might've had room to worry about things happening much closer to home.

Sterling accurately interprets my silence as the slow boil of rage. "On the bright side, now we know for certain that the ghosts are connected to Shine. You dispelled it with a touch. Exactly like Shine."

"Her," I say. "Not it!"

Sterling and Abigail share a brief look as we turn up the drive to Heath's fortress and stop, headlights off. I guess taking a stand at Gage's party didn't work as well as they'd hoped.

"How did you know it was Mad Mary Sweet?" Abigail asks.

"The song she was singing. Didn't you hear it?" They shake their heads. Sterling isn't a surprise. I have no idea where she stood when everything happened, but Abigail was close. I thought close enough. "Well, it was Mary's song."

Just mentioning it sends a fresh chorus through my mind, but without the crashing, out-of-control feeling it had last night. I let it spin like a merry-go-round for a minute, the end feeding seamlessly into the beginning until it's time for the ride to stop and I pull the plug.

"Also," I add, "my parents gave Mr. King permission to use the footage of my unholy event in his rotten show."

Sterling offers me a consoling frown, but I can tell that she still doesn't agree that this is a bad thing for the town. Abigail, though, has the intelligence to be horrified on my behalf.

She says, "I guess you'll be making nice with the Kings, then."

It's just like Abigail to find the friendly solution to a problem. Of course she's right. If I want to keep my face away from public view, I need to cozy up to Mr. King.

Heath finally jogs down the driveway and joins our jolly band. Then we're off. The sun suffers beneath the trees, giving way to a clear, dark sky. Perfect for a night at the track.

The Chevelle may be a beautiful ride, but it's not the most comfortable. It rocks us back and forth as we make the slow climb through the wooded dirt road. By the time we park, my back's sore from a stubborn spring in the seat and I smell like leather conditioner. It won't matter for long. The sky is lit with floodlights and headlights, I smell smoke and exhaust and dirt, and the air is warm on my skin. This is a perfect night.

"A little pre-race courage?" I ask, swirling the bottle of vodka.

Sterling and Heath decline, but Abigail snatches the bottle and takes a double shot. Sterling pins me with an accusing look, as though I shouldn't have offered my vodka to Abigail when I knew she was nervous, but I'm not her mother. I reach for the bottle before she can take a third hit.

"Leave some for the rest of us," I tease, taking my own healthy swig before tossing the bottle into the Chevelle.

By the time we make it into the bleachers, my head's gone a little fuzzy and I feel warm all over. Sterling and Heath wind up to the top and pick a spot near the end. I like it. It's good to control the way in and out and we can see the entire track from here—a single paved loop lined with concrete median barriers on the bleacher side. The pavement was originally laid in the 1950s by Mr. Wawheece's father as a gift to his son. The story is that Mr. Wawheece once held dreams of escaping Sticks as a professional racecar driver and he practiced on this track from dawn till dusk. But one day, when the rain was a little too light and his tires a little too bald, he flipped and barely walked away with his life. He hasn't run the track since.

It still sits on Wawheece land and the town maintains it just well enough to keep it functional, but Mr. Wawheece has mostly lost interest in this piece of his kingdom.

I lean backward over the rails, letting my fuzzy head get a little fuzzier while the stars swim above. A hand lands on my knee, holding me steady. I don't much care whose it is. I lean farther back until I can see the tips of the pine trees spearing the sky.

"Candy," Sterling whines. "Stop it."

The hand on my knee tightens. Long, strong fingers. Heath.

I relent, lifting my head so quickly the world spins beneath my feet. It's not an unpleasant feeling. The air is sharp with sugar and smoke, and right now, surrounded by all the bad habits of Sticks, I love this little town.

Abigail stands super tall on the top bleacher. Her eyes scan the crowd below, hunting while trying to appear as though she's not.

Sterling and Heath have huddled again. She leans into his shoulder, ready to fall asleep even in the midst of all this.

Abigail fidgets. Her eyes are stuck on a clump of girls who've just come around the corner. It takes me a minute to spot Shannon. There she is, strawberry-blond hair cinched in a ponytail, dark eyes skittering over the bleachers. She finds Abigail and immediately looks away, a warm smile pressing at her cheeks. It's all so tediously coy.

"Abigail," I urge, "go talk to her."

"I don't know what to say," she says so softly it's almost lost in a sudden rev of engines.

Sterling reaches for Abigail's hand. "How does she look tonight?"

"Like the last minute of sunset," comes Abigail's murmured response.

A smile muscles its way onto my resistant face. "Start

153

with that. Or start with 'hello,' but for the love of Pete, start with something. I can't take this much longer."

"Do you want me to go with you?" Sterling offers.

For a moment, it seems Abigail's become a statue. We've reached the limit of her capacity for emotional expression and this will be yet another missed opportunity, but then she shakes herself.

"No," she says. "I'm going to say hi."

We watch her descend the steps and slip into the crowd. Even from this distance I can tell she's moving without her usual confidence. I've never understood why the promise of love has the power to make a perfectly reasonable person feel like they're incomplete without it, to get weak in the knees, or act a fool. If someone made me that nervous, I'd hightail it in the other direction faster than they could spit. Give me a high-impact love that makes me stronger than I already am. Or give me nothing at all.

Abigail and Shannon make agonizingly slow progress. I turn my attention to the track, where a few of the shiniest cars in town are parked side by side. Clustered around them are the drivers. Sharing cigarettes and psyching one another out before the first race. Directly across the track, there's a row of cars waiting in the wings. They'll come out in sets, each group getting five laps to determine the winning car. At the end, those winners will race. Everyone watches the last race. Even those who come for the darkness of the field will emerge for the final event and the shouts will be heard in town.

Quentin Stokes'll be with them, but not good for much until after. He doesn't get too bunched up about winning or losing. He likes the rush of the race and the rush of a postrace kiss. I'm fond enough of the second that I'm willing to wait for it.

Checking in on the floor show, I see Abigail and Shannon have moved away from Shannon's crew of friends and are sharing a moment a few feet from the bleachers. It's as private as it gets unless they suddenly go from zero to sixty and head for the field, which is less likely than snow.

Abigail's been mooning after Shannon since freshman year, but she's never been brave enough to make anything that might be construed as a move. I can't blame her. Sticks isn't what you'd call metropolitan. And it's not as though her family's suddenly going to support their daughter's sinful leanings. I don't know how she's been coping with that sort of pressure, but whatever her strategy was, it's changed. Abigail Beale has made a small, but significant move.

And here I am, the fifth wheel.

"I'm going back to the car for another sip. Anyone want?" I ask, but Sterling's eyelids barely flutter. "Never mind."

Heath digs the keys from Sterling's pocket and tosses them over. By the time I hit the ground, cars are revving their engines and a screech of a cheer breaks across the crowd. It's seconds before the pistol fires and the cars fly into action. I pick my way through the throng of specta-tors toward the nonracing cars. Here the air smells less like sweat and smoke and more like a warm summer night.

I fish my vodka from the backseat of the Chevelle and take a sip. It's tepid and burns as it slides down my throat. I lean against the car, waiting for the liquid to work its magic and lift me from the trenches of fifth wheels and Shine-less eyes.

"Candy, Candy," a voice drawls. "I'll take a piece of you any day."

Laughter. Not what I was hoping for.

I open my eyes to a swirl of stars and slowly turn to see my assailant. Or several assailants. A group of boys approaches from the end of the parking field. Eyes on me. Prowling. Led by the Wawheece brothers, Riley and Lamont.

I don't bother to move from the car. "The only piece of me you'll get is a taste of my fist if you come too close."

Lamont cackles. He's not much for verbal communi-cation. I'm fairly certain any mental gifts they may have received were not evenly split.

"Whatcha drinkin'?" Riley asks, stepping closer to swipe the bottle from my hand. "It's polite to share."

"It's polite to ask, you ass." I reach for the bottle and miss as he dodges. "Or didn't your mama raise you right?"

"Tsk, tsk, Candy Cane. It's too early to bring my mama

156

into anything. But now that you've done it, it was thoughtful of yours to prepare you for your career on the pole." He unscrews the cap of my vodka and tosses it back, taking an overly large gulp.

"Hey!" snaps a voice from within the pack, quickly followed by the Prince of Ghosts himself, Gage King. "I didn't hear her offer, man." His eyes are fixed on Riley, unrelenting, and he's stepped up so that he's partly between us.

They make an odd pairing, but I suspect Gage knows only the boys who've been working on his new house this summer. I'll give him a pass on hanging with Riley Wawheece until school starts.

"She was about to. Candy likes to give it up. You wanna pull?" Riley's grin is loose, his gaze already glassy. He goes to raise the bottle again, eyes shifting back to Gage.

This isn't about me anymore.

Gage waits until Riley lowers the bottle. Then he leans in and says, "Return what doesn't belong to you or I'll do it for you."

The air shivers with the distant roar of cars.

I can't look away, yet every muscle in my body is ready to move. Riley's eyes narrow. That boy was born spoiling for a fight. There's no way for Gage to know it, no way for him to know that the Wawheece boys are 20 percent of Doc Payola's practice. It's the not knowing that impresses me.

"You sure about this, *Gage*?" The bottle lowers. And

with that movement it goes from beverage to weapon.

"C'mon," I say. "Everyone just relax."

Gage says, "I'm relaxed," and the calm that settles over him is practiced—a perfectly confident aggression that chips away at careless smirks on the faces behind Riley. If I don't do anything, this is going to get stupid.

Stepping forward, I snatch the open bottle from Riley's grip.

"Thanks," I say, shaking spilled drops of vodka from my hand. "You're a peach."

Guys have this way of communicating with glares and wide nostrils and bloated pectorals they think girls don't understand. But the exchange between Gage and Riley isn't complicated. It's reducible to one simple thing: dominance. One of them will leave this place with more than the other.

"Whatever," Riley says, melting into his pack.

Gage hasn't taken his eyes off Riley and it's making the boy twitchy. It's not an unpleasant thing to witness. "Coming?" Riley asks.

"In a minute," Gage says, dismissing everyone like they're *his* pack of miscreants. Bravo to him. "I'll find you."

I'd swear it was a threat. If the flinch on Riley's face is any indication, he thinks so, too. He recovers, but his retreat is too quick. And that's when I realize I'm alone with Gage.

The roar from the track climbs to a pitch as the first race ends. The first winner is called through a bullhorn to an approving crowd. When the boys are out of earshot, Gage finally turns his dark eyes on me.

I say, "Five minutes in town and you're already running with the worst. I don't know if I should compliment you or condemn you."

"Five minutes in my company and you've got me figured?" he retorts. "I don't know if I should compliment you or promise to prove you wrong."

Points for responding with wit and humor.

I set the contaminated bottle of vodka on the trunk of the car. The cap's long gone and I'm definitely not putting my mouth where Riley's has been. Sighing, I tip the remaining liquid into the grass.

Gage frowns.

"Don't you need to catch up with your friends?" I ask. "They'll be giving someone else trouble before long."

"I will," he says, casting a glance over his shoulder. Then, sounding alarmed, he asks, "Are you here alone?"

That makes me laugh and wins a crippling smile from Gage. My head swims as the alcohol pulls me into a more complicated dance. Here is Gage King, thumbs pushed through belt loops, the glint of a silver chain beneath his shirt.

"I should've guessed you wouldn't be anywhere alone," he says, subdued.

And once again, before I can stop myself, I cross the line

from composed to overeager simply by opening my mouth. "Not with a guy."

I see the twitch of a grin at his mouth. Victorious and grating. Damned vodka in my brain.

"Do you believe in ghosts?" I blurt.

His smile hardens. Light catches on his heavy brow, turning his face into jagged edges of light and shadow. "That's what we're starting with?" he asks.

I shrug. "Seems like a pretty good place to me."

"Is it important?"

"Damned important."

He nods like it was the answer he expected, then squints at the lights over the track. The crowd's no louder than a hum now. This is the quiet lull between races. Gage is just as quiet as he searches the distance, considering his answer. If he'll give one. He seems both grim and confident standing there in jeans and a black collared shirt with the top buttons open, the sleeves rolled up, and a wide mess of leather bracelets. Though I can't see them clearly, his shoes appear to be both nice and leather. Too much fashion for Sticks. I'd bet good money his wardrobe downshifts after a few weeks. And that'll be a shame.

I'm startled to find his eyes on me when I look up again. How long was I studying his shoes? How long was he studying me studying his shoes? Doesn't matter. I asked a question.

"Well?" I prompt.

"I'd rather not."

"What? Believe or answer?"

This time his pause is brief and resolute. "Either," he says. "Both. I wish you'd ask me anything else."

It's an invitation. I could agree, ask him how he's liking Sticks or what his hobbies are or if he wants to come hang with my friends. We could move straight past the tough stuff and onto something more fun. I'm supposed to be making nice, after all.

He takes a step closer, repeating the invitation with a small, hopeful smile. Those lips. I wouldn't be opposed to something that ended in the backseat of a car or at the far edge of the field.

"Let's forget about ghosts," he suggests.

I laugh. "How is that even possible for someone like you?"

Disappointment falls down his face. In two seconds he's gone from playful to something quite the opposite.

"You're right," he says with a resigned sigh. "I can't."

And with that, he turns and walks away from me toward the roaring crowd.

As I watch him go, I realize just how much I wanted him to stay. He was offering something uncomplicated, and I'm the one who made it about ghosts. Once again, I'm letting these stories drive me and now I'm standing alone in this parking lot when I might have been doing something much more interesting.

I consider returning to the bleachers where my friends wait. I consider loitering around Quentin Stokes's car until I can claim him at the end of the night.

Neither appeals. Instead, I crawl into the back of the Chevelle and let the familiar noises lull me to sleep until my friends return.

Junior year. I've waited for this day all summer and now that it's here, I wish I could do anything else. The first day of a new year should be like a birthday. Everyone I care to see should be happy to see me, full of superficial compliments about my hair, my clothes, my boots, and my magnificent smile.

Instead, everyone wants to know how I banished Mad Mary Sweet, or they want to call me a freak, or they want me to come over and dispel the ghost they swear they saw hanging in their closet. All day, I practice derailing conversations with the threat of all the secrets I know. There's a currency to shame, and I never intend to pay any of it out. Sarah Menard backs down when I remind her that I know her purity ring's just for show, Cade Vincent caves when I reveal I know he's dealing from the back of his car, and Sonny Patin blanches at the phrase "backwoods bed wetter . . ."

The only person to treat me with any diplomacy is Quentin Stokes, who leans against my locker with a cocky smile and a pouting, "Missed you Saturday night." That, at least, feels normal, since I felt too weird after my parking lot Gage encounter to stick around after the race and hang out with Stokes. I tell him, "Yeah, you did." And as I strut my stuff to the girls bathroom, he calls, "Not for long, though." He likes the game, but he doesn't like to lose, which is one of the things I actually like about him. He's more flame than spark. But I have enough fire to deal with today.

To top things off, there's a story floating around about how there was a woman crying in a church pew after services on Sunday. Father O'Connor went to comfort her and she stood, wandering straight through the pews with long, black hair streaming behind her.

Father O'Connor never would have said a word. The story comes from Mrs. Calhoun, who stays late to pick up.

With so few details, I can't tell if this one echoes a swamp story, but Mrs. Calhoun isn't one for embellishment. If I had to bet, I'd say this was yet another true sighting.

According to plan, Abigail, Sterling, and I have nearly

identical schedules. We rotate through the day, claiming our seats in a triangle of three in every class with the exception of Madame Evan's class, where we're ruled by the cruel tyranny of the alphabet. Nova King turns up in half of our classes. The first is advanced European history with Mr. Berry. Nova walks in wearing that flawless bob and pink smile and, spotting us, heads straight over to turn our triangle into a square. No sign of new-school jitters. I have to admire that.

"Hey, girls," Nova says, dropping a messenger bag by the desk and sitting. "Mind if I join you?"

"Only if you don't ask me about Friday night," I say.

She gives me a shrewd smile. "I know you don't know me very well, but trust me, I've got an idea what you're going through."

"Welcome to the collective," I say, relieved.

By the time lunch rolls around, the rumors about me and my ghostly counterpart are in full swing. I know it'll blow over. I know it's 100 percent temporary, but it's hellish and I don't like it, and if I think this is bad, I can't wait to see what my spot on *Local Haunts* generates.

Heath joins us at lunch and so does Nova, which for her consists of an apple, a chocolate bar, and a diet soda. If I tried to subsist on that, I'd keel over five minutes into practice, but I suppose nonathletes don't need to be much other than conscious and coherent.

"I heard you were at the racetrack Saturday night, Candy," Nova says, biting into her apple. "I thought it would be sort of an all-testosterone scene, but girls go, too?"

I know how she heard it and I'm surprised that the memory of that conversation with Gage is tinged with something like apprehension.

"It's basically the only scene," I say apologetically, but she doesn't shrink away.

"Sounds fun." She smiles around another bite. "Guess that's where I'll be next time. Do you guys just meet up there? Or is there some sort of introduction protocol? I don't want to misstep so soon in a new town."

She's nice, smart, not openly critical of my town, and I like her. Which, now that I think about it, I'm pretty sure I decided before committing grand theft equine with her.

"How are you dealing with the house?" Sterling asks, brazenly ignoring Nova's questions. "You must be suffering without air-conditioning."

Nova rolls her eyes, breezing past the slight. "It's not awesome, but my room is pretty amazing. Or it's going to be. You guys should come check it out. Maybe help me decide where to put what. I'm horrible with decoration."

This is perfect. If I have any chance of convincing Mr. King not to use that footage, it's by cozying up to his daughter. In the space of a minute, we've agreed to hang with

Nova King in the Lillard House after volleyball practice.

The day continues to surprise. At the end of lunch, Riley Wawheece calls my name and doesn't follow it up with anything obnoxious or harassing. "Candy. Hey. Wait up," is all he says. Which, of course, I don't. But he continues his pursuit with some of his infamous charm. "Goddamn it, Candy, I'm trying to give you something. Just wait a goddamn minute."

Heath and Sterling usher me forward while Abigail turns to run interference, which is usually enough of a deterrent for anyone looking for trouble, but Riley persists.

"Just," he starts to shout, but thinks better of it and lowers his voice, "I just need to talk to you for a fucking second."

I stop and turn to face him. On one side of me, Heath bristles. On the other, Sterling utters a sigh of displeasure. They're not usually so aggressive, but the Wawheece boys occupy a special place in all our hearts. Even without the abbreviated story I told them about Saturday night at the Chevelle, they'd resent any attention he directed our way.

"What do you want?"

He takes a few hulking steps forward. Being so close to him under regular light, it's difficult not to express disgust. He has a face like a rockslide, eyes and mouth crowding his large nose. His shorn head is pocked with old scars, and his lips are big and wet. It's no wonder he's angry. I'd almost feel sorry for him if he wasn't also mean. But he stands there with his shoulders hunched and without his posse, looking almost contrite.

"It's no big deal, I just wanted to give you this." He digs into his bag and produces a puffy plastic sack. It crinkles when he pushes it into my hands. "And to say I'm sorry I acted like a dick."

"You'll have to be more specific." I laugh, but he doesn't, and Abigail shoots me a critical look.

"I'm apologizing, for Chrissake." He tugs at the back of his neck with fat-knuckled, paint-spattered hands. "Just. I'm sorry, all right? That's all I'm saying. *Sorry.* Are we cool?"

This time he looks me right in the eye. His "sorry" is delivered both forcefully and with a hint of desperation. It's unsettling.

"Yeah," I say. "We're cool, Wawheece, we're cool."

"Great," he says with a nod of his head. And with an awkward wave, he turns and skulks the opposite way down the hall.

The four of us stand still for a moment, watching him cut a path without even trying.

"You wanna tell us what that was about?" Heath asks.

"I have no idea."

Abigail nudges me with her elbow. "Not true. Look in the bag. But . . . maybe hold it away from your face."

"That's what she said," I mutter, gingerly peeling open the bag.

Inside the plastic is a crumpled brown paper bag, and inside that is a bottle of vodka. New, unopened, and exactly like the one I abandoned at the track.

"Is he hitting on you?" Sterling asks with justified alarm.

"It's not a box of condoms," Abigail answers, totally deadpan.

"Jezuz," Heath breathes, walking away with his chivalrous sensibilities.

"No, it's actually an apology," I muse, wrapping the bottle and stashing it in my bag before a teacher comes by.

"What's happening?" Sterling asks. "Do you think he's dying?"

"Maybe he's had a change of heart?" Abigail suggests. "Trying civility for a while?"

I shake my head, unsure what to think. He's not the apologizing type. Neither of the Wawheece boys are, and if Riley suddenly decided to make amends on all his past wrongs, what chance is there he'd start with me for a transgression as small as stealing my liquor? Not much.

The bell shrieks overhead and the hallway goes from calm to frenzied. Sterling rushes to Choir with Heath at her side, Abigail heads to Government, but I stand still and follow a thought. Throwing down enough cash for a bottle of vodka he wouldn't get to taste couldn't have been fun for Riley. There's no way he made this decision on his own. Someone else must have put him up to it. No one among his usual crew. Even if one of them had enough of a conscience to suggest it, they wouldn't have the chops to enforce it.

There's really only one possibility.

The warning bell rings. Sixty seconds to get across campus to Journalism. But looking up, I see I'm not alone in my near-tardiness. Along with five or six harried freshmen, there's a figure leaning against the lockers at the far end of the hallway. Button-down shirt with rolled sleeves and a swath of bands around one wrist. When I spot him he stands, gives a little salute, and disappears behind a classroom doorway.

Lord help me, I recognize him from a distance: Gage King.

THAT EVENING, SUNSET MURDERS THE top half of the Lillard House.

Nova answers the door in bare feet. Her smile greets us along with a puff of paint thinner or something just as pungent.

"Sorry about the smell," she says, wrinkling her nose. "They painted the upstairs after the party and it reeks. I've got the windows open in my room. It helps, I promise."

"How are you not high all the time?" I ask, stepping into the cavernous foyer.

"Who's to say I'm not?" she teases with a laugh. "Call it a bonus."

Without the press of a crowd, and the dazzling sight of Gage King in a three-piece suit, I see more of this transformed foyer than I did during the gala. The floor is cool, smooth marble, and an enormous chandelier hangs from the dome of the ceiling. Rich wallpaper of burgundy and gold rushes to meet white molding halfway down the height of the tall walls. The two stairways that curl around the foyer are carpeted in red, and the whole space has been decorated with gold accents and light. It's like stepping into a painting.

"Wow." Sterling stares up at the chandelier. "This is— this is really—"

"Ostentatious?" Nova offers. "Grandiose? Pretentious?"

Clever, self-deprecating, funny. She was meant to be my friend.

"It's gorgeous," Abigail offers solemnly. "Your home is gorgeous."

"I just live here," Nova says with a shrug. "But thanks. My dad will appreciate the compliment."

She leads us up one of the curling staircases and down a long hall to a corner room at the back of the house. Her room. As promised, the old-fashioned floor-to-ceiling windows are open with gauzy purple curtains ruffling in the breeze. It's warmer up here on the second floor, sticky warm. The breeze helps keep things tolerable. Not an ideal way to live, but any self-respecting southerner can stand a little warmth.

Nova's walls have been painted the color of pumpkins. A bold choice, one she's softened with white trim and purple accents. The windows overlook the hill in the backyard and the oak forest north of the house. I peer out the latter, hunting for any sign of that little shack we visited last time, but the oaks are dense and guarded.

Stacked on the foot of her bed are a pile of her intended decorations. They range from glittery Venetian masks to mirrors to prints of vibrant paintings by no one I recognize. We start by turning on some music—her room, her choice, and she chooses some completely inoffensive pop—and spreading the items out one at a time.

"We move so often," she explains, "it just makes me feel better if my room is always mine. These help."

"Where did you get these?" Sterling raises a mask to her face—a pointy-chinned blue mask with purple and green feathers sprouting around the top and a spade painted on one cheek.

"Oh," Nova says, and pauses, as though deciding whether or not to tell the truth. "My father took us to Italy a few years ago to investigate some old haunted church."

"Your Venetian masks are actually from Venice?" Abigail asks, wonder in her voice.

"I bought them there," Nova answers. "But for all I know, they're made in China like everything else."

"Have you been anywhere else?" Abigail presses with a

new light in her eyes. New Orleans does nothing for her, but I'm glad to see she's not blind to the idea that the rest of the world might have something to offer her.

"A few places." Nova holds up by her dresser a painting of a girl who might be drowning. I'll never understand the urge to make death beautiful. "Dad likes to film on location as much as possible, of course, and he likes to take us with him."

"Nice to have a dad who cares," Sterling says without a hint of bitterness or jealousy. I'm proud of her for clearly thinking of her stepfather, Darold, and not her sperm-papa.

Nova only shrugs and moves to place a painting on the wall. "Here?"

"You weren't kidding about needing help with this stuff," I say, reaching to take the painting from her hands. "At least you picked great colors, but you'd better leave the decorating to us."

We spend the next hour and a half piecing together her room. As we work, she shares little stories behind each piece. A tacky boomerang she picked up in Australia for a boyfriend who dumped her while she was away—she keeps it for the irony of knowing things don't always come back, a pastel obi covered in flying cranes and mountains given to her by an old Japanese woman on their trip to a haunted fishing spot in Hakone, prints of paintings she bought at the MoMA or the Louvre or some other amazing place I'll be lucky to see for myself. By the end of it, Abigail's gone quieter than usual, and Sterling might be realizing there's a world outside of Louisiana for the first time in her life.

Now that the sun's done and gone, the breeze through the windows has a hint of coolness to it. Humidity begins to loosen its hold so that it's practically comfortable if you aren't climbing on chairs and straining to hold a frame in place while Abigail marks the spot for the nail.

"Nova!" The voice of Mr. King comes from somewhere in the house.

Nova hops off her bed. "Be right back," she says, skating out the door.

As her footsteps recede down the stairs, I take a peek inside her closet. Abigail makes a sharp noise but doesn't move to stop me. Which is basically the same thing as turning a blind eye.

Tugging on the light string, I find Nova's fashion sense displayed before me. Not all of it is relevant to the South, but it is all enviable. Leather jackets, adorable dresses, tops I'd have to drive to New Orleans to have any hope of finding. On the floor, unopened boxes are stacked neatly, and on the back of the door hangs an impressive shoe caddy.

I push the door closed just as Nova reenters the room. She definitely saw me but says nothing about the fact that I was snooping in her private business. Instead, she holds the door open and invites us downstairs.

"Dad's made daiquiris," she says. "Virgin but still awesome. Anybody allergic to strawberries?"

"Not today," Sterling says, sparing a glance for me.

Nova leads us downstairs to the back porch. On our way, we pass what is now the family room, where Thad crouches with a controller in his hands in front of a TV large enough to crush him. He jumps as something on screen explodes, whooping and stabbing the air with his little fist.

"Nice move, Thad," I call, leaning through the door and doing a quick search for Gage. Not here. Probably not home, which should be a relief.

Thad spins and his heavy little face breaks into a grin. "Candy! Hi!" he calls, then hops up, shrugging his shoulders roughly, and adds, "I mean, hello, Miss Candace."

"It's okay if you call me Candy. We're friends, right?"

His smile softens as he nods once. So sure and serious. I return the nod, then, waving, I follow Sterling and Abigail to the porch.

They've plunked down on the steps, each leaning against one of the tall columns supporting the high roof. Before us, the grass is depressed in a large square, but that's the only lingering evidence of Friday night's gala. The dance floor, the bandstand, and every errant champagne flute has been removed so it's just us and a straight shot down the hill to the swamp.

For a minute it's the beginning of summer again, and I'm about to go into the swamp at Sterling's side to find her brother. We didn't know that the only way to win him back would be to leave Lenora May behind. She died beneath that everblooming cherry tree and when she did, the entire town forgot her. Except for us. We remember her because we were there. That's the reason I started to believe any of this. This damn swamp changed how I understand my world.

The notes of Thad's video game crash through the open living room windows, anchoring me safely in the present. Nova appears at the door bearing a tray of tall glasses filled with deep pink. She hands them around, places a basket of pistachios between us, and settles cross-legged on the floor.

The daiquiris are amazing. We barely speak until we're slurping the dregs of strawberry seeds and ice from the bottom of our glasses.

"Your dad missed his calling," I say.

"Right?" Nova asks with a grin when we lean back with full bellies and cold tongues.

"If he ever gets tired of chasing ghosts, he's got a future in frozen drinks," I say. "But it doesn't look like the ghost business is treating him too poorly."

"Doesn't look like it," Nova says, her eyes trained on the swamp at the bottom of the hill.

It's too dark to see the fence and too late in the season for fireflies. The swamp's just black and ugly and filled with shrieking bugs.

"Any of you ever been inside?" Nova asks.

"Inside where?" Sterling sits up a little straighter, looking between Nova and the swamp.

"That swamp. Where all your ghosts come from."

"How do you know that?" I ask, more sharply than I should have.

Nova narrows her eyes a bit. "Where else would they come from?"

"All of us," says Abigail as though Nova and I weren't talking. I shoot her a look meant to caution against this much truth, but either she can't see my expression or she doesn't care, because she continues with, "I've spent more time than I even thought possible inside that swamp and if I don't return before I go to my grave, it'll be too soon."

Nova prods, "What happened to you?"

For sure, I think Abigail will shake her head as she has so often this summer, with regret and embarrassment and an ocean of silence behind it, but she speaks again. "I was lured inside by music and dreams, and once it had me, it transformed me into a beast. My mind wasn't my own. Not all of it. Not enough of it—it was like my mind was a song I didn't know."

Abigail never wants to talk about what happened this

summer, how she ate a swamp berry and was lured inside by the same spirit who held Sterling's brother, how he transformed her into a gatorgirl and made the rest of us forget her. I'm reeling from Abigail's uncharacteristic sincerity when Sterling starts.

"Just a few months ago, the swamp took my brother. Or, not the swamp exactly, but a spirit inside the swamp did. And there was a girl who took his place in town and no one knew the difference but me. Her name was Lenora May and her brother, Fisher, demanded that we return her to the swamp or he'd kill my brother. We barely got him back."

I feel my mouth open and have to focus to shut it again. Somehow we've gone from harmless chatter about the merits of ice drinks to confessional hour at the Lillard House. These are things Abigail and Sterling have discussed only a handful of times since they happened, and only ever behind closed doors with just the three of us and Heath. And here they are spilling secrets for someone we met last week?

"Did you ever see the spirit?" Nova turns on Sterling. "Personally?"

Sterling laughs. "More than that. I met him multiple times. Had conversations with him. Touched him."

"Touched him?" Nova's eyes are eager. "You mean, you've felt the magic?"

"I feel it every day. I love the Wasting Shine," Sterling answers.

Talking openly about Shine is a bit too much for comfort. Time to speak up. I wave a hand in front of both of them. "Um, y'all, maybe we should talk about something else. *Anything* else."

"What happened to you in the swamp, Candy?" Nova ignores my plea. My name is too sweet on her lips.

"Nothing. Not a damn thing." I cross my arms over my chest. "Can we stop talking about this now? Unless you want to tell us why you're so interested? Maybe you'd like to spill a few closely guarded secrets?"

"Dad's probably going to start exploring it soon," Nova continues. "He says that in a place like this, there's likely a focal point for all the activity, something that roots the power to this place."

"There is," says Sterling. "It's—"

"Hey!" I snap, gripping her arm, spinning her to look at my face. "Does this seem like a bright idea to you?"

She pauses. "Not particularly, no." Her blue eyes struggle to focus on me, a small crease appearing in her brow. Not a common look for Sterling but one I recognize easily enough.

"I thought you said these were virgin daiquiris," I say to Nova. "What the hell did you put in them?"

She holds up her hands, adopting an innocent expression. "Nothing. I swear. There wasn't a drop of alcohol in them. Just berries, ice, cream, and mint."

I push to my feet. "I think you're lying."

She follows, pleading, "If I were lying, don't you think you'd know?"

It's true. Maybe it's true. My head's as clear as a freaking windowpane. If she'd spiked the drinks, I'd feel it.

"You did *something*, Nova King, and I don't take kindly to people messing with my friends."

She does a stellar impression of distress. "Candy, I—"

"What's going on out here?"

I jump and turn to see Mr. King standing in the dusky doorway. Had the door been open this entire time? When had Thad stopped playing his game and how long has Mr. King been within earshot?

"Nothing, Dad," Nova says, gathering the empty glasses on the tray. "We're just chatting about the swamp," Nova offers so blithely I could slap her. I will if she gives up anything more than that, but she stops there at the tip of all our secrets.

Mr. King's reaction is difficult to gauge. His eyes flit between us quick as a hummingbird. "I could've sworn I heard someone call you a liar." His knowing eyes settle on me like a net. "You girls having a problem?"

"Nope," Nova says brightly. "And we were just heading inside. The bugs are getting vicious."

"In that case," he says, and turns all his attention to me. "Candace, I was hoping you and I could have a quick talk."

This is a talk I need to have. But not with two loose-lipped friends in tow.

"Actually, we were leaving," I say. "Abigail has a medieval curfew and we're her ride. So. Thanks for the drink."

Without bothering to wait for a reply, I herd glossy-eyed Sterling and Abigail around the outside of the house. Seems a safer route than cutting through it again. I only pray we don't meet Gage on our way to the car. I don't think I can navigate another King encounter tonight.

Luck is with me. I get the girls into the backseat without any interference other than Abigail's long, unwieldy legs.

"If either of you vomits, you're paying for the shampoo," I say to the two dark figures in the rearview. They lean their heads together like they're ready to sleep off whatever the hell it is that just happened to them. Abigail's head rests on top of Sterling's like they're a nested pair. It would be sweet if it wasn't freaking me out.

I can't take either of them home in this condition. Sterling might get away with it, but Abigail will be grounded for a month because there's no justice in the Beale house that doesn't come down hardest on her. Damn it. I pull over by the river, dig my cell phone from my purse, and dial a number I've only ever dialed once before.

"Please, pick up," I mutter when the phone reaches its third ring. "Please."

"Please, what?"

"Hey, Heath. I've got a little problem."

Heath's room is its own world—above the garage and totally separate from the main house with its own bathroom. There's a bed tucked in beneath a skylight, a desk sort of dividing the room in two, and an entertainment system with plush sofas arranged in an L. There's so much space he could probably host a concert up here and his parents would never know. Tonight, though, they've gone to Alexandria to see some opera production and Heath's a very convenient bachelor.

On his bed, Sterling and Abigail sleep as soundly as they have since we got them up here nearly two hours ago. I sit on the sofa with Heath, watching the end of yet another episode of *Local Haunts*. We'd been ready to put on one of the old *Alien* movies when I found the marathon running on one of the Discovery channels. It seemed like necessary research at the time, but all I've really learned by the end of three episodes is that Mr. King—Roz, as he's endearingly called by everyone else on the show—has an alarmingly likeable stage presence. He travels from town to town, following ghost stories, and even when people greet him with a cold shoulder, by the end, they're shaking his hand and wiping their eyes at some emotional tripe he's spinning.

He's the scariest thing about the whole show. But it's his daughter who drugged my friends and pried their secrets from them.

"How long till curfew?" Heath asks, though he's checking his own watch.

I illuminate my phone. "Twenty minutes. Maybe we should try to wake them?"

He moves to Sterling's side of the bed and I take Abigail's, shaking her shoulder gently. I don't realize I've been holding my breath until her eyelids flutter.

"Abigail? You feeling okay?"

"Yeah," she mumbles.

She blinks and slowly sits up, looking around her in confusion. On the other side of the bed, Sterling's doing the same.

"Good. You've got to wake up if we're going to get you home in time."

"What time is it?" she asks at the same moment Sterling asks, "What happened?"

Heath meets my eyes and I shake my head. Not yet. Twenty minutes won't be enough.

"Go splash some water on your face. We'll figure it out later," I say.

"Figure it out?" Abigail pauses on her way to Heath's private bathroom. "What's there to figure out?"

"Good question. It's nine forty-two."

Abigail abandons all confusion. She freshens her makeup, rinses her mouth, and hurries us to the car in the space of ten minutes. Heath joins us and I tell them everything that happened at the King house on the drive to the Beale residence.

"We said all that? Are you sure?" Abigail's panic is sharper than Sterling's. "Maybe you were messed up, too? Maybe you misheard?"

"I didn't." I reach her driveway with five minutes to spare. "I swear, I was completely unaffected." I pause to make sure Heath still agrees with my assessment. He nods. "Shine. She must have dosed the drinks to make you share things you otherwise wouldn't."

Sterling nods.

Abigail says, "Oh God," and stares out the window as though having this conversation so close to her prison will elicit some sort of terrible retribution. "I have to go."

The porch light brightens at her approach, warming over her black skin, and we watch her ease her key into the front door and slip inside like a fugitive.

"That girl is afraid of everything," I say, mournful.

"I don't think that's true," Heath responds quickly, probably before he had occasion to notice what his mouth was doing.

"You think you know her better than I do?"

With a shrug, he drapes one elbow out the window. "I think you don't always know as much as you think."

Sterling giggles from the backseat.

"We weren't talking about me," I bite, throwing the car into reverse. "We're talking about how it was that Nova dosed these fools with Shine and played Twenty Questions."

"And it didn't affect you because Shine just doesn't."

"Right. I am the great dead zone, but I thought you all wore charms to protect you."

"We do." Sterling perks up, plucking at the thin leather band on her wrist. "But they only help us think straight when Shine's around. All bets are off when you ingest the stuff. And if she gave it a command before we ate it? Like 'tell the truth,' or something? Then we'd have answered whatever she asked."

"*If* it was her," Heath adds.

"What do you mean, 'if'?" I ask.

"You said she wasn't the only one around, right? That her dad made them?"

I pause and review everything that happened between Mr. King calling Nova down and our graceless departure. He's right. Nova left the room, came back, and brought us down for drinks. She'd had every opportunity to doctor them with something. It had been Nova, after all, who sent us ahead while she prepared the tray. Nova who handed out glasses instead of letting us pick our own. But the more

I think of it, the less certain I am that she's to blame. She brought the drinks, but it had been Mr. King who made them. Mr. King who snuck up to the doorway in a dark hallway to listen in on our conversation. Mr. King who defended his daughter's honor when I called her a liar.

And isn't it Mr. King who's so interested in getting at the secrets of the swamp? But if it was him, how did Nova know what questions to ask? Did he cast a separate spell on her? Had her eyes looked glassy? Or is she a willing participant? Too many questions.

Roz or Nova.

Whichever it was, they've just made sure I won't take my eyes off them.

"Well," I say, killing my headlights as we creep into Heath's driveway just in case his parents have come home since we left. "We have one advantage."

"We know you're an advantage, Candy," Sterling says with a roll of her eyes.

"Thank you, but that's not what I meant. I mean, I know what they're after." I smile, feeling satisfied with myself even as Sterling knocks my shoulder with her fist and demands, "What is it, Pickens?!"

"The tree."

I have just enough time to feel superior to the Kings when Heath brings it all crashing down with one word: "Why?"

Silence fills the car as we realize there's no good reason anyone outside of our small group should know or care about the everblooming cherry tree.

"This just keeps getting better," Heath says, climbing out of the car. "Night, y'all." He gives Sterling a too-sweet peck on the lips before jogging up the long drive.

It's not until I'm finally home in my own bed that one more thread of this web comes into view: whether it was Nova or Mr. King, if they used Shine once, they'll do it again. And now they know we've been to the source.

I WAKE TUESDAY MORNING HEAVY with dread. It puts me in a foul mood. I prefer emotions with a sense of movement like courage or desire or fury. Dread is useless and sloppy, like walking across a carpet in sopping-wet jeans.

Not even my peppiest of playlists lightens my mood, so I dress to match it—thin black leggings, slouching blouse, bulky necklace, and lips dressed to pout.

It feels like it's been more than two weeks since my birthday. So much has changed since then. I've seen a ghost, discovered I'm a barren husk of a girl, and will soon be an unwilling television star. Sometimes it's hard to remember that all I wanted from my junior year was a set of straight

As, a taste of Clary hooch, and to demolish some boy's innocence.

Now I dread facing my mother, I dread my next ghost encounter, and I dread whatever threat the Kings represent.

And I'd like to remove at least one of those from my plate as pronto as possible.

Nova King sits in front of me in Euro history, looking as severe and intentional as ever. At once, Sterling and Abigail lean in on either side of me like wings. But Nova beats me to the opening parry. Spinning in her seat, she presses her hands on my desk and without any sort of preamble, jumps right in.

She says, "We need to talk."

"No shit."

If Nova is fazed by my sharpness, she doesn't let on. "After class."

We all nod as Mr. Berry pulls us into the months leading up to World War I. He likes to be dramatic and starts with a poem by Siegfried Sassoon about ghosts and soldiers and fields of bloodred poppies.

The lunch bell rings along with a clap of thunder so loud it may as well be the first sign of the apocalypse. Within minutes the hallways are thick with the smell of rain and the constant squeak of sneakers on tile. Nova follows us to Sterling's locker.

"You don't need to ask," she says. "I know I messed up

last night. And I know you know."

"It was *you*? And you *know* you dosed us with Shine?" Sterling spits, almost forgetting to whisper.

"Shine is what you call the magic here, right? Yes." Nova's admission is far from remorseful. "But you have to understand—"

"That's not exactly how you want to start this," Abigail interrupts, causing even me to take a small step back.

"Sorry," Nova says, raising her hands in what is now a true apologetic gesture. "I'm not usually around people who know much of anything, and Shine just tends to be the fastest way to get at any real information, and I really am sorry I did it, but Candace . . ." She pauses for breath, her eyebrows lift so high her bangs nearly obscure her eyes. "I've never met anyone like you."

"Anyone like me?"

"Someone who wasn't affected! You weren't, were you? And you can't see Shine? And it's repelled by your touch? I know what you are!"

Her excitement is specifically unnerving.

It's the word *what* that drills into my brain. Not *who*, but *what*.

"And I'll tell you everything. Will you come over again? I promise, nothing hanky, just talking."

I find myself nodding dumbly. "Yeah."

"No!" Abigail cuts between us as Sterling pinches me.

"No way is she coming over to your place again."

They're right, of course. This is not a great plan.

"Well, I could come to you, but there are some things I'd like to show you at home and Dad'll know if they're gone."

She's said the exact right thing to intrigue me. With a look for each of my friends, I say, "Okay. Your place."

"How does four p.m. Saturday sound? Good? Good." She turns to face Abigail. "And I'm really sorry. Really." She shifts again to face Sterling and the recently arrived Heath. "Really." And then she's gone.

"You can't seriously be intending to go to her house again." Abigail's all blades and quiet fury. "There's no way you can trust her."

"I know, but she can't do anything to me the way she can to you, and I want answers, so . . ."

They can't argue against it, so they don't, but I sort of wish they would. I don't relish the thought of descending into the lion's den on my own.

The second sign of the apocalypse arrives in the form of Riley Wawheece. Blundering forth with his cadre of unwashed followers, he slings his eyes over to me and mutters, "Hey, Candy."

That's all. Just a hey and my name lobbed like a grenade. Everyone around us stops to stare as he continues on his way.

"What did you do to that boy?" Abigail ducks her head to ask.

I have no answer for her other than some irrational anger that he's no longer treating me the way he treats everyone else in this school. This isn't a power I want any piece of, and I'd invite him to take it back if it didn't involve complex conversation.

"Whatever it is, if you could bottle it, I'd bet you could retire by graduation," Heath says with equal parts amusement and envy.

"Who knows what's going on in that boy's head at any given time?" I say, aiming for indifference and finding something oddly stirring in its place. "He's probably confused me for—well, he's probably just confused."

Not my best, but a kind or nonaggressive word from a Wawheece will throw anyone off their game. A kind glance from those pale eyes and I am understandably floundering. I shake it off and head for the lunchroom.

Rain pummels the roof, the full force of the storm releasing suddenly and all at once. I wish I could do the same.

When we're a mere ten feet from the cafeteria doors, we hear a shriek followed by the sound of a hundred pairs of feet moving all at once. We hurry forward, pressing through the double doors and down the short flight of stairs to where everyone has shifted to the side of the room where windows look out over the football field and the swamp beyond.

Outside, rain falls in heavy, opaque sheets. The crowd is near the windows, but several feet back, leaning away as one. They're mostly students, but I spot a few teachers mixed in. A dozen or so more cowardly souls have huddled at the other side of the room and are whispering, shivering, praying—doing all they can to keep from looking.

With Sterling and Abigail on my heels, I push through the crowd. There's real fear written in the faces of those nearest and I hear clips and phrases as I make my way through: "Do you see?" and "What do they want?" and "How many are there?"

I don't have to ask what they're talking about. Every person I pass has their eyes trained on a point beyond the glass. Lightning flashes over their features, all locked in some form of horror or pain or exhilaration. I feel the familiar stirring in my chest—ghosts.

But reaching the front of the crowd, I see only rain and the hollow reflections of my peers.

Like everyone else, Sterling and Abigail adopt expressions of wonder. Abigail's hand flies to her pendant, but Sterling raises a hand to the glass. Her eyes go mournful.

"What do you see?" I ask, remarkably disappointed. Obviously whatever magic let me see Mad Mary at the gala has worn off.

Sterling hesitates a moment, but it's not because she's afraid. Her lips move silently and I realize she's counting. With each number, her eyes fall a little more.

"Thirteen," she says in a voice just above a whisper. "There are thirteen of them."

"Of what?"

She turns, her eyes finding me, but not really focusing. "Children," she says.

"The Baker's Dozen," I say, taken aback by my own realization. "They were starving, their families were starving because of a five-year blight. Insects invaded the region and as soon as any crop began to grow, it was stripped. Destroyed. People were dying. So the oldest kids from thirteen different families decided that something had to be done. They made a pact and one night all of them left home in the middle of the night. They walked into the swamp to die so that their families would live."

The cafeteria is silent now but for my voice and the sound of rain pelting above our heads. Even the teachers listen to my tale, their eyes watering and darting away.

My mind churns like the storm outside. Another swamp story has come to us.

The teachers on cafeteria duty finally collect their wits enough to start hollering. They tell everyone to move away from the windows, but no one does. How could they, with thirteen child spirits staring at them?

"She can make them go away," someone calls. "Candace Pickens can."

The crowd parts to reveal the speaker, hater Hallie Rhodes with no hint of her usual malice. She's as frightened as everyone else and now they all look to me.

The crowd speaks at once with too many voices to decipher—"That's right!" "She got rid of that other one!" "Candy, you have to do something!" "Do it!" "Fix it!" "You have to!"

Sterling, Abigail, and Heath form a rigid triangle around me, refusing to budge under this strange assault. I try to sort the faces surrounding me, but they become a blur of trembling lips and waving hands.

"Get off her back!" I recognize the commanding tenor of Quentin Stokes and catch his blue eyes as they carve a little breathing room around us.

But the pleading remains. My strange stigma has become the thing they want most from me. Like it or not, this is something I can do and if it's going to be public knowledge, I may as well do it on purpose.

I place my thumb and index finger between my teeth and rip one of the ear-splitting whistles I learned from Aunt Sarah. Sterling and Heath share a gasp and grab their ears. Abigail's back stays tall.

"All right!" I shout. "Keep your panties on. I'll do it."

Handing my bag to Abigail, I ask, "Where are they?"

"You really can't see them?" Sterling asks, every bit as confused as I am.

"Apparently, Mad Mary was an isolated incident." I try not to sound bitter. I remind myself that I never wanted to see ghosts in the first place, but it feels like yet another failure, one more thing that's out of my hands.

"About four feet back from the windows," Abigail answers my original question. "Mostly in a row, but a few are two deep."

"Thanks."

No one tries to stop me. I look straight at Mrs. Gwaltney and Principal Barlow, the latter of whom clearly ran to get here and is sweating and puffing around his gut, but neither of them does anything to indicate I shouldn't walk outside in this dreadful rain.

The cafeteria door is at the far end of the room. I walk along the front of the crowd, between the windows and tables, where I should be sitting with my food. Then, all alone, I push through the heavy door and out into the rain.

Water slicks down my neck, cutting a cold path all the way down my spine. I'm drenched before I can draw a full breath. This is the sort of rain that obliterates the world—there's no color but blurred grays and blues, no sound but the hammering of rain, no smell but the cold scent of water. I shield my eyes.

Four feet back from the school, I see nothing. I imagine

what everyone else must see: a line of hollow-cheeked children with ragged clothing and hungry frowns. I step forward and tell myself that the cold feeling against my neck is only the rain.

Two deep, Abigail said some of them stood two deep, so I open my arms and try to hold my shoulders tall as I walk forward again.

"Why can't I see you?" I whisper as I walk. But there is no answer, only the pounding of rain and the threatening crash of thunder.

When the lightning flashes, I catch the faces watching from the other side of the windows. Fearsomely watching, while I'm frigidly doing.

I wonder how many dead children I've walked through by now. I should've asked someone to count, to pound on the glass when I've completed my duty.

Cold seeps into my fingertips. I shouldn't be this cold in August. I shouldn't be starting to *shiver, shiver, shiver.*

Blood pounds in my ears like rain. My arms grow heavy, my steps slow, and I begin to wonder if I will drown here in this blooming *river, river, river.*

My head sings, my skin sings, my bones sing.

A tree grows up through my legs and branches into my arms and head, all vibrating with this same, sweet melody. *The tree it took her for its own, own, own; fond and jealous of her bones, bones, bones.*

My hand jerks. Pain flares briefly through my fingers. I turn toward it and there stands Gage King, drenched and frowning in the storm.

"Candace," he has to shout to be heard. "Candace!"

"What?" I shout.

"Are you okay?"

Now I frown. "Why wouldn't I be?"

He sweeps one arm out, gesturing to the flooded field in which we stand, and then to the school very far away at the top of the hill. I have no memory of walking down that hill. None whatsoever.

He sees the confusion in my face and with a tug of my hand begins to walk. Not toward the school, but toward the student parking lot. Our feet sink deeper and deeper into the pummeled field as we splash toward firmer ground.

Gage leads us to a car I'd recognize as a dense black Mustang in any rain. He hits the automatic locks and I climb into the passenger seat as fast as possible. He turns the keys in the ignition, but only to blast the heat. Only a fool would try to drive anywhere in a deluge like this.

He offers me a towel.

"I just have the one," he says as an apology. "We'll have to share."

He's as soaked as I am, all clothing plastered against his skin. It's kind of him to offer me first go at the towel and I'm in no mood to play the "who's more polite" game. I take the towel and use it to pat my face, squeeze my hair, and do a quick, hopefully surreptitious nipple check.

"Thanks," I say, returning the towel and angling the heater vents more directly at my chest. "No offense, but why are you here and not Saucier or Beale?"

He laughs once. "Right after you left, Principal Barlow forced everyone away from the door and back to class. I saw your little posse caught right up front."

"And you came after me because . . . ?"

This time he doesn't laugh. "You walked through that whole line of ghost kids and they vanished the second you touched them. I was at the far end of the cafeteria. I could see your face the whole time and right at the end, you sort of blanked out and wandered off." He pauses, remembering to pat himself dry with the towel. "I was worried."

Blanked out. That's not how it felt. But if he hadn't come after me, who knows where I'd be by now? "Thanks," I mutter.

The car warms up fast and even though the windshield is fogging like the river, Gage turns the wipers on full. They do nothing against the storm except remind us it's the victor in this situation.

Gage sits angled toward me, water soaking into the black cloth of the seat and smoothing his not-from-around-here henley against his chest.

Everything about this car is slick. The dash and dials are

all polished like gems, I spot three pair of black sunglasses placed strategically around the cabin, each more battered than the last, and Gage rests his hand casually on the steering wheel as though the car is a beast that requires his touch to keep calm. It's magazine slick, James Bond slick, against the laws of decency slick.

"You guys really do rain down here. These storms don't mess around." He peers through the windshield before flipping the wipers off, convinced they're useless.

"I thought you were from Washington. Doesn't it rain all the time there?"

"Yes, but not like this. It's more of a committed drizzle. Just enough to make you question if you were supposed to be born a fish." A smile creeps up one cheek. "You've been checking up on me?"

"Due diligence," I say, leaning toward the heat vents. I'm warming up, but not fast enough. Grateful as I am to be somewhere dry, I'm pretty sure I shouldn't be here. I should be somewhere quiet and alone, where I can think straight thoughts about whatever keeps happening to my head.

"You okay?" Gage asks after a minute.

"I'm just kind of confused."

"Do you want to talk about it?" Gage speaks against the rain. In comparison his voice is musical.

"Not really."

Lightning flashes through the downpour a second before

thunder vibrates the car. Gage taps the wheel with his index finger and studies me. I study him right back and feel the chill drain right out of my bones.

"Me, either," he says. "But I like you, so I think we should."

I'm floored by his honesty. I nod. This thing exists between us and there's no getting around it so we might as well barrel through.

"You don't see them. Ghosts." It's a statement, not a question. Like Nova, he seems to know more than the rest of Sticks combined.

I shrug. "I don't know. No, I suppose, but I saw the one behind your house, so I must just get spotty reception or something."

"You saw that woman?" His confusion suggests a wealth of knowledge I'd really like to have. "That's good."

"What? Why?" My questions and frustrations mount with equal speed.

"There's something here we need," he responds, casually ignoring my questions. "And when we find it, my father will take it. He won't have a choice."

Immediately, I think of Nova's questions about the source. He's talking about the everblooming cherry tree.

"Why?" I ask.

"Because my mother is very sick," he says simply.

The storm fills the silence that follows. Gage fills nothing except his lungs, breathing in and out while his fingers tighten against the steering wheel. I want to put my hand on his and ease his pain, but it feels intrusive.

"I'm sorry," I say.

"My dad thinks you know something," he blurts, leaning forward with one hand now braced on the seat above my shoulder. "He and Nova."

I start to nod, but he cuts me off again.

"Don't tell him anything," he says, and now his hands grip my shoulders.

"But—"

"No. Don't tell him anything. Don't tell her anything. Don't tell *me* anything. Just . . . don't, Candace, please," he pleads.

"Okay, I won't."

He breathes a sigh of relief. "Good," he says.

But before he relaxes too much, I add, "Then you have to tell *me* something. Tell me what you know. Tell me why what *I* know is such a big deal."

"I can't," he says, remorseful but unbending.

"Then tell me *something*. Give me a reason to trust you."

The look on his face hovers somewhere between regret and defiance when he says, "You shouldn't."

I can't believe how accepting he is of this, how cowardly it is to simply warn me away as though that's enough. If you see someone moving down a dangerous path, you don't tell them that the signs are unreliable, you tell them that the road ends in water or fire or ghosts. The thing he doesn't seem to get is this: if he blocks my way on this path, I'll just make another because I'm not afraid.

But I guess he is.

"No problem," I say, thrusting the door open amid a cathartic rumble of thunder. And this time, I leave him and walk out under the roaring sky.

THE NEXT MORNING, I WAKE to find five texts from folks asking me to please come banish a ghost from their bedroom/shed/kitchen/truck/pants. The last is from none other than Quentin Stokes and it, at least, makes me laugh. The rest, I ignore.

At school, people no longer look at me like I might banish them with a touch. Now they look at me like I've become a superhero, which is better but too pandering for my taste. People expect things from superheroes, they feel entitled to their gifts and powers, and they'll turn on them in a heartbeat if they don't have full access to them. Well, to that, I say no, thank you very much! I'd much rather be the girl I was before. The one people gossiped to and listened to, the one who controlled the crowd and not the other way around.

I spend all of Wednesday brushing off any compliments about my superpowers with a laugh, a flip of my hair, and a roll of my eyes. Anything to suggest it's no big deal and maybe anybody could do it if they'd just try. Sterling and Abigail prop me up, but I know they're worried. Hell, I'm worried, I just don't know what to do about it.

Thursday morning, I wake to the surprising news that school is closed. It doesn't take long to find out the reason is that Featherhead Fred was driving through town not long after volleyball ended on Wednesday evening when he encountered an entire regiment of the Confederate Army marching down the road. He was bleary-eyed and spooked and he swerved to avoid hitting them. His efforts took him right smack into the side of Sticks High.

Sterling, Abigail, and I decide to use the day to our advantage and do as little as possible. They arrive midmorning and we spend our time listening to Abigail's music, painting our nails, and trying not to talk about anything related to ghosts.

Around noon, we hit up Nanny for some sweet tea and take a leisurely stroll through wilting backyards to her house at the edge of my own neighborhood. It's nothing fancy, but a respectable brick house on twenty-seven acres including one small pond, one abused trampoline, and our beloved family graveyard. The good thing about Nanny's house being so large is that it's easy to slip in and out without ever being seen. And with her legendary sweet tea waiting in the fridge, the risk is always worth it.

When we emerge from our shortcut through the woods, there's a shiny red pickup truck in the driveway, bleeding in the sunlight.

"What's Old Lady Clary doing here?" Sterling wonders aloud.

"She and Nanny have started swapping gossip," I answer.

It's actually a good thing. Having company at this time of day means Nanny's likely to be on the front porch or in the sitting room at the front of the house. If we go in through the back porch, we're good as golden.

We've done this a hundred times over the years. Sterling and Abigail know as well as I do where to step and how to avoid being seen. We switch our phones to silent, ditch our shoes on the porch, and slip inside like the thieves we are, walking on the balls of our feet. Abigail reaches for three glasses while I ease the fridge door open and grab the pitcher of tea. Sterling creeps up to the corner where the kitchen wraps around to the foyer and flaps her hands to indicate that the grannies are inside and not on the front porch.

We move as quickly as absolute silence allows, but Old

Lady Clary's voice travels just far enough to be heard as she says, "Something's wrong with Candace."

The girls heard it, too, and for a second our eyes connect. An impulse flashes through me, to scream and stop Nanny from sharing my secret with the town megaphone, to rush the girls from this kitchen so I can be the one to tell them, but instead, I freeze.

"Don't you blame my granddaughter for this, Ida Clary." Nanny's voice rises to meet Old Lady Clary's.

The adrenaline rushing through my ears gives way to curiosity. There's no chance we're leaving now.

We set our glasses on the island countertop and move farther into the kitchen, where we'll be close enough to hear better but still hidden from view.

"I know it ain't her fault, but you know as well as I do what she is."

"That clap is *your* business, not mine. Candace is just a girl like any other."

Old Lady Clary makes a noise I can only call a scoff. "You know that isn't true. Do you think it's coincidence that these ghost sightings are following in her wake?"

My mouth falls open as I realize she's right. All the real ghost sightings have occurred in places I've been or been recently—Calhoun Creek, my birthday party, the Flying J, the locker room, the Kings' house, and the list only goes on from there.

"I'm sure I don't know what you mean, Ida," Nanny says the same way she might warn Carol or Irene away from fresh cookies.

But Old Lady Clary's not intimidated. She continues right on. "You know how I can tell who's telling a true story and who's callin' the dog? Because Candace was present right before each of the real sightings—behind the school, twice at the racetrack, and in the field by the Stokes' house where the kids like to—"

"Stories! And nothing to them but imagination," Nanny cuts in.

"You of all people should know better, Margery Craven. Kids could have been hurt if Fred's accident had happened even an hour earlier, and Candace can stop all of this."

That sends a shock through the three of us. Most of all me. Old Bat Clary must be drinking more than tea to think I can do a blessed thing about these ghosts. How can I do anything about ghosts I can't see? It must shock Nanny, too, because all is quiet for about a solid minute.

"How, do you reckon?" Nanny asks begrudgingly.

"That, I'm afraid, is still a mystery to me. But she's the Shine Child. She's the only one of us who *can* do something."

Sterling throws her hands up and rages silently for a moment. She finds Old Lady Clary a source of pure frustration, but really the answer isn't surprising. Old Lady Clary is two parts mystery and grandeur and one part mysterious shrugs and coffee. She and Sterling have a history of unanswered questions.

"Then you leave my granddaughter out of it, hear me? Until you have something useful to say, you leave Candace alone."

We hear the creak of a chair as Nanny stands up to bid Old Lady Clary a good afternoon, and with that, we steal through the kitchen to collect our sweating glasses of sweet tea and retreat through the back porch.

From the front of the house, we hear Old Lady Clary's truck rev and drive away. We cross the yard and climb into the sagging cradle of the old trampoline to drink our somewhat tainted rewards.

It's a while before anyone speaks. My phone lights up with yet another request. I let it stay where it is at the center of the trampoline. Fred's accident has people understandably worried, but I can't be expected to race across town every time someone thinks they've seen a ghost.

"So," Sterling begins. "Shine Child?"

I knew what it was the second Old Lady Clary said the words. I just never thought to connect it to me. "It's one of the Clary Tales," I explain. "It's the story of a young man who could walk through the swamp unharmed and did so all his life. That's basically the whole story except that there was a girl who was sweet on him and one day followed him into the swamp. The boy was busy collecting flowers or hunting ducks and didn't hear when the swamp sucked her under. She died and he was sad, but he got married sometime later and was given fat, happy babies by his wife."

"So he was kind of like you?" Sterling asks. "Immune to Shine?"

"But why would that make her think you can stop this?" Abigail asks.

There's nothing so horrible as not having an answer. I down my tea and drop the glass to the ground three feet below. Sterling and Abigail watch me with expressions of veiled concern and unveiled interest.

With a sigh, I prepare to let them down. I say, "I have no freaking clue, but I'm pretty tired of everyone else knowing more about me than I do."

"Do you want to ask Lady Clary?" Sterling asks, reluctant.

"What are the chances she tells us anything we don't already know?" I ask, feeling defeated. "I'd rather take my chances with Nova. At least she seems to *want* to tell me things."

When the sun's a less brilliant ball in the west, we deposit our empty glasses inside the porch and head home. As we emerge from the Thurmans' backyard and pick our way along my street, I see a dark SUV parked in the street in front of my house.

Just as we're close enough to see it has Washington State

plates, my front door opens and out steps Mr. King. My mother says something obviously cheerful and he laughs before waving and fixing his big white Stetson on top of his head. Oblivious to our presence, Mom shuts the door and Mr. King crosses the front yard toward his car.

Seeing him causes whatever small degree of patience I had left to snap. I make a beeline for him. He turns and, seeing me, waits.

"Evening, Miss Candace," he offers.

"Look," I say, "I know my parents gave you permission to use that footage, but I *don't* give you permission. In fact, I give you the exact opposite of permission."

His smile is condescending. "I'm afraid they've signed all the paperwork already." He raises one hand with what I assume must be the offending papers. "It's a done deal."

I consider my next words carefully but decide I won't be giving him anything he doesn't already know. "Do you want to know how many people have asked me to come banish their ghosts today alone? If I were a priest, I could turn a pretty penny for my services, but I have no desire to be a priest and if you put that footage in your show, things will only get worse. You're ruining my life."

His eyes shift to my left and right. Abigail and Sterling, I assume, backing me up.

"You're asking me to give up the finest footage I've ever

captured," he admits. "What are you going to offer me in return?"

I pause. He wants the tree, that much I know, but without knowing why, there's no way in hell I'll tell him where it is.

From behind me, Sterling says, "I'll give you an interview. All the swamp lore you want, *and* I'll tell you what happened to me and my brother."

"Saucier!" I snap.

Mr. King perks up at the offer. He rolls the contract between his palms as he considers, weighing my future celebrity against the unknown but enticing offer of Sterling's firsthand account of encountering the swamp.

The streetlights click on, painting our illicit dealings in sickly orange.

"All right," Mr. King says now that he's had a good think. "You come have a chat with me, Miss Sterling, and I'll hand over the contract."

"Deal," Sterling says, stepping up to shake the hand of Mr. King.

"Nice doing business with you."

We don't return the sentiment, but that doesn't seem to bother Mr. King at all. He treats us to one of his winning smiles then slides into his SUV and leaves us alone on the street.

"You don't have to do it, Saucier," I say.

"I know," she answers. "But I might have done it anyway."

"You're a damn fool," I counter. Sterling may think there's no harm in talking openly about the swamp—at least not when she's aware she's talking openly about the swamp—but I think she's dead wrong.

And I decide right then that if there's any truth to the notion that I can stop these ghosts from haunting my town, that I'll do it. If there's nothing for Mr. King to shoot, there's no show, and if there's no show, there's no reason for Mr. King to stick around asking uncomfortable questions.

By Friday, I've become a collection of sharp edges. School is back in session, but with three classrooms out of commission. The classes are redistributed to the lesser-used spaces like the cafeteria, the auditorium, and the library. That works until the ghosts of three girls in dated prom dresses run shrieking across the stage. They weren't there long enough for anyone to force me into yet another banishing, but for the rest of the day people huddled uncomfortably close to me.

When I get home from school, I find Mom in my room with a laundry basket and an agenda. I'm so on edge, it takes all the patience I can muster to keep from sinking my teeth into her.

"Can we talk?" she asks. "No research," she promises. "Just talk."

Even this has cost her. All her usual shields are down. She's trying, and that means I should, too.

I lean against the edge of my desk and she takes the bed. Her eyes scan the walls, which chronicle my greatest achievements from my seventeen years of life in certificates, group pictures, award ribbons, and trophies. My room is a shrine, a tribute to the version of me I need to be in order to leave Sticks. I suspect it gives Mom a different sort of satisfaction than it gives me.

"I've never told you how hard it was for me to get pregnant. No, don't freak out. I'm not going to go into detail, I just need you to know that I didn't know how important these kinds of things were until it wasn't easy." She pauses, having taken us over that first hurdle, and waits to see if I'll bolt like the green filly I've become.

I hold my ground. If there's one thing I know about my mother, it's that she'll say her piece over and over again until she's convinced she's been heard. The surest method out of this is to take the Band-Aid approach. So it's about time I take it.

"You will hate me for saying this, but you can't know what you'll want in five or ten years. I'd hate to see you make choices now that you'll regret later."

I nod. "I know. But they're still my choices and I'm not interested in turning my body into a science experiment on some infinitesimal chance that it'll change something."

"I know what you're going through. I know you're angry and disappointed and confused, but we have options. We can try to fix this."

"I don't need fixing," I snap, suddenly protective of my biological failures.

"Candace, I need you to really think about this. Don't just react, think. You're such an achiever—you're used to being able to do everything really well and you shut down when you can't. I don't want you to wake up one day and realize you've cheated yourself out of something."

I can hear everything she's not saying and it fills me with a cold passion. I want to strike back.

"You don't have to worry because finding out I'm a reproductive dead end was probably the best thing I've ever heard. Do you realize how much sex I can have?"

"Candace!" Her shock smells like fear. "Be serious."

"Oh, but I am." I let cruelty into my smile. "Babies are out of the picture. All I have to worry about are diseases and assholes."

I recognize the degree of control it takes for her not to respond immediately. It's satisfying to know I've planted a seed of worry. If she'll believe that I'm a reckless, angry child ready to drown my woes and seduce half the town, then it serves her right.

She clears her throat and lifts her chin. "I know you're angry. I know this is unfair. There's a lot about life that isn't fair, and sometimes we can't do anything about it, but sometimes we can."

"Don't try to pretend this is about anything other than your own disappointments, *Mom*. You passed your faulty genes to me and now you're suffering because no one will ever call you Grandma. Well, you know what? *Poor you!*"

She stands with the laundry basket pressed to her hip. "Okay, Candace. I won't bring it up again. But if you change your mind—"

"Don't hold your breath."

"If you change your mind, I'll be ready to help."

She closes the door behind her and I scream into my pillow.

I don't want to be fixed. I don't want to spend hours thinking about whether or not I need to be fixed. How am I supposed to know what will make me happy? Or unhappy, for that matter? I know what makes me unhappy right now and it's my mother looking at me like I'm broken.

In the midst of what could quickly become an ugly pity spiral, I text Red and Leo and bully them into holding an impromptu party. There's no real chance they'd refuse, but it costs me twenty bucks and a box of shotgun shells just the same.

Their place is perfect for this sort of thing. They live in an old trailer on the back half of Uncle Jack's acreage. The lawn is maintained by frequent parties full of trampling feet, an outdoor fridge is constantly occupied by a keg, and they keep a firing range stocked with cans and rotting fruit.

With a few well-placed texts and phone calls, I ignite the party. Cars begin rolling up no more than fifteen minutes after my first lure went out. It's satisfying to see. With so little effort on my part, these fifty people will enjoy something less mundane than they'd have come up with on their own. I get a distraction that will keep me busy until I can get some info out of Nova tomorrow. And Mom gets to wait at home and wonder what her precious daughter is up to.

While we wait for the crowd to thicken, we start the night off right with pumpkin carving. It may not feel like fall, but soon the weather'll turn and we'll break out exciting wardrobe pieces like flannel and lightweight leather jackets and scarves.

Leo sets five pumpkins at the end of the range. Red loads fresh clips into a collection of .22 rifles and hands one to me. He saves two for himself and Leo and hands the other two to Heath, who looks like he'd rather not, and Quentin

Stokes, who was the first to respond to my call and shoulders the rifle with a cocky sort of confidence.

Red calls us to the line and we stand a few feet apart with our eyes on the pumpkins.

"Hey, Candy," Stokes says in my ear, flirting. "You want me to help you with that? I don't mind showing you how to grip it."

Stokes is the perfect combination of attributes—he's just pretty enough, just smart enough, just easy enough to be entertaining without inspiring feelings of true love. There are at least thirty copies of him in our grade alone. They're all Ken doll, salt-of-the-earth types who aspire to be exactly what they are. Which makes them easy targets.

I ask, "Your grip gets a lot of practice, does it?"

I fire. He laughs and for the next ten minutes, we all become completely focused on our pumpkins. I take my time, lining up my sights, exhaling when I shoot. Red hollers when the last shot is fired. The air smells like gun smoke and competition.

Leo collects the pumpkins in a wheelbarrow and carts them to us for display. Each one bears the rough approximation of a jack-o'-lantern smile except for mine. Leo raises my pumpkin and an eyebrow.

"It's for Stokes," I say.

"Subtle," says Leo, holding the gutted fruit up for everyone to see.

It's definitely rough, but I have to admire my handiwork. There, in ten bullet holes, are the letters *F U.*

Stokes says, "Any time," and I give him my most satisfied smile.

The night picks up speed after that. Nearly every junior, senior, and recent graduate shows up at one point or another. The notable exception being the King kids. They stay blessedly absent.

This sort of setting is where I do my finest work. I slip in and out of circles, listening and waiting for someone to look at me with a twinge in their eye. Everyone has a tell: Sterling tucks her chin, Abigail avoids eye contact, everything about Heath is a tell. It's more complicated with people I don't care to spend recreational time with, but I've collected more than a few tells in my tenure as a lowly underclassman.

I scan the crowd for any bit of gossip that doesn't have to do with me or the swamp. Beneath a low-leaning pine tree, I spot Max Thames and Tara Taylor bending around each other in some misguided attempt to define the word *lewd.* Max's little sister Kelly has no love for Tara and watches them with her hands strangling her cup. There's something gossip-worthy there. I don't know that I care, but it's better than nothing.

I start to head toward Kelly when Riley Wawheece appears out of nowhere. He's just suddenly here, standing beside me with a plastic cup in one hand, the other shoved into his pocket. When he bobs his head in greeting, I notice how the shadows sculpt his shoulders and chest into something attractive, how here he stands upright and confident where usually he hulks like a crab. Our eyes connect and I notice how a small smile bends his lips just for me.

And then I notice how my first reaction to his presence was nothing like normal.

*Head in the game, Pickens*, I chide myself.

I'm already haunted by swamp ghosts; adding Riley Wawheece to the mix just seems cruel.

"What are you doing, Wawheece?" I ask.

"Just came to say hey," he says, defensive. "Can't a guy say hey?"

"Sure, but a girl doesn't have to listen."

I don't even feel a little bad as I stalk away to find someone more agreeable. But Sterling and Abigail have disappeared too early. Sterling with Heath. Abigail with Shannon. They've both fallen into forbidden romances and they plan to use every stolen minute they can. And good for them. I'm glad for them, but the later it gets, the more the crowd thins until those left around the fire are either the die-hards or the too-drunks.

And I am alone. I called this entire party into being and I'm still alone. While everyone else hooks up or blisses out, I'm startlingly sober and standing here like the parsley on a plate of fried chicken. This is what my mom is afraid of. What boy will want the girl who can't give him kids? What do I have to offer if I can't offer family? I'll end up a ghost before I've died.

I fill my cup with cheap beer and tip my head back to guzzle it in one go. This isn't fair. I'm not ready to think about this. I shouldn't have to think about this. I'm done thinking about this.

I spot a cut figure in the firelight near my cousins. That's the one. The boy of my mother's fears. He's blond hair, thick biceps, and easy manner. He's uncomplicated. He comes with no strings attached and he's exactly what I want.

I stride across the yard, press my hands against his chest, and lean to whisper against his skin, "C'mon, Stokes."

Someone whistles. I don't care who.

Quentin captures the tips of my fingers with his and tugs me into the shadows. My head swirls with anticipation and the beer I downed too fast.

This is what I want—reckless, easy kisses and not a single care for my biology or ghosts. This is what I want.

Stokes pulls me against him, presses my back to a pine tree, and drops his mouth to mine like a ton of bricks. He wants control, so I give it. His mouth barely breaks contact with my skin as it travels from my lips, down my neck, and over the top of my shirt.

My head spins like the sky above.

If my mother only knew what her precious girl was up to. I wish she did. Maybe I'll tell her. I want her disappointment to be legendary.

I grip Stokes by the shirt and turn him so it's his back against the tree. I let my kiss carry all of my fury and then I reach for his belt. He reaches for the button of my jeans, but I move his hands firmly away.

His eyes flare with a question. I answer by tugging again at his belt. His fingers overtake mine fumbling between us until his pants drop to the ground.

"Condom," he says, husky and excited.

I laugh, suddenly flooded with a sense of power and freedom. I lean in to him and whisper, "Here's my secret, Stokes. You can't get me pregnant."

"You on the pill?"

"Nope," I say without a care in the world. "I just can't get pregnant. Ever."

I see the moment he fully comprehends what this means. I feel it in the grip of his hands at my waist, suddenly rushed and greedy. But I don't care. Not right now, not while these careless kisses are burning my neck.

Again, my mind twists, the ground suddenly becomes unstable, and I stumble against Stokes. He's happy to support me, pull me close, drown me with a kiss while the wind whispers in my ear, *the tree it took her for its own, own, own; fond and jealous of her bones, bones, bones.*

Leaves unfurl in my mind, blossoms open pink and wanting, roots shred through my veins and I feel a shiver race through my skin. I feel myself falling into this madness again, I feel my mind spinning with words that aren't my own. I hear a voice not my own and it sings, *They took all she had, had, had, and left her mad, mad, mad.*

What, what, what is happening? I squeeze my eyes shut, but that song continues to spin through my mind.

And then pain. Stokes bites my lip bringing me firmly back to this moment where I am not a tree.

I push against him. "Shit. Stop."

His response is a plea. "What?"

"Sorry," I say, stepping away. "I'm not okay."

That should be code to any boy with sense that stopping is a good thing, but he responds with venom. "You're shitting me."

He's a picture of disbelief with his pants pooled around his boots, plaid boxers glowing in the moonlight, and a dumbstruck expression on his face. My stomach twists. This was a bad idea from the start.

I say, "Not even a little. Sorry, Stokes."

There's not an ounce of grace about him as he gathers his pants to his waist and zips himself in. "Bitch," he spits, then strides toward the trailer with all the pomp he can muster.

I lean against the pine tree. Bark catches my hair and the scent of Stokes is cleansed with the warmth of a summer night, pine, smoke, the sweet hint of honeysuckle. I watch until Stokes passes through the light of the fire and around the edge of the trailer.

My gaze drifts through the patches of night sky between the pines to the constellations there—stars like families, drawn together by proximity and stories.

And here am I, the North Star. Brilliant and isolated, orienting everyone but connecting to no one. I am all I'll ever be and I don't know what that means anymore.

I've never been the girl who imagines her wedding or anticipates a family like it's a given that I'll have both, but I've never considered that neither would be in the cards.

But I've also never imagined myself alone. And right now, that's all I see in my future. Me.

And me alone.

I USED TO THINK SLEEPING in was overrated. There's nothing worse than the feeling of waking with the sun fully alive and present inside your room. Your eyes feel assaulted and heavy, half the day is gone, and sleep becomes a tangible thing you take with you through the rest of the day. I don't like it.

But the morning after the party, I love it. I pull the covers over my head, ignore the call of my parents from the kitchen, and sleep, sleep, sleep until my body revolts and says, *Get up, or pee in the bed.*

By the time I've made myself presentable for the late afternoon tryst with Nova King, my parents have gone off to do whatever it is they do on weekends, and Abigail has called my phone five times. Which is every bit as unusual as me sleeping in, which is how I know she means it. I dial her number.

"Candy," she says.

"Beale," I say.

"When are you meeting Nova?"

I check the time. Already after noon. Gross. "In a few hours," I answer.

I hear the measure of her breath on the other end. "Do you want me to go with you?"

"Thanks, but I do think it's better if it's only me, and I'll be fine. Unless she's secretly a cannibal and is planning something culinary, she can't hurt me. Shine can't hurt me."

While Abigail decides how to react, I pad through my empty house and dig some cold pizza out of the fridge. It makes a more than decent brunch.

"Okay," she says, unhappy. "But call me the minute you're done."

"Yes, Mom."

"Call me whatever you want," she says. "Just call me."

"Promise."

We hang up and I eat the rest of my pizza at the empty kitchen table, thinking that a friend is someone who reminds you who you are and who you want to be. Abigail reminds me that I'm not alone even when I have to do things by

228

myself, because she's out there, waiting for my phone call. Just knowing that bolsters me to get moving.

It's late afternoon when I turn up the drive to the Lillard House. I pause to marvel at how much it's changed. The stretch of the oak tunnel is dark, but at the end, the Lillard House is bright and fearless in the sun. Though I'm here begrudgingly, a part of me looks forward to spending more time inside it.

Nova meets me at the door.

"Hungry?" she asks, first thing.

I hesitate, but the truth is I can always eat.

"There's still leftover cake from the party," she explains. "A lot, actually. We need help eating it."

She's right. There's enough cake to feed half the senior class, or two starving girls. We cut pieces as large as our heads and take them into the living room. Everything in this house is still and quiet. Even with most of the windows open, the abandoned feeling of the old Lillard bones lingers beneath the veneer of curtains and fresh paint. I search for any hint of a mother figure, but other than a family portrait posted over the mantel, in which their mom is a thumbnail with a smile and brown hair, there's nothing. No mom purse, no matronly jackets slung over the couch, nothing feminine that doesn't point directly to Nova.

"What's wrong with your mom?" I ask.

Nova's fork pauses in the air. Then she shrugs and answers

without meeting my eyes. "Back pain. It's hard for her to get out of bed most days."

We keep eating, but I resist the urge to be lured into a sense of comfort. "You were going to—to share some information with me?"

She leans in. "I am."

I don't know how to react, so I don't. I just sit there, staring at her over my chocolate cake, wishing Sterling or Abigail were here to react for me.

Finally, I manage, "Ready when you are."

She laughs. "Okay, but you can't look at me like I'm nuts when I tell you."

I wonder if my face does anything other than look at people like they're nuts when they talk about Shine. "Promise," I say.

With a gesture that I should follow, Nova sets her cake on the coffee table and jumps up. Several of these ground-floor rooms are as empty as they were for the party. They look barren and sad in daylight, but we don't stop in any of them. She continues through the house, down a side hall to rooms I haven't seen since they were in ruins. This portion of the house is bare with only a runner carpet and a few ancient paintings on the walls. All the doors hang open, revealing smaller rooms with unpacked boxes or sparse furniture in them. Lonely rooms.

We stop at the only closed door on the hall. Nova knocks

softly, listens, then retrieves a key from the molding over the door opposite this one, and lets us into a dark room.

"Dad's out filming in the swamp, but the house is so big, I always have to double-check," she whispers.

The room is cool and smells like old wood and a spice I can't name. Nova presses the door closed so quietly I know only because the room is suddenly even darker. I hear her moving. Then there's a click and a small desk lamp casts a green glow around the room. As if this weren't eerie enough.

I don't have to ask where we are. Clearly, this is Mr. King's secret lair.

This room comes from the recent dark ages, the time before telephones and computers. There's nothing here to connect it to the outside world. The desk is cluttered with stacks of books and papers. All unremarkable in their chaos. Behind the desk are two tall shelves packed to the gills with additional books, some of which look old enough to be my very great, very dead grandparents.

On either side of the desk, the walls bear paintings. One of Joan of Arc, her face stuck in one of those possessed expressions with the spirit of God behind her, one of a man kneeling at the feet of a kingly ghost, and one that's clearly Chinese or Japanese of a child cowering before a horde of terrifying creatures. It might be the way the green light makes everything look sick, but I shudder at that one.

Nova ducks behind the desk, opens the bottom drawer,

and begins to empty it. She stacks everything precisely on the floor in reverse order, taking care to remove items one at a time.

On the corner of the desk is a small gilded frame with a picture of a woman in a cowboy hat with dirt on her face. Her smile is resigned and directed at whoever it was holding the camera. It's the dark hair that gives her away as the elusive Mrs. King, which means someone clearly thought Mr. King was worth his salt once upon a time.

"Your dad doesn't seem like he'd notice if two of those folders were reversed." I crouch next to Nova, straightening the edges of her pile.

"This drawer, he would notice," she says with surety. "Believe me."

When she's pulled everything out, she presses her fingertips against a barely noticeable impression at the farthest edge of the drawer. There's a soft *click* then the floor lifts away in her hand, revealing a compartment beneath that's half as deep as the drawer. A sharp scent attacks my nose and I sneeze once violently. It's not a stealthy sound and Nova glares her displeasure.

"Sorry," I whisper, rubbing another itch out of my nose.

Inside the secret drawer are a journal and a collection of leather pouches. Nova reaches for the journal, and together we squeeze onto Mr. King's desk chair with the book on our laps. It, at least, isn't ancient. It looks like a standard leather journal you could find at any bookstore, assuming you have a bookstore and not the "Books and Barbecue" trailer that sits in the parking lot of the Flying J gas station. You'd be hard-pressed to find something like this in Sticks.

Nova unties the cord and quickly flips through pages of handwritten notes, illustrations, and clippings from newspapers and magazines, coming to a stop about halfway through. The page is dated March 22, 1977—Seal Harbor, WA. Below that a yellowed newspaper clipping is glued flat and reads:

### Strange Sighting in Seal Harbor

In the usually owlish community of Seal Harbor, sightings of what can only be described as spirits have become commonplace. Residents report being aware that the area was "a little different," but things seem to have taken a turn for the dramatic of late.

Said Heather Skiff, a longtime resident of Seal Harbor, "We've got spirits and who knows why, but we always have. Sometimes they're just brighter than others. We aren't worried." That was the general sentiment around town, and in fact the town has experienced several recurrences of supernatural activity in the past. This reporter was able to dig up fourteen similar occurrences dating back to the early 1800s.

Below the article, Mr. King has made careful notes about the little mountain town. Seal Harbor is pushed halfway up the edges of the Olympic Mountains in Washington State. He notes what sort of vegetation is normal, what sort of geography is normal, and below that he's drawn a sketch of the same damn cherry tree that's hiding in our swamp.

"The hell?" I peer at the word scribbled beneath the drawing: *Source?*

"You recognize it?" Nova asks.

"Yeah," I say. "Yeah, we've got one just like it."

She bobs her head, all of her hair swinging by her chin. "I thought as much. Do you know where it is?"

I shrug.

Nova leans in close, her eyes eager. "Your friends do. Do you think they'd take me to it?"

It's the eagerness that does it, sets my caution on edge. "No."

I can always tell when people are hiding something and in this moment, Nova is definitely hiding something. Her lips pinch against a desire to argue and she takes a second to analyze the commitment in my face. I hold steady and after she's realized this truck ain't for sale, she returns her attention to the journal.

"Here, this is what I wanted to show you."

She presses her finger to the opposite page, where Mr. King has written a series of questions and answers. The one that captures my attention is, *All power requires balance, so what's the balance here?* Then, a word underlined five times: *Child?*

"I don't understand," I say, my mouth going dry.

"He describes it down here," she says, dragging her finger down a paragraph of text. "There was some old sha-man type in town who talked about how these occasions of power in the world always create a site for it to root and a counterbalance. The tree is the source and the child, called the Blind Bone, is the counterbalance. They both must always exist or neither of them will."

"I still don't understand. Why are you showing me this?"

"Because," Nova says, searching out my eyes with her own. "You're the Blind Bone."

I stare at her for a second in disbelief. Then I simply say, "Bullshit."

Nova grins and snaps the book shut. "I don't think so."

"Then explain, because I'm not going to believe it just because you *say* it's true."

Nova sighs. "C'mon. Not here."

She fits the journal into the hidden compartment, then just as carefully as she removed them, replaces the stack of folders, papers, and pamphlets meant to throw snoopers off the right track. When she's satisfied there's no distinguish-able difference between now and when we found it, she closes the drawer and switches off the light.

Wrapped in darkness once again, we make our way to the door and into the hallway. This must be the benefit of having such a large house. There's still no one in sight. We make it down the hallway and through the back door without encountering a single person. I'm mildly disappointed.

Nova strides into the grass, making straight for the scrubby hill that rolls into the swamp. The one Mad Mary Sweet climbed.

"Do we have to go down there?" I ask.

Nova pauses. She's so unlike Sticks. I've always resented the notion that it's possible to tell when someone's not from your neck of the woods. Mostly because when I do finally pick a school and leave this place, I want my new city to embrace me as if I've merely been away for a few years. But Nova is all sharp lines and angles where Sticks is all blurred edges and coils.

"No," she decides, returning to me.

We settle on the back porch with our legs dangling over the edge.

"Okay," I say. "Explain."

She crosses her legs and leans in. "Like you saw in that article, Sticks isn't unique. Shine exists in . . . well, we don't know how many places, but in all of them there is a person, a Blind Bone, who balances that power. That's you. You can always tell who the Blind Bone is because they naturally dispel Shine with a touch."

"I'd really appreciate if you stopped referring to me as the Blind Bone."

Her laugh is short. "Just Bone, then?"

"Candy," I say. "It's worked this long. But why am I the swamp's dedicated buzzkill?"

"You're not a buzzkill," Nova says with an amused smile, one that shrinks her eyes and mouth all at once. "You're the natural balance. You exist to keep the Shine in check—to keep it from running wild through the town or even farther. You're like Congress."

"Oh my sweet baby Jesus, please pick another metaphor," I plead, automatically flashing back to Mrs. Thompson's class on the branches of government and the time I was forced to dress up like a bill and parade around the class. I couldn't remember what I was supposed to say when, and all I remember from that day is the snickering giggles of all my classmates.

"Fine," she says, nodding. "How about a virus?"

I can't imagine where this is going. "So long as you're not leading up to a sex joke."

She snorts. "You're not the virus, you're the vaccine. Think about the source of Shine as a sort of constantly proliferating virus."

This would be easier if I'd ever seen Shine, but I recall Sterling's descriptions of the everblooming cherry tree the way she sees it. How the Wasting Shine spreads out from it in a twisted web that connects all the living things of the swamp.

"Go on."

"You're the naturally occurring vaccine that keeps that virus in check."

"I'm not sure I follow. . . ."

"Focus, Candy," she says sharply. Too sharply? "You are the boundary around the swamp, and you're just as powerful as that source, wherever it is."

"No, the fence is the boundary around the swamp." I distinctly remember Sterling explaining that Fisher and Lenora May couldn't cross the fence without assistance. That was the boundary for them because it was the boundary of the swamp. Nothing still connected to Shine could pass it.

But Nova shakes her head. "That fence has never done more than deter the people of this town from treading where they shouldn't. Believe me."

"But the ghosts didn't start appearing until Sterling and Phin broke the fence and stuck a gate in it."

"Candy." She says my name with importance. "That fence worked because you believed it would. It was the story you grew up with, right?"

"Yes, it was a story. A fiction. A thing that isn't real."

"Sometimes, we believe things without meaning to," she says.

"Bull," I say.

But she doesn't believe me, and the more I think about it, neither do I. Before this summer, I would have sworn on my life and the lives of my family that something had to be seen and proved in order to be believed. But I was wrong. Sometimes, belief isn't a matter of fact and proof; sometimes it's a matter of trust. I've never seen the Shine, but I believe it's real because I trust my friends.

"You heal fast, don't you," Nova states, breaking into my thoughts. "Not immediately or perfectly, but faster than you should."

Instinctively, I rub the scar in my left palm. But it was an aberration, wasn't it? Or was it only the first injury bad enough for me to notice? The cuts on my knuckles I earned from shattering my diploma should have stung much longer than they did. But they've been gone for days.

Nova takes my silence as an answer. "I thought so. Bone children usually do, but there's always a trade-off. Some are blind. Some have a single deadly allergy. Some lose their minds. Whatever it is, there's always a trade-off."

*Some lose their minds.* The thought leaves me nauseated. I push to my feet, very ready to be done with this entire conversation.

"Two more things." I hold up a finger. "Why did I suddenly see that ghost at Gage's party when I haven't seen any of the others?"

She shrugs. "I'm not an expert, but it's probably something you did."

"I didn't do—" The memory of shedding blood into the roots of the damned cherry tree halts my denial. "Maybe." I raise a second finger. "Two. I am not immortal, which means there must have been a . . ." It pains me to speak the words. ". . . Blind Bone before me."

"I love how smart you are, Candace Pickens." Her smile is admiring. "Yes. It's a cycle: when one dies, another is born."

"What?"

I didn't actually need her to repeat it, but she does anyway.

"When one dies, another is born. Always on the same day, sometimes down to the minute. It's like the passing of the torch."

A chill slips down the entire length of my body.

"Or a curse."

I LEAVE. I MUMBLE AN excuse and run down the long corridor of oaks. I don't feel the wind on my skin, the gravel beneath my feet, I don't even see my way clearly, I just run.

The curse is real. The Craven Curse I've mocked my entire life as the worst sort of family nonsense is real.

*Maybe more real than I am.*

My head spins. My breath stumbles. I have to stop running and press the meat of my fake hands into my fake eyes until some semblance of stability returns.

Wild thoughts flood my mind. I don't know what I did to my junior year to make it come at me with such a vengeance, but I wish with every fiber of my being I could take it back. I wish with every fiber of my being the Kings had never come to town, that Sterling had never opened my eyes to the reality of the swamp, that I hadn't been born to such a small, odious place as Sticks. *Odious.* The word feels good.

If I'd been born anywhere else, maybe I wouldn't have to worry about things like fertility and Shine. Instead, I've won the lottery. I'm a *thing* with a *name* and the ability to heal faster than normal people do. All it cost me was what? My sanity? My fertility? Was I lucky enough to win two trade-offs, as Nova called them?

What possible prize could be worth either of those things? Nothing. Absolutely nothing.

I kick at the large gravel on the side of the road. The Mississippi River snakes by, dragging sunset on its back. I stoop, gather rocks in my hand, and hurl them into the water. Sunset fractures and it's satisfying to destroy something so beautiful, even temporarily. That means I can destroy it again and again. And I do.

Ahead, I hear the low growl of an engine. A modern Mustang—the sort so popular you can't go a mile without spotting one on the highway—rolls into view at the curve of the road. It's dark, gunmetal gray, and absorbing the light of the setting sun.

Gage.

I back into the grass, waiting to see if he'll pause or smile or in some way acknowledge my presence.

He doesn't.

Though his window's down and he passes near enough that I can see the time on his dash, he doesn't even do me the courtesy of the one-handed wave. He passes and continues as though I'm not standing here.

All my frustration takes shape inside my chest.

I rip off my shoe and hurl it as hard as I can. It smacks against the rear windshield and the brake lights flare angry red.

The door opens and Gage emerges, deliberate and stalking toward me. Sunset cuts him in half. He is half light, half dark, walking like a tempest. He stoops to retrieve my shoe without breaking his stride. His eyes pin me.

I lift my chin.

"You dropped this." He thrusts the shoe between us. His words are controlled.

"No," I say. Chin up, chin up, chin up. "I threw it. At you."

His eyes narrow before they explode. "Why?"

The shout is welcome. "Because you were rude!"

"Rude? *I* was rude? And what's throwing your shoe at someone's car?"

"Necessary."

"Which brings me back to *why*?" He's not shouting anymore. But his anger is in the flush of his skin.

"Because you ignored me just now and you won't talk to me. Neither of those is acceptable in my book."

His laugh is humorless. "Acceptable." He repeats the word.

That saps some of my backbone. I feel it drain right down to my toes, leaving my stomach vaguely sick. "I know you like me. You said it. So talk to me."

This time when he pauses, he lifts his eyes and takes a slow, deep breath. "I'm . . . That was all a mistake," he says, then starts to retreat.

My toes tingle and my gut churns. There is nothing else. I'll stand here until the sun has set on this fretful day. I'll wake in the morning to my mother's cry of "The crows are in the corn!" still watching Gage's taillights burn a path down the road.

He's nearly to his car before I feel my legs again.

"The hell it was."

I rush to him. Press my hands to his chest, push him against the car, and lift my lips to his. His mouth is hot and resistant, but only for a second. I pull his bottom lip between mine, his hands fall to my waist, then his arms crush me.

Our kisses aren't shy but furious and hurried.

He lifts me and turns my back against the car, kissing me until my lips burn and I don't remember ever touching the ground.

I don't know which of us takes a breath first, but finally we part and my toes remember what they're for.

It's dusk. The sun has abandoned every part of the sky and the cliffs of Gage's face are painted in watercolor. I run my fingers through his hair, over his forehead, down his neck. He lets me explore, until I'm ready for another kiss. He catches my hands with his, putting a little more distance between us.

"Okay," he says, his voice on unsteady legs. "I lied."

"I know," I say, stepping forward, but he holds out his hands.

"But it doesn't change anything."

At some point, his car got tired of the door hanging open. The air pings repeatedly with its irritation. I know how it feels.

"What is that supposed to mean?"

"It means—" He stops, but this time he doesn't look down or up or away at the running river; he looks right at me. "We can't do this."

"Why?" My anger starts boiling again. "Stop being such a coward and tell me *why*!"

"No!"

"I know what I am! You know why? Because *your sister* told me. What I don't understand is why you all care so damn much. So I'm this Bone, so what?!"

It's nearly dark, but I'm pretty sure the expression on his

face is what you would call stunned. Instead of answering, he scoops up my shoe and pushes it into my hands.

"I told you not to tell her anything. You need to stay away from us. All of us. Please, Candace, for your own good."

The sting is sharper than I expect. I fire back, "You want to know what pisses me off? People who think they know what's good for me. What is it about boys and parents that makes them think they can tell me what's good for me without offering evidence? I know what it is, piss and arrogance." My anger has momentum now; there's no stopping the storm that is me. "Girls can't possibly keep sense in their pretty heads, right? We need authority figures to guide us along the safe path. Well, you know what I say to that? I say f—"

Gage rushes forward, stopping my mouth with his. It's as fierce as I've ever wanted any kiss to be, fierce and desperate and fraught.

I push him away. "That's not the way this goes."

He nods like he knows. Again, there's a gulf between us, a span of space that both holds me back and tempts me forward. Between us are questions and answers that would change everything if only we'd uncover them.

"Keeping people in the dark never goes well. You say I should stay away from some vague threat. Well, that's not how I deal with threats."

"I'm trying to help you."

"Well, you suck at it."

He flings himself back and, raising his hands, shouts, "I know!"

Night has become as dark as this conversation. There's no clarity here other than the light streaming from Gage's headlights, and they only illuminate what he chooses.

"I'm not going to play this game with you anymore," I promise.

"You shouldn't," he says heavily.

I deny my watering eyes. With a curt good night, I jog out of his taillights and as far as I can possibly go. I'm halfway home when I remember I drove to the Kings' and have to return for my damn car.

There's no traffic in this part of town. It's just me and all the dying summer bugs as I jog along the river. The oak tunnel feels especially cavernous tonight, oppressively cavernous. I miss the closed-in warmth of my bed. There is too much room for madness here.

My car is parked to the side of the house. Right next to Gage's Mustang. Nice of him to come give me a ride back to the house. If he had, I might have made good on my promise to throw my second shoe.

Which is probably why he didn't come.

I walk softly across the gravel, mindful of any noise that might give me away. I hear nothing but the gentle grating of stone beneath my feet, the chirp of crickets, and the distant shushing of the river.

But then, above all of that, a cry that raises the hair along my arms.

It drifts along a single pitch then stutters into a sob and I realize it's a female voice keening from somewhere within the Lillard House.

With a shiver, I dive into my car and peel away.

NANNY LIKES ABIGAIL. NO IDEA why, but ever since I first introduced them, they've been fast friends. Honestly, I think it makes Nanny feel cosmopolitan to tell people her granddaughter has black friends. It doesn't usually come so in handy, until I need to distract Nanny.

First thing after church I call Abigail and Sterling. I explain what happened with Nova as concisely as possible and end by shamelessly begging them to help with my biweekly internment as Nanny's Sunday-afternoon minion. Why? Because she's the keeper of the family tome and I need to know more about the Craven Curse and the Blind Bone.

We dust and vacuum and scrub for the better part of three hours.

"Tea!" Nanny calls, inviting us to pause in our toil. She has a pitcher of sweet tea and a basket of fried cheese sticks on the front porch.

Abigail protests that she'd rather keep cleaning and get the work done, but Nanny's having none of it. We'll take our tea or risk offending her down to her hard-as-opal bones.

The tea is Nanny's signature perfect sweet tea—just the right ratio of tea to sweet with a sprig of mint to cool it off. We only get the sprig of mint when we aren't filching it. Add the spice of her cheese straws and not one of us bothers to make conversation.

This, it turns out, is a tactical error.

"Girls," Nanny sings. "Won't you convince Candace, here, that it's a good idea to see a doctor about her . . . troubles? She won't listen to her mother."

Years of bracing for Nanny's subtle attacks is the only reason my jaw doesn't drop. I do nothing to indicate surprise or hurt. I sit and I sip my tea, letting Nanny's words wash over me like a cold shower.

Sterling is the one to give me away. Always, always Sterling. While Abigail is a statue, Sterling reveals everything with the shape of her eyes.

"Don't tell me she didn't tell you two?" Nanny feigns

surprise but is clearly delighted to be stirring the pot. "I thought for sure she'd have told her best friends."

"I didn't because it's not a big deal," I say, unable to resist this bait.

"Not a big deal? But of course it is, hon; you're just too young to recognize it. Mark my words, it won't be long before you care and then you'll sincerely regret not seeking treatment."

I grind my teeth. I know what she wants. She wants to goad me into a public argument with her in which my friends will be guilted into taking her side because she's old.

"Thanks for the tea," I say. "It's exactly what I needed to keep going."

Sterling and Abigail follow my lead and we return to the living room, where Grandpa Craven's picture sits above the taxidermied head of the one and only gator he ever killed. The story is that he was duck hunting with friends when they spotted a gator in the tall swamp grass. He'd never hunted a gator before, but he was full of gumption that day and somehow convinced his friends it'd be a great idea. Sometimes I think it's my favorite thing about Nanny's house.

"You want to tell us what that was about?" Sterling asks, inquisitive without prodding.

Abigail doesn't say a word. Of course, Abigail already knows.

"No," I say, but I do. "You know how I never got my period? Well, the doctors say I'm not . . . fertile. And in my mother's eyes and in Nanny's eyes, that makes me less than a woman, but it's no big deal."

Pity can be so quiet and so needling. I feel it from both sides and it makes my skin itch.

"Oh, Candy," Sterling breathes. "I don't even know what to say."

Abigail surprises us all by pulling me into the biggest, most amazing hug I've ever experienced. Sterling joins, wrapping her thin arms as far as they'll go around both of us, and I start to feel an uncomfortable pinching in the back of my throat.

I had no idea how sad I was until this moment. Until my friends hugged me instead of trying to fix me. Until I didn't feel like it was a matter of being broken, but a matter of being different.

"It's no big deal," I repeat, struggling to keep my voice steady. It's never okay to cry at Nanny's house, so I push them away. "Let's finish and get out of here."

They're reluctant to let go. Sterling steps back and awkwardly twists her hands together, fretting. Abigail slides her palms down my arms to squeeze my hands in hers.

She looks me dead in the eye and says, "There ain't nothing about you that makes you *less*."

I feel the well of my eyes start to fill. "I love you, Abigail

Beale, but Lord help me, I will never forgive you if I spill a tear right now."

She cracks a grin. "Then nut up, Pickens."

"Would you just guard the door?"

I find the tome Uncle Jack uses to torture us every year on the shelf by Nanny's bed. She keeps it in a locked box but leaves the key lying on top. Uncle Jack gets after her for leaving valuables out in the open like that, but she always argues that if someone wanted in a locked box badly enough, the lack of a key wouldn't stop them.

It's ancient, leather bound with crispy pages and a smell like history. Sterling crouches behind me, her chin on my shoulder.

An elaborate drawing of the family tree spans the first pages. Someone with a careful hand did this in the days before ballpoint pens. Curling cursive letters tumble out of the leaves one after another, growing more fruitful the closer they get to the bottom. There's something very affirming about this tree. I may not carry the line forward, but this past seems very, very alive.

I finger the blue satin ribbon tucked between pages and flip to it. Here is where the Craven Curse gets going. The words *The Peculiar Case of the Cravens* are elegantly carved in black ink. In all the years of Uncle Jack's readings, I've never once laid eyes on the actual text. It feels forbidden.

I flip the page.

It begins with a narrative about who first noticed the trend of synchronized birth and death among family members all the way back when our family first settled in these parts. The stories were passed down orally for a time until Sarah Sissy Craven thought they deserved ink and paper. She began the chronicle and passed the book down to whoever was the next link in this "curious chain."

"What are we looking for?" Sterling whispers. She's known about the curse for as long as I have, but neither of us thought it was worth believing in until Nova unwittingly connected it to Shine.

"Anything odd," I suggest. "Anything that confirms what Nova is saying."

I have no idea what that will look like. I suppose we'll know it when we see it and not a minute before.

We stay hunched and unmoving, flipping pages as quickly as we can read them, making torturously slow progress. Cursive truly is a dying art and it's one neither of us is fluent in. Every time Nanny Craven makes a noise, I'm certain she's coming through her bedroom door ready to smite me for snooping in her things. Never mind the fact that I'm supposedly next in line to inherit this thing. And when that happens, the scanner will be my best friend.

The stories all start with the name of the curse bearer, the person's spouse, parents, children, and who the curse landed on next. It's a tight little lineage, but rarely a straight one. I search for a pattern and find none: it has no loyalty to either gender, it doesn't have a special preference for the children or grandchildren of the current bearer, and it doesn't follow a set number of years. For all intents and purposes, it appears to be completely random.

The only thing I do notice is how many of the female curse bearers were as childless as I'll be. Every so often, there's a couple with no child. Their branch of the tree stunts while others flourish around them. I feel a kinship to these women already.

"Go back!" Sterling flaps her hand. "There. Read this one."

I follow her finger to an entry that barely takes up half a page. It's such a familiar story I didn't even have to read it. Poor, sweet Annemarie Craven who went mad and died in the swamp.

"What about it?"

Sterling's expression suggests I've missed something major. I follow her finger to a faint notation made off to the side. "Mary," she says. "Mad Mary . . ."

"Sweet," I breathe, astonished.

I'm a direct descendent of the very ghost I confronted the night of the gala.

I'VE COMPLETELY FORGOTTEN THE PARTY at my cousins' by the time school starts on Monday. If I needed a measure for how twisted my priorities have become, that's it.

No one else forgot about it, though. Everyone who did go is talking about it with smug smiles, and everyone who didn't go is trying to figure out how to get themselves invited next time. But the glory of the moment is tainted by what accompanies those stories—ghosts encountered by lovers in the woods, ghosts following people home from the party, ghosts in the streets and fields and trees.

My name is rarely spoken without the word *ghost* or *spirit* or *haint* hanging in the surrounding sentences.

When Nova slips into her seat in front of me for European history, all I can think of is how I'm apparently the Blind Bone of Sticks, but I don't know what that really means, and how I'm related to Mad Mary Sweet. It makes focusing on anything else a challenge I'm primed to fail.

I stare into the crease of my textbook as Mr. Berry gets rolling. On either side, words stretch away, but I focus on the sliver of a shadow running down the center of my book. It grows darker the longer I look at it, dark like the *river, river, river.*

The bell rings. I look up, ready to follow Mr. Berry into whatever lesson he has planned, but everyone around me is standing up, gathering their books as though class is over.

Because class *is* over. The clock tells me so, and so does Abigail's concerned nudge.

I pack up, shaking off whatever it is that just happened and focus on not letting it happen again for the rest of the day. But it nags at the back of my head through every class and all through lunch. That voice was back, *her* voice was back, pulling my mind into a deadly dance I didn't even realize I was in.

I'm so distracted that I miss the first evil glare from Quentin.

"What's his deal?" Abigail asks.

I look up in time to see him leaving the cafeteria with a glare.

"I, uh, sort of turned him down Friday night."

"With a face like that, I'd have expected you shot his dog."

I shrug. It's not an inaccurate description of what happened between us, but it can't be the first time he's faced rejection.

By the end of the day, Quentin's decided to make a scene. He's waiting for me when Abigail and I return to my locker. Normally, I'd approve of any aggressive gesture from his broad shoulders, but not today. And not like this.

"I know your secret," he says just loudly enough to be heard by myself and Abigail. He leans against the locker next to mine, invading my space with a predatory grin. Once upon a time, I'd have found something tempting in that grin. It's the sort that promises dangerous kisses in dark corners, the sort that makes you feel like you're falling over.

I defy him with my balance. "Which one?"

His lip curls. "And you owe me."

"Owe you?" I snap. "What exactly do I owe you?"

He closes the distance between us and drops his mouth to my ear. "For you to finish what you started."

"Or what?"

"Or I tell everyone how it doesn't matter what you do to her, Candy Cane can't get pregnant."

And just like that he's crossed the line. I give him a swift shove right in the pecs. He flies back, surprise and anger making an ape of his face. The fact that there's any surprise at all is a testament to how much of an ape he is. The fact that I'm surprised is a testament to how poorly I judged his character.

The hallway should be clearing out by now, but traffic's become conveniently sluggish and students are clumping like sheep.

"Slut." He lobs the word like a bomb.

I take a second to consider if this is worth the escalation. There's too much of an audience for anything else, and the blood-burn of conflict is already alive in my chest.

"Who cares if I'm a slut? At least I don't have to blackmail girls into getting on their knees."

Our audience suggests I've won this exchange. But Quentin doesn't like their opinion. There's violence in his eyes when he starts to advance, but Abigail moves behind him and slips a foot into his path. He's too focused on me to notice and trips neatly over it. He hits his knees with a crack.

"You gonna let your pet dyke fight your battles for you?" Quentin sneers, spotting Abigail.

Now Abigail freezes. Her wish to become invisible breaks across her face as the same people who cheered my insult of Quentin now snicker at his insult of her. Fickle recreants.

I stride over and take her hand, turning to challenge Quentin with, "Way to rock an insult like it's the twentieth century, you ass. You shame your family with insults that old."

"You a dyke, too, now, Candy?"

My peers are as dumb as he is, gasping like that comment had a single cutting blade. Abigail's fingers are cold, but she's not dumb. She's afraid. And that pisses me off.

"And what if I am? What if Abigail and I are lovers? Afraid to learn girls are better kissers than you are? Here's a shocker: I'll bet a dog's a better kisser than you."

The curses he drops are the foulest sort. Colorful as stained glass, but strung together so poorly, the result is a mess.

I laugh in his reddening face. "Now that we've exhausted your vocabulary—"

He lunges.

The crowd cinches at my back. I have a split second to decide if I'm going to dance or flee.

I raise my fists and easily deflect Quentin's jab. He's not fooling around. That punch was full force. Made for knocking teeth out of grins and lights out of eyes. My opinion of him improves for the fact that he's willing to fight a girl.

Our crowd is pleased. Every other hand is holding a cell phone; every eye is alight with the thrill.

Quentin jabs again. This time, he follows it with a faster

hook than I'd given him credit for. I'm not fast enough. The blow glances off my shoulder.

Bastard.

In my head, Leo's voice is steady as a wind: *Pain is weakness leaving the body. Keep your hands up, use your knees.*

There's no way I can overpower someone like Quentin. I have to be quicker and smarter. Sharper.

I ram my knee into Quentin's thigh and when he crumples just a bit, I follow up with an elbow strike to his cheek.

In my peripheral vision, I see Abigail right where I left her, standing inside our ring of spectators, a twist of anger and fear frozen on her face. Not everyone can be good in a fight, but I didn't expect her to be quite so bad.

The glance cost me. Quentin shoves his fist into my gut and I buckle. I know what happens now: a knee to the face, an elbow to the back of my head, anything to drop me hard and fast. I've done this a thousand times with Red and Leo but never with such ferocity. The next blow will be unforgiving. I brace for pain.

Then a growl from behind and another colorful profanity from ahead. The smack of fist against skin is unmistakable, and when I stand, I find Riley Wawheece huffing over the bent form of Quentin. Everyone else is still and silent.

"We done here?" Riley hulks. The skin on his knuckles split from the impact, but he shows no pain.

Quentin spits blood at Riley's shoes.

Before either of them can make another move, Principal Barlow barks, "Break it up!" He pushes through the disintegrating crowd, arriving red-faced and frowning, a pen strangled in one tight fist. "Quentin Stokes. Riley Wawheece. Why am I not surprised?"

He doesn't even look at me. Everyone else does, and I'm infuriated for more reasons than I can name.

I step forward with a brazen confession on my lips, but Riley cuts me off. He says, "The only surprise'd be if Quentin threw a decent punch."

Quentin rises to the bait. He pulls all of Barlow's focus with a new string of curses. Riley uses the distraction to catch my eyes. The look he gives me is more eloquent than he's ever been with words. He says, *Let me do this.* And I swear he even says, *Please.*

It's so chivalrous I stand there stunned. His hands fall out of fists and his body somehow transforms from hunched for a fight to confident. He's so familiar with the punishment in store for him that it's provided some strange sort of comfort.

I'm not enamored with the idea of being rescued from a good fight, but I'm also not enamored with the idea of being benched until the end of volleyball season.

Principal Barlow leads them away, completely ignorant of my involvement, and I let them go.

Everyone will know this story inside of ten minutes. If

I'm lucky, someone will decide Riley was the self-sacrificing hero and I was the hotheaded damsel who got in over her head. If I'm not, the reigning story will be that I started a fight I couldn't finish and took advantage of dim-witted Wawheece. Since Riley's never been the heroic type and I've never been the damsel type, I suspect I know which will win.

It only sort of matters. Neither will capture the bizarre complexity of what just happened.

And what *did* just happen here? Quentin got a small taste of justice, Abigail's honor was defended, and I escaped a wicked knockout—those things are certain. It's the other piece that makes me question the way of the world. Did I actually share a significant, *sincere* moment with Wawheece? In this case, I'm not convinced the truth makes a better story. And I'm not convinced I want to spend any more time pondering Wawheece the Bald and his unsettling act of kindness.

Any stragglers have lost interest now that the boys have been carted off. The carcass has been picked clean and now the flies are peeling away one by one, texting as they go, spreading my shame like disease.

Abigail stands exactly where she's stood this whole time. Her arms crossed tight against her chest, shoulders hunched as though blocking a winter wind.

"Let's get the hell out of here," I say, reaching to tug her along.

She jerks away from my touch, and stalks down the hall without a word.

I pause, allowing this new twist in the fabric of my life to fully register. Abigail hadn't moved an inch since the fight started. Abigail just huffed away. Abigail . . . is upset. But why?

Long legs give Abigail an edge over me when it comes to speed, but she's not running. She's stalking. Angrily. I catch up. Confusedly.

"Beale! What?" I ask, trotting across the parking lot.

She doesn't stop until she reaches her temporarily-running-again car. She rips the door open and thrusts her bag inside. Then she spins and there's an unexpected sheen of tears in her brown eyes. She says, "How could you do that to me, Candace?"

"What are you talking about?" I plant my hands on my hips and for the first time feel the bruise on my elbow. "I just fought Quentin Stokes for you!"

"No. You didn't." Her voice is a whip holding me back. "You did it *for* you. But you did it *to* me."

This does nothing to ease my confusion. I cast through the very fresh memory of doing battle with Stokes, looking for any egregious act that might have upset Abigail, and find none. "You're not making any sense!" I grip my hip bones to keep from flinging my arms at her. If I move, I will explode.

"I don't expect you to understand," she quips, and now I do explode a little.

"Oh no. That's a cop-out. That's a cheap parental cop-out and it's not what friends do. You tell me what you think I did wrong, Abigail Beale. You tell me right now."

For a brief moment, her eyes close and her face becomes placid. I'll never understand how she buries herself like that, folding the truth of herself away under the story she wants us all to believe. I think it must hurt.

When she opens her eyes, they're still wet, but the look in them is controlled.

She says, "You know how you didn't want the world to see what happened that night at Gage's birthday party? How you felt about Quentin sharing your secret? Well, you turned around and did the same thing to me."

"In what universe does that make any sense?! He was attacking you!"

"Yes, he was, and everyone knows he's an arrogant sack of lies, but *you*, you used me, Candy. You made a joke about who I am and said it loud enough for everyone to hear."

"But—"

She interrupts my protest. "When they hear it from you, they believe it. That's the way it is. That's your gift, and I don't want anyone thinking they know the first thing about my life."

Now I understand. She's afraid I've given away her secret.

"But everyone knows, Beale," I say. It takes real effort to keep my voice gentle and not flush with the frustration I feel. "It hasn't been a secret for a long time."

"There's a difference between something being known and something being said. Especially around here."

"Okay. I get that, but the people who matter don't care. It's not important anymore. Even here."

Something falls from her eyes. Tears, and a sadness so quiet I almost miss it. But it's there in the press of her lips, in the protective bend of her arms, in the way she's so certain I won't understand.

"I wish that were true," she says, defeated. "Just . . . leave it alone."

We don't speak again. She retrieves her gym bag and returns to school for practice. I should follow. Coach will start whether I'm there or not and I'll be benched for show-ing up late. But I don't move. I stand in the first real chill of autumn in the mostly empty lot and watch my friend. Tall and stately, dark skin aglow in the warm light, she walks as though something haunts her. It drags at her shoulders and weights her steps, tugs her chin down and casts a thick shadow over her back.

In the stories that make up Abigail, she's always the understated, unlikely hero. For three weeks in the seventh grade she secretly slipped her own lunch into Ben Craig's backpack when his parents fell on harder-than-usual times.

To this day, he doesn't know it was Abigail. The only reason I know is because she needed his locker combination and I'm terribly resourceful. She swore me to secrecy and since it's a well-known fact that a broken promise is the first step toward chaos, I kept my mouth shut and split my lunch with her every day for three weeks.

All the stories of Abigail's kindness are similarly self-sacrificing. She notices some breech of justice, finds a way to correct it, and does so without anyone the wiser. I used to think she was irritatingly humble or allergic to attention.

The truth of the matter is much less endearing and it hits me like a years-overdue train. She's not avoiding recognition. She's atoning for her shame.

And I'm the asshole who used that shame like my own personal weapon.

I FEEL LIKE I'VE KILLED my best friend.

We don't speak for the rest of the afternoon. We go to volleyball practice and get yelled at over and over again by Coach because something's off and she can't figure out what. My gut hurts twice over: once from Quentin's punch, and once from emotional rot. The combination leads to a supremely shitty performance on my part. I don't have the heart to tell Coach it's my fault that Abigail and I are out of sync and creating a domino effect through the team.

I spend a sleepless night trying to find the words that will fix us, but I end up replaying the fight in my head. She looked at me like I'd destroyed her and I don't know how I can do anything to repair that.

My alarm sounds, rescuing me from another devastating analysis of all the ways I failed Abigail Beale. I get ready for school without any zeal whatsoever.

Hot showers are a good remedy for most hurts, but mine does very little. I stare into the swirling drain and even though the water is nearly hot enough to scald, there's a cold inside me that makes me *shiver, shiver, shiver.*

"Candy!" Mom shouts, banging on the door. "Candace Pickens, you're about to be late!"

Late? I had an hour when I got in the shower.

Turning off the faucet, I realize the skin of my fingers is pruney and the bathroom is choked with steam. I race to get dressed and when I reach for my phone I see that Mom is right. I spent nearly an hour in the bathroom and I'm ten minutes from a tardy slip.

Mom adopts a look of concern when she sees me, tentatively asking, "Everything all right?"

My stomach is now a solid knot of bruise and regret so at least I'm not lying when I say, "Stomachache."

Her eyes drift from my face to my stomach to a bit lower, where for just a second I catch wild hope in her expression. "Oh, honey, I'll heat some milk and honey."

The familiar press of anger rises in my chest, but it's dull. Dull enough for me to feel a twinge of sympathy for my mom. "That's okay. Thanks, though," I say.

By the time I leave my house, I feel so far from normal I may as well be in another state.

There's a difference between knowing something and living it. I *know* I'd make a great president just like I know the earth rotates constantly, but I can't say what it's like to sit in the Oval Office or feel the pull of the moon against the ocean.

I knew my town was small. I knew it was bound together like a solar system, with opposing forces and physics and moonshine. I knew how events on one side of the system affected movements clear at the other end because I was a part of it and sort of apart from it, too.

Today, I know my town is small because I'm suffocating inside it. Everyone looks at me like I'm an alien. In the absence of Riley and Quentin, who both received three days' suspension, I'm all they have to look at.

All anyone wants to talk about is the fight. From the minute I get to school to the minute the final bell rings, I'm stalked by whispers and rumors, none of which are about my new superpowers. I never thought I'd prefer questions about my spirit-banishing talents to anything, but the third time someone suggests I'm Riley Wawheece's one true love, I'm ready to reevaluate my priorities.

Sterling missed practice yesterday and today she can't contain her horror, fluctuating between fury at Quentin for being a dick and confusion over the tension between me and Abigail. Heath simmers whenever anyone dares to speak Quentin's name, Nova regards me with a mixture of curiosity and admiration, and Gage has the most maddening reaction of all. He drops everything when he spots me and rushes to my side. He stops just short of touching my chin and we end up in a strangled moment, a wordless encounter in which he studies my face and clenches his jaw but ultimately convinces himself I'm all right and walks away.

Abigail regards me not at all. Not in class, not at lunch, not at practice.

For the next two days, everything exists on the edge of a knife. Sterling tries to be all things to both me and Abigail. She encourages me to apologize, but anytime I get close to bringing it up, Abigail repeats, "Leave it alone."

So I do.

When Riley ambushes me at my locker on Friday, things go from bad to worse. He stands there in a canvas jacket over a T-shirt and distressed jeans, his bald head made shiny by the fluorescent lights. The expression on his face lacks any of its usual aggression, which is disturbing enough, but the absolute worst thing about his appearance at my side is the fact that he's obviously gone to some effort to clean himself. He doesn't smell of sweat and grime, and everything from the shine of his head to the state of his fingernails looks *cared* for.

He says, "Hey."

And that's when I know I'm in hell.

"What?" I respond.

He stutters, but is inured to such mild abuse. "Once again, I'm just saying hey."

I regard him coolly. There's no world in which this can be a good thing. He probably wants to hear me say "thank you" or apologize for the suspension he suffered. But there's no reason he needs to act friendly first. I can already imagine how this will exacerbate the rumors of our unearthly courtship.

He smiles. A genuine "I'm a nice guy" sort of smile without a hint of its signature cruelty. It makes his face look more human. In fact, it makes all his features fit together seamlessly: his wide lips are supported by a broad jawline, his nose has room to display all the tragedies his life has wrought, and his eyes are the clear blue of a swimming pool.

As I consider whether they've always been so blue, they crinkle in amusement and I experience a sinking sensation as I realize how deeply entranced I've been by Riley's eyes.

"What?" I say. Again.

His chuckle is self-satisfied. "I just asked if you caught any shit for Monday. At home, or anything."

*He was thinking about me? He was worried about me?* The thought throws me off my game.

As far as fights go, I got off easy. No visible bruises to explain or attempt to cover with makeup. The worst blow I took was in my gut and if anyone saw me naked they'd know it was given with malice, but the only person who sees me naked is me.

"Oh, um, no. No shit on my end. You?"

I regret the question immediately. Riley's been catching shit at home for ages whether he did anything to earn it or not. His answer is a rehearsed shrug, a darkening of the eyes, and an involuntary clench of the fists. There's a brick wall between us where before there was a freakish field of daisies and sunshine and eyes a perfect watercolor blue.

"Well, thanks," I say, suddenly eager to smooth things over. "It wasn't necessary, but thanks."

"Yeah, I know." He leans away, then with a smirk adds, "Candy Cane."

A second passes before it registers that the nickname didn't bother me. Two seconds pass before it registers that people are watching me. And a whole three seconds pass before I'm witty enough to wipe the smile from my face.

Lord save me from myself.

By the end of the day I feel like getting a tattoo or piercing my skin or drinking my weight in Old Lady Clary's hooch. Something, *anything* as long as it's destructive. There's only one of those I can get away with in the long run, so I needle Red to get one of his legal friends to buy me a bucket of booze until he relents. It only costs me a promise to come over and clean the bathroom in the trailer. He wanted the kitchen, too, but gave me a pass on account of giving Quentin Stokes more love than he gave me.

Clary hooch is the strongest stuff around that won't make you go blind. Grandpa Craven loved it and that's why it's been the drink of choice on my birthday for as long as I can remember. It's illegal as sin, but the last person in Sticks likely to do anything about it is our very own Sheriff Felder. The story is that the Felder family owes the Clarys a life-debt that goes back to the very early days of Sticks's history.

So when she cooks up batches of corn liquor, he looks the other way.

And I get a mason jar of crystal-clear delirium to help me unremember this week.

The list of friends to share it with is shorter than it should be. I try my best not to get totally lit in front of Sterling, and the temperature between Abigail and me is still frosty. There's the B-string, but I'm not in a mood for sycophants.

I'm also not in the mood for solitude. Sitting alone in my room while Mom and Dad fall asleep to a movie in the living room is definitely the worst way to end this week. I need someone who doesn't bore me and doesn't adore me.

One name occurs to me. It might not be a smart name, but she's the closest thing to an ally I have anymore. At least with her, I know where I stand. And maybe she has more information to share.

I tap a quick text to Nova: *have hooch, will travel.*

In the five minutes that pass before her response, I entertain the idea of taking this week from bad to worse and going to have a nice long heart-to-heart with the swamp. I've only seen the one haint. It's the outlier, the exception to the rule that I, Candace Craven Pickens, do not do crazy. But if what Nova says is true, if the Blind Bone always has a weakness, then crazy might be very much in my future. There's no other explanation for seeing Mad Mary Sweet and only her, for hearing her dizzying song in my mind on so many occasions. Maybe I should take my jar and go camp at the base of that damnable cherry tree until the sun rises. If insanity is going to happen, why not hasten its approach?

It's a horrible idea, but I can feel the resolve forming in my chest.

I'm saved from myself by Nova's text: *pack a bag and come over. how would you like to get revenge on stokes lol.*

I can't get to the Lillard House fast enough. In the driveway, I pause long enough to search for Gage's Mustang. It's the first stroke of luck I've had all week that it's conspicuously missing. That probably means he's out helping his dad harvest all the swamp stories this town has to offer, but right now, I don't really care.

Nova greets me with a half-full bag of chips and a tray of cupcakes.

"I could kiss you," I say, making myself at home in her worldly temple of a room. I kick my shoes to the corner and settle into the sleeping bag she prepared for me.

"I wouldn't turn you down," she sings. "What is that?"

I can't help my laugh. "*This* is a bottle of Sticks's finest home brew."

She takes the jar from my hand, wrinkling her long nose as she reads the label—a mailing label printed on the Clarys' home machine, circa 1985. "When it's red, you're dead, but Clary burns clear?"

"Moonshiner wisdom. You don't drink any old hooch, you have to test it to make sure it's not full of poisons. The test is simple, burn it. If the flame turns red, drink it, you're dead. If the flame is clear, drink it, you're still here."

Her grip on the bottle turns delicate. "You're sure we should drink it?"

"Nope," I admit. "But I'm not in a mood for things I 'should' do. I won't be offended if you keep it sober."

She ponders the jar in her hand. When her gaze finds me, it's topped up with mischief.

"Great," I say and twist off the top.

It doesn't take long before my head swims in that perfect place between being able to list the presidents in chronological order and not caring when I forget Howard Taft.

That's when Nova springs to her feet. "Are we in a revenge-having mood?"

It's hard to imagine Sterling or Abigail ever indulging me like this. In our trio, I am the mastermind. Having another one around feels decadent. I willingly give her the reins. Quentin may have gotten in trouble for the fight, but I sense things between us are far from over. There's no way I can get my secret back from him.

"I'm in whatever kind of mood you want me to be."

Nova's smile spreads like butter and before I know it, we're outside beneath a glittering black sky.

I should know by now that my friends will always, always lead me to the swamp. At least this time, I'm in jeans and feeling extremely agreeable. Nova leads us down her pre-ferred path to the fence and a short ways beyond. We trip and giggle as the ground gets softer and softer.

"According to Mr. Calhoun, there's a herd of wild boar somewhereabouts," I warn when something crashes nearby.

"The same Mr. Calhoun who wears Velcro-strap shoes and mismatched socks?" Nova asks, skeptical.

That makes me laugh. "Good point."

"Of course, with my luck recently, they're probably wereboars who hunt young girls instead of truffles, have bad breath, and a fetish for tusks."

Nova pauses to give me a bewildered look.

I shrug. "Blame it on the hooch."

After a few more minutes, Nova stops. All around, the swamp is settling in for autumn. A few bugs snap, but for the most part, everything is quieting down. The trees are making room for more sky, and the ground is collecting a winter coat. In my growing expertise on all things swamp, I have to admit this is my favorite excursion yet. It feels so calm, there's almost a sense of order.

"I just need a little bit of Shine," she says after a few more minutes. "It's always stronger if you can get it closer to the source."

I wait for the question that naturally follows that statement: *Will you take me to the tree?* But it doesn't come. Progress. Maybe whatever preoccupation the Kings have with the swamp isn't as dire as Gage implies, and Nova and I can be real friends instead of convenient ones.

She goes through the motions of a priest blessing the host or wine. I don't hear what she says, but for a moment, I imagine I can see what she sees—the soft, ruddy glow of Shine against the dark of the swamp. Light flashing against her skin like a cigarette. I close my eyes and see the flash against my eyelids. It flares, bright as a motion sensor.

I imagine the swamp is carpeted in light, the brilliance of Shine carving veins and arteries through the meat of the swamp, turning the mud, the brush, and every single tree into part of its body. Every single thread leading to the same place. Every single thread searching for me. Me, the middling magician, the Mary, the mad, mad, mad me.

None of my thoughts make sense. Tipsy. This is a serious hooch-soaked tipsy.

I look down and find my feet are ringed in Shine. I see it. *Do I see it?* I stand in the black-hole center of millions of little tendrils, all thrumming with the pulse of the swamp. It fills my ears and arrests my heart, forcing it to *tha-dump, tha-dump, tha-dump* like a good little soldier.

Nova's voice layers over our heartbeat. "Perfect. Time to go."

She grips my hand in her icy one. Or is mine icy? I follow when she tugs, reluctant to leave this unique and heady sight of the swamp.

I hear laughter—Nova's—as she trips her way toward the fence. When I look down again, the swamp is black and thick and dull.

We emerge into crisp air and a black sky full of stars. I feel no pain. I feel perfect as we race up the hill and climb into Nova's car.

There's no way she should be driving.

"There's no way you should be driving," I say.

She presses a reassuring hand against my thigh. "I didn't have as much as you, remember?"

I think back. How much did we have? Not much. I'd only been in her room for a few minutes before we set out for revenge. One small glass. Each. There must have been more. But I don't remember more, I remember being *mad, mad, mad, she's so very bad.*

My heart roars with the engine, roars like furious water filling my lungs, roars like the voice trapped beneath.

Nova guns it down the driveway and up the side road. I open the window so the cool air can sharpen my senses and convince me that there's nothing wrong. Because there is nothing wrong. I repeat the phrase in my head, breathing deeply.

By the time Nova stops the car, I almost believe it. But the night swirls around my ankles like snakes.

*I am Candy Cane Pickens.* No. *I am Candace Marie Craven.* No. *I am mad, mad, mad.* No.

"Candace Craven Pickens!"

"You okay over there?" Nova asks.

I pinch my own thigh. Hard. It'll bruise, but the pain is just bracing enough. The only voice in my head is my own.

"Just psyching myself up," I lie.

We hop out of the car and Nova meets me at the nose. "You wait here. I'll be right back."

I blink and she's back. With Quentin Stokes.

Behind them, I finally take a minute to notice that we're parked in front of the Stokes' house—a double-wide with ten cars representing as many decades parked in the yard. We're all the way across town.

Quentin approaches warily. Good for him. Even so, he

looks dangerous in a destroyed way. He's in a destroyed red hoodie and an equally destroyed pair of jeans. His hair, similarly, is a devastation of blond spikes, sharp as gator teeth. Beside him, Nova flashes me a devious grin. Whatever she has planned, I'm suddenly very eager.

"What do you want?" Quentin asks, prickly.

Nova says, "Candy's brought you a peace offering, haven't you, Candy?"

I have no idea what she's talking about, but she nods meaningfully at my hands and I find I'm holding a smaller jam jar of Clary hooch. When did that happen?

"Um, yes." I lift the jar and offer it to Quentin. I guess I'm apologizing. "Sorry, Stokes. No hard feelings?"

He takes the jar, as uncertain as I am about what's happening here. "Whatever."

"Have a sip," Nova urges.

The image of four strawberry daiquiris comes to mind. The jar of moonshine glitters in Quentin's hand. But it's not just moonshine, it's Wasting Shine. And I realize that this won't be a typical revenge scenario. I weigh my curiosity against the discomfort I feel in this moment. It's not right to use Shine against people like this, but it'll serve Quentin right for being such a dick.

Quentin takes a sip with a placating smile for Nova. "Great. It's great. Now this is getting weird so . . ."

"Not so fast." Nova whips out her phone and begins

flipping through the applications. "I have a request to make of you, Quentin Stokes."

"I don't have time for this shit."

When he turns to go, Nova says a single word: "Obey."

I expect Quentin to argue, I think even he expects to argue, but as soon as his mouth opens, his expression relaxes. His eyes go glossy.

Nova is pleased. She steps closer to Quentin and says, "Candy is going to ask you who you secretly wish you could kiss and when she does, you're going to say Riley Wawheece and then you're going to explain that is why you're so jealous of her. Got it?"

He nods.

Nova lifts her phone, ready to film. "Your turn, Candy."

I think I should be horrified—I know I should—but it's delight I feel. If not for Quentin, all of my problems would be cut in half. Or, at least in thirds, because I wouldn't be in this gut-rotting fight with Abigail. This will feel good.

"Stokes," I say, briefly wondering how theatric this should be. I decide not much. Blackmail material doesn't have to be pretty, just present. "Who do you have a crush on?"

He shakes his head but is compelled to speak. "Riley. Riley Wawheece. But he likes you and that pisses me off."

"Tragic," I say.

The laugh that comes from Nova is teasing and sharp.

She pats Quentin once on the cheek, whispers something in his ear, then trots to the car. There's a sense of urgency now and when I look again at Stokes, I see why. A wash of emotions is dawning on his face. Whatever it is she did to him, it's expiring.

Just as we're peeling down the driveway, his shouting assails the night. Nova tosses the phone into my lap. Mine, I realize. She's made the recording on my own phone, not hers.

As soon as we're safe once again in Nova's room, she raises the jar of moonshine. "Here's to giving assholes exactly what they deserve!"

Together we laugh and sip at the clear liquid. I'm really no better at it now than I was on my birthday. Just a sip brings tears to my eyes and tempts me to cough. It doesn't matter. I make it a healthy sip.

Nova uses my moment of weakness to snatch my phone. She says, "Time to make this tragic love famous."

"Wait, what?" A sober feeling comes over me. "No! You can't post that."

"Why not? I thought you wanted revenge." She presses play again. "This, my friend, is what revenge looks like. If we post it, he's ruined."

And suddenly, all my delight flees. I know what it's like to have this sort of threat hanging over your head—if Sterling doesn't go chat with Mr. King next weekend, I'll know what it's like to have that video posted. No way can I do this to another person.

"It's not only him, it's them. Wawheece is involved now, too, and I've got no beef with him." Abigail's words ring in my mind. Posting this kind of thing would hurt her, too. Not because there's anything wrong with boys loving boys or girls loving girls, but because using the video like this implies that there is.

I get it. Exactly what Abigail was trying to say to me. I get it and I wish to high heaven that alone was enough to repair the damaged bridge between us.

I say, "Look, you may not have spent a lot of time in the South, but this is the sort of thing that'll bring hell down on those boys. The fact that Stokes knows I have it is more than enough." This video ensures that Stokes won't tell a soul about my reproductive issues. My secret is safe, I had a little fun, and that's more than I expected to get out of this. "We have to delete it."

We sit in the small pool of light cast by her bedside lamp. It pushes shadows up the walls, where they fill every crevice of her Venetian masks, making them sinister.

"Here's the thing, Candy, I want something from you." Now Nova smiles and her face shifts from playful to dangerous. She holds my phone close to her.

"What?" Shock brings me to my feet. "Give me my phone."

The room tilts ever so slightly. I panic. Either I'm tipsy, or about to blank out for a tremendously awkward hour. *Focus, Pickens.*

"Sure." Nova tosses her head, making the feather by her ear flutter. "Take me to the tree and I will."

"No."

"Take me to the tree, or I post this video."

"Are you threatening me?" My own voice is choked with a sudden rush of anger.

"I tried to be nice, but I think you need an incentive." Nova waits, her thumb poised and ready to post. "I want the tree."

I step forward and deliver a sharp kick to her shin, catching my hostage phone as she drops it.

"I don't really give a damn what you want." I snatch up my bag and head for the door. "I'll never take you to that tree."

I slam the door and head downstairs. It's late and quiet and I'm just tipsy enough that driving is a bad idea. I slip into the living room and curl up on the sofa. The video glows on my phone. Just looking at it brings on a fresh wash of anger.

I sweep my thumb across the trash can, deleting the video forever.

MY DREAMS ROCK AND ROCK and rock. In them, I'm on one of my cousins' four-wheelers, stuck in the mud and pulling the whole thing back and forth to work it free. It's the end of the season. The cypress trees are beginning to rust between stubborn, green pines, and the air is just nippy enough to make my skin prickle. Mud coats my legs. It's warm against the wind. I can hear Leo and Red haranguing me, making cracks about how my arms aren't man enough for the job.

Back and forth, back and forth, the rocking gets more pronounced, but there's no hint of the give I should feel as the wheels come free of the mud. Instead, the water begins to move in a circle, faster and faster until I'm pulled along with it and I spin and spin and spin.

I wake to whispers. No, not whispers. The rub of metal on metal. Knives. I wake to the sound of knives being sharpened. It seems perfectly reasonable for the few seconds it takes my brain to reconnect all of its circuits. The sound fades and I feel a small puff of wind against my cheek.

When I blink, the house is dark and unfamiliar. The ceilings are smoother than mine would be, the windows taller and lacking the pinpoint glare of my neighbor's always-on security light. Not my room. Not my house. I'm lying on the Kings' sofa because I wasn't ready to drive. Right.

The floor heaves when I roll to my side and the whole room tilts on its axis. I feel drunk. Bad drunk. And in desperate need of a gallon of water.

My feet aren't convinced that I should use them. It takes me a minute to feel secure in a standing position, one hand on the wall for balance. The distance between me and the kitchen is intimidating. I take my time, keeping each step small and quiet. My balance increases with each one.

I didn't drink enough hooch to be this drunk. A few sips before the incident with Quentin, a few after, certainly not enough to cause this kind of feeling.

My steps are softened by the thick runner carpet, but

I feel cold and exposed. The only sounds are the very faint hum of some appliance and a struggling moan from above.

I pause and listen. The moan falls and I decide it must have been the wind. Once in the kitchen I get blessedly lucky and find the Kings' glasses in the first cabinet I try.

There is nothing so sweet as water. I guzzle glass after cool glass until my stomach reminds me it's in a mood to be delicate. I stand, leaning my back against the counter, willing sobriety into my head. Afraid this tipping sensation is not a drunk feeling, but a crazy feeling.

More water. My stomach resists, but I gulp, hoping that by filling myself with water, I'll feel more solid. I lean against the counter and take a few steadying breaths. Then it's time to go.

The King house is more cavernous than usual in the dark. Now that my sense isn't being dominated by a primal need for hydration, I can appreciate how truly eerie it is to be walking through their elegant living room in my thin cotton pants and tank top. Floorboards cackle beneath my feet. The moans from above gain a little volume and a shiver passes down my arms. I should leave. Slip through the front door and race home to my own sweet bed, but I see a sliver of light down the hallway that holds President King's secret lair.

I take a few cautious steps toward it and stop, because now there are voices. Harried, urgent, whispered voices.

I move closer.

The first voice I hear is tinged with panic. "—we shouldn't even *be* here. If she dies, it's *your* fault."

"Don't you think I know that?" This voice, though still whispered, is somehow more substantial and mature. Mr. President King himself, I'd wager. "But we don't have a choice anymore."

There's a pause. It feels weighty and important. I wish I could see the faces that carry it. Then the first voice speaks again. "Yes, we do. It's just not a good one."

Again, silence. This one is painful in length.

"Right now, my main concern is Candace," Mr. King says, falling out of a whisper. "We need to—"

"I know," Gage responds heavily. "But Nova won't quit, Dad; she's not thinking right."

My head spins. I press a hand to the wall for balance. *What, what, what are they talking about?* I'm torn between the impulse to barge through the door or run away.

Run away. I think running is the smarter choice. Run now, confront later. When I'm dressed and less hazy and the sun is up.

I back away from the door. Above me, the moan comes again, wending its way through the walls and down the stairs. The hallway feels colder now than it did a moment ago, the moan more insistent. I follow the sound, climbing back up the twisted staircase and treading softly down the hall, away from the end with Nova's room.

A few of the doors stand open, which makes it easy to see when they're empty. I pass one that must belong to Gage, going by the tossed bed and stacks of books in need of a shelf. I take special note of the telescope by the window: it's larger than any I've ever seen and actually pointed at the sky—not the typical use of telescopes around here. Guess his interest in astronomy goes deeper than constellations.

The next open door surely leads to Mr. King's abode. There's a small voice in my head reminding me that waltzing into someone's bedroom, but especially *this* bedroom, is a piss-poor idea. I do it anyway.

Through the windows the sky is cloudless, the moon a bold capital *D* over the swamp, and not a single pine shuffles in the breeze. It's calm as death outside. And from above, another moan, louder this time, glides through the house.

This room is a shrine in the worst way: elaborately framed pictures hang on every wall, all of the same woman I saw in the picture he keeps in his secret lair. In one, she's young and laughing with her hair tossed out behind her. In another, she stands in her wedding dress, balanced on a brick wall with the long train of her dress dropping to the earth like a column. In yet another, she's surrounded by the cradle of her three children, a tired but no less spirited smile on her face. And in yet another, she gazes at the camera with very little expression at all. It's not fancy. She's wearing a flannel shirt and there's a smudge of dirt on her chin, but the look in her eyes draws me farther into the room. The others are so clearly a documentary of her life, but this one . . . this one is so personal I can't look away.

The final picture is actually a tall painting mounted between the bed and the wall. It's clearly a rendering of Mrs. King in her happiest days. She stands in a long dark dress before a cherry tree in full bloom with a wistful smile on her rosy pink lips.

Missing entirely is any sign of Mrs. King herself.

"Where are you?" I hear myself saying.

A sound makes me spin and for a moment I hold my breath and listen for any suggestion that Mr. King and Gage are on the move again. But all is silent.

Except for the quiet rasp of breath.

Not my breath.

But close enough to stir the hair at my neck.

I spin and there stands a woman with hollow cheeks and wide, mournful eyes. She's the negative of the vibrant woman in the painting. A pale and withering Mrs. King. Behind her, the painting swings on hinges revealing a dimly lit staircase.

She's so close I can see the crest of blue veins beneath the pallid sheen of her cheeks. The look in her eyes is both empty and entirely focused on me.

I inch backward. "Um, Mrs. King?" And I recall the curling script of the gala invitation. "Ruth? Mrs. Ruth?"

A sound begins in her throat. Her jaw worries up and down and then the word finds shape. She lists toward me. "Bonnnnnnes."

"What?" I ask, inching back again, fighting the urge to flee this spectral woman.

"Bonnnnes," she repeats and now she seems to find her strength because her voice rises. "Bones, bones, bones!"

She lurches then, mouth gaping, arms out, nails scraping at my flesh.

I scream, flailing to escape her grasp.

"Mom!" I hear Gage bark.

"Ruth!" I hear Mr. King shout.

Then there are hands pulling us apart.

"What are you doing in here?" Mr. King demands, struggling to contain his distressed wife. He continues, "You have no business being in here, Miss Candace."

"I—" I search for the lie that isn't too much a lie. "I thought I heard something."

"Get her out of here," he says to Gage curtly.

"What's wrong with her?" I ask.

But no one answers me. Gage's arms are a vice around my shoulders. He steers me to the door and into the hallway, where he pauses.

"Are you okay?" he asks, looking me up and down.

I fold my arms over my chest and note that he's barefoot and smells like swamp.

"I'm fine."

Even in the dim of the night, his face is bright with conflict as he says, "You have to go. You have to go and *never* come around us again. Do you understand me?"

"Perfectly." I step away from him. My hands shake when I unclench them, so I keep them tight against me. "What's wrong with her?"

He sighs sharply. "She's sick."

"I can see that, but why is she here instead of a hospital?"

Nova's voice sounds from the other end of the hallway. "Everything okay?" She stands in the soft light of Thad's bedroom, the boy clinging to her like a static-filled sock. "The shouting woke Thad."

"Go back to bed," Gage snaps, and I suspect a little of that anger is actually for Nova.

"You can have my bed if you want, Candy," Nova offers kindly, as if our fight never happened. "I'll bunk with Thad."

At the same moment, Gage and I answer her.

"I'm going home," I say, while he says, "She's going home."

Nova shrugs and slips away to rest with Thad and that's as much of this family as I can take.

At some point, Gage's hand reasserted its grip on my elbow. I pull away and head for the stairs. He follows. Silent. Guarding. Brooding. Until I've gathered my things and reached the front door.

At the threshold I stop, unable to resist a snipe. "You know what? Whatever it is you're trying to hide here? It's gonna come out. Secrets have a way of doing that around here."

Then I leave. I march myself straight through the front door into the chill of night.

My breath comes in little white puffs. The cold sinks right through my thin pj's and reasserts the injustice of being thrust out in the middle of a September night. I fumble my keys, drop my bag, and break a nail all in the course of trying to get inside my car. When I finally do, I start the engine, blast the heat, and lean my head against the seat until I can feel the tip of my nose begin to warm.

And right as I begin to reverse, I see a light flicker in the narrow gabled windows above the second floor. A figure ghosts past and back again, pausing to press a thin hand against the pane.

I strain to see more, but the hand fades and even through

the layers of glass between her and me, her moan fills the night.

Nova said Mrs. King suffered from back pain, but that's not what I saw. I saw a woman who'd lost her mind.

And I shudder because part of me also saw my future in her madness.

TOWN PICK-UP DAY WASN'T A real thing before this year. With the arrival of television cameras and the promise of fame, the town's decided to sand off the uglier edges of Main Street: Clary General's getting a fresh pour of gravel for the parking lot and new seat covers for the rocking chairs; the Flying J's getting a new coat of paint and home-made signs that say things like "Stop here for cold beer!" instead of the disintegrating cardboard advertisement for Coors that's been in the window since I was born; and Miss Kristy of Kristy's Kountry Stitchin' has made red-and-white gingham bows for every streetlamp from the school to Clary General. She says we'll add sprigs of holly after

Thanksgiving for some holiday flair.

The filming officially got under way at the now infamous gala, so it might be said that we missed the boat. But as Nanny says, it's never too late for a face-lift. Mr. King's planning some lingering shots of the heart of Sticks, and the town is eager to maintain the illusion that we have more to offer than beer and boogans.

Though I'm exhausted after my night at the Kings', I meet Sterling and Abigail at the crack of ten a.m. With direction from recalcitrant Mr. Clary, we take up the task of smoothing pine needles around the porch garden of Clary General. There's a strange tension in the air, as though everyone is supremely excited to be out painting and buffing and decorating.

Abigail—still mad—picks a spot on the opposite end of the porch to work. I decide to let it ride until she warms enough for an apology. There are more important things to discuss than my past insensitivities.

We work to the strains of country music and the familiar shouts of men. There are clumps of boys and girls our age and younger peppered all up and down Main Street. We've all learned that it's far better to obey our parents' demands and put in our time. The film crew is already here, cameras laid out beneath the shade of old oaks, interviewing folk about their close encounters with spirits. According to Old Lady Clary, a good half of them are just spinning yarn.

Sterling adopts an unusual role as peacekeeper, swinging between us like a confused pendulum. Our conversation is light, but there's something off about her tone. She's trying too hard.

On her fourth trip to me, I stop her. "You're going to pass out if you don't just say what's on your mind, Saucier."

I can see I've disappointed her by being so astute. You'd think she'd be used to it by now.

With a nervous glance at Abigail, she settles in closer. "What were you thinking, Candy? She's really pissed. And I mean *really*."

"I know, but I'm sorry! I know why what I did was wrong and I'd apologize if she weren't cutting me down with those glares."

Sterling squints with her whole face. "What do you think we're talking about?"

From across the lawn, my name charges ahead of Quentin Stokes. Dread descends like a storm. I know what happened. The video was posted.

He arrives, face flushed and creased with fury. He grips my arm, but releases me just as quickly.

"How— Why—" He spits, unable to shape his rage. Sunlight flashes over a fresh reddening bruise on his ear. "Dammit, Candace! I thought we were good! Why would you do that?"

"I didn't. I deleted it." My protests sound weak even to me, and I know they're true.

"Not before you *posted* it," he roars, putting us at the very center of attention.

Guilt is quick to rot my insides. Horror follows as I realize what must have happened. Nova. She had plenty of time to forward herself a copy or post it herself before giving me back my phone.

"It wasn't me," I say.

"Oh yeah, then who was it?" he asks. "I'm not stupid. We were the only two people there!"

"What? No, Nov—"

"I should tell everyone your little secret now." He's desperate, eyes wild with fear.

"I swear to you, Stokes, it wasn't me." How can he not remember Nova was there?

"Who was it, then?" His gaze flies past me, hardening on a new target. "Your girlfriend?"

Dread, guilt, patience, they all freeze beneath the wrath that wakes in me. I step forward and push a finger into his chest. "You listen to me, Stokes. Abigail Beale's a better person than most of the people in this town. This has nothing to do with her and you'll leave her out of it."

His anger works itself through his jaw and when he turns his head, I see the bruise again. Someone walloped him good right in the ear. Recently.

"I'm sorry," I say, genuinely regretful. "I didn't mean for it to get out. I should have been more careful."

"Yeah, you shoulda been."

That was probably a threat. He'll probably share my secret with the entire town now, and I can't even hold that against him. My feet are too sick to move. I watch the back of his head as he huffs away.

All eyes are on me. They feel like knowing eyes. Like judging eyes. They feel like the same eyes that have been watching me since I was born, the same eyes that know more about my business than is decent, the same eyes that do or don't see what our swamp is, depending on the weather. I don't like this sensation of not knowing what thoughts meander behind those eyes.

Sterling bumps an elbow into mine and raises a questioning eyebrow.

"I'm okay," I say. Quentin's out of sight now. Crawling away to lick his wounds and probably plot my demise.

"Oh, I know you're okay," Sterling says. "I was suggesting that you put two and two together and figure out why Abigail's pissed."

Abigail's words from last week are seared into the tender flesh of my brain. *You used me.*

I did it again. Only this time, it's worse because I tried to do the right thing and failed.

I may not have pulled the trigger, but I knew the gun was there.

I ask, "Does everyone know?"

"It went Sticks viral last night," she confirms. "Anonymous, but you're the only two visible in the video, so . . . How could you do something like that?"

The answer to that question is uncomfortable—because I wasn't the one posting, because I wasn't paying attention, because I trusted someone I shouldn't have.

Nova.

Not even Quentin remembers she was there, and that can only mean that when she whispered her Shine-induced command into his ear, she told him to forget she was there. It'll be my word against hers. Right now, my words are the only ones that matter.

"Is there anything I can possibly say that won't make it worse?" I ask.

Sterling makes a sound that's something like a snort. "Making things worse is what you do. But you have to do that before you can even start to make it better, so . . . giddy up."

Abigail is still hard at work, smoothing a pine needle flower bed that's smooth as can be. Her determination is meant to insult.

"I'm an ass," I say.

The needles in her hand suffer a crushing death. "That supposed to be news?"

"No." I crouch next to her. Blaming Nova feels like a cop-out even if it's partly true. I was there and I didn't stop it from happening in the first place so I start with the basics. "I'm sorry, Abigail. It was stupid and I wasn't thinking and I'm ashamed to have been a part of it."

She stands, dusting her hands on the legs of her work pants. "Thanks for the apology," she says without making eye contact. Then she turns to walk away.

"Abigail?"

She ignores me at first. I call again and she spins on her heel, marching straight to me with a finger pointed at my nose.

"Don't you dare call me that. You call me Beale, like you always do. Don't try to soften my heart toward you because I promise you it won't work. You've betrayed me. Twice. And I don't trust people who betray me because they're self-centered and thoughtless."

I'm stunned to silence. Abigail's rage is wet in her eyes and tight on her lips.

"You call me Beale or nothing at all. Got it?"

A lump rises in my throat. I nod. She nods. And then she's gone.

Sterling brushes a hand down my arm.

"I didn't do it," I say, pleading.

She shrugs, toes digging in the dirt. "You sorta did."

She's as right as she is wrong, and I can't find it in me to argue. "You should go make sure she's okay," I say.

Sterling hesitates, reaching out to grip my hand in hers. I will myself not to cry, not to keep her to myself when I'm the one who did wrong. I nudge her.

"Go."

And she does.

IT TAKES TWO SECONDS TO find the text Nova sent to herself from my phone with the video attached. It's the damning evidence I need, but it's also useless. Quentin doesn't remember that she was there and she never speaks on film. I'm also unsure it matters to anyone but me. But it definitely matters to me so I text Nova on the same thread: *i know what you did.*

She takes her sweet time sending her response: *that was nothing. imagine what else I can do. take me to the tree.*

Seeing those words raises my blood. I feel gullible and stupid and threatened. It makes me so angry I could spit.

After an hour, I follow up: *delete this number.*

There's no response. This, too, raises my blood. I hate her for tricking me so easily, for helping me to make everything so much worse, for smiling and pretending we could be friends.

It all makes me feel helpless and if there's one thing I hate, it's feeling helpless. I decide there's at least one thing I can do.

I have to be quick. Weekends are prime time for the Wawheece boys. I've probably got until the end of lunch to catch Riley where I want him.

With the windows down, I drive the speed limit through town to the catered streets of Heath's neighborhood, which is more accurately the Wawheece neighborhood, since they're responsible for its development. Like so many things in Sticks, these roads lead to the family with the deepest pockets.

Looking at Riley and Lamont, you'd never expect their house. Not in a million years would you expect those grubby, bedraggled boys to dwell inside something so beautiful and stately, but their house is exactly that. Built in the Greek revival style so common to the South, it proudly exhibits tall columns along a broad face of windows and mini balconies. Their trucks are still parked in the long detached garage, which likely means lunch is ongoing.

I ponder what it would be like to knock on the Wawheece front door and ask for Riley. Character suicide, that's what it would be like. It's much wiser to sit out here like a stalker and wait for Riley's shiny head to appear before making my approach.

A coward's move, that's what that is.

Smoothing my vintage Spice Girls T-shirt, I walk confidently to the door and press the bell.

It takes a second, but I hear footsteps approaching and then the door opens on the face of Mrs. Wawheece. Her hair is poofed like any gilded halo, she wears a crawdad-covered apron over the ample curves of her body, and she welcomes me with a smile.

"Well, Candace Pickens, this *is* a surprise. What can I do for you, sweet pea?"

"I'm, um, I'm here to see Riley. If he's home," I say.

The house smells strongly of sweet meats, salty beans, and very fresh corn bread. My mouth waters, but I couldn't eat if I tried.

"Ri!" Mrs. Wawheece tosses over her shoulder. "Someone here for you, Ri! It sure is nice to see you," she adds, her smile becoming sweeter than sugar.

Heavier footsteps head in our direction. *Sweet Lord, let them be Riley's*, I think as I say, "Yes, you, too, ma'am."

"Candy?" Riley says, coming around his mom. "I . . . Hey."

Mrs. Wawheece's retreat is deliberately slow. Riley ushers me out onto the front porch and pulls the door closed behind us. For that, I'm more than a little grateful.

"Hey," I say.

Then I pause. I know what I have to do, but how to get it done is suddenly a mystery.

"I see the irony in what I'm about to say," he starts, "but what are you doing here?"

Moving past the shock of a guy like Riley knowing how to correctly use the word *irony* in a sentence, I clear my throat. "It's about that video."

Before I say anything else, he shakes his head. "Don't worry about it."

"What?" I ask.

"I said don't worry about it."

I study him as all of my assumptions about the sort of boy Riley Wawheece is begin to fracture. His family is dirty rich, emphasis on the dirty, and Riley and his brother have been the brutes of our generation since kindergarten. There's no way this guy is telling me not to worry about a video in which another guy confessed love for him.

"I just wanted to apologize," I say. "Posting it was unintentional and I'm sorry if it caused you any trouble."

Mr. Wawheece chooses that moment to holler Riley's name from the garage. "Get a move on or ya ain't getting paid, hear?"

Riley's smile is grim. "I can handle trouble. But thanks."

"O . . . kay." I take a step back. This was my mission.

307

I shouldn't question how it was accomplished, just that it was. But this is too strange to let lie. "Wait, why don't you care?"

Again, his dad shouts from the garage. That's a man with more temper than patience. He's exactly what I expect to find in the Wawheece house.

"I do care, just not the way you think I do," Riley explains, hands braced on his hips. "Look, I got no problem with Stokes saying he likes me. I mean, so what?"

"O . . . kay," I repeat, unsure how to proceed. "Stokes is pretty bent out of shape about it."

"Yeah, it's probably more his dad than him."

Once again, I feel that overwhelming dread pulling down from my shoulders and knees. I was a part of this. I am part of this problem.

"I didn't post it," I say, suddenly desperate for it not to be my fault.

Riley nods. "It'll blow over. Everything always does."

In what world does Riley Wawheece offer me a comforting word?

"See ya, Candy." With a half hearted smile, he leaves me standing on his oversized porch while his dad gripes from the garage. He's catching hell for wasting time. His dad's a terror, shouting and taking quick shots at Riley's head, but Riley bears it in silence. Just climbs into the bed of their rig and crouches while his dad guns it out of the driveway.

And I'll be damned, but I think I just felt something fond for the boy who's been nothing but a hair-pulling cur for all my life.

In church on Sunday, I sit next to Sterling, which is normal. I always sit with Sterling for the sermon. The part that isn't normal are the sideways glances I get from my peers and their parents. My own parents tiptoe around the issue. Mom says, "If there's anything you want to talk about, I got a recommendation for a lady therapist in Alexandria. Think about it?" Dad says, "It's okay to be angry, Possum. Try to be angry in the right direction." That's the only indication I have that they've either seen or heard about the video.

While Father O'Connor speaks, I let my thoughts occupy the high ceilings above my head. How was it possible that I got things so wrong? No, I know how. I can't fool myself into thinking my actions were anything other than selfish. The part I don't understand is why knowing it was wrong didn't stop me.

I used to think it was silly to assume that birthdays made you older, that age had anything to do with your intelligence. I still think that's true.

What I didn't know until right this very minute was how growing up happens in little surges. We grow up in moments—when we encounter such stupidities in ourselves that our only choice is to grow past them or into them.

Maybe that's why some kids grow up too fast and others not at all.

Two days ago, I was an entirely different Candace Pickens than I am today. Two days ago, I was a girl who was incapable of admitting fault. Today, I am very, very wrong and I can either burrow into it or change. The video lit a wildfire. It got Stokes punished, added fuel to my preexisting problems with Abigail, and probably soiled my good name. I can't undo all the damage it's done, but it's my responsibility to try.

Father O'Connor sits back in his velvety chair and the congregation raises their voices. I know the words, but I don't sing. I stand and let all those voices wash over me. It's my favorite part of any church service. I can't sing worth a lick, but neither can half of these people and that's never stopped them.

There are plenty of things in Sticks I'd like to escape, but there's something about these musty pews, these tattered Bibles, these eccentric people that feels like home. And you don't burn down your home just because you want to go someplace else.

The song of the choir spirals around me. I tip my head back and relax into the vibration. One minute without feeling or thinking is all I need. One minute of complete silence between my head and my heart. I concentrate on nothing but the notes, letting my mind follow the instinctual language of music, rising and falling like a feather on the breeze. Rising and falling. Rising and falling.

Rising and falling.

Rising and

falling,

falling,

falling

into the *river,*

*river,*

*river.*

Sterling pinches my thigh. It stings and I hiss involuntarily, but when I turn to punish her for it, her forehead is a committed frown.

"What?" I ask.

"Are you okay?" She stands because that's what everyone else is doing. The service is over. But it had only just begun. Hadn't it?

And then I know it's happened again. My mind lost itself in that swirling song and time passed without my permission. How many times is that? Four? Five? Too many. My innards turn spiky and uncomfortable at the thought.

Sterling tugs my hand and I follow her out into the parking lot. The sun is warm on my skin and that's the only reason I realize I have gooseflesh and am shivering.

"This has been happening to you more and more," Sterling insists, sounding confident and knowledgeable.

"Abigail and I have been watching you and at least once a day you zone out like this."

I open my mouth to respond, but she jumps right back in.

"Don't you dare try to deny it, Candace Pickens. Something is happening to you and it's your duty to tell me what."

"Okay, okay," I say. "But only because I like it when you're pushy." I pull her away from the crowd and try to convince my innards to release this uncomfortable confession. "You remember what Nova told me about being this Blind Bone? That I balance the swamp magic and I heal quickly because of it? Well, she also said there's always a trade-off."

"Like, in payment?"

"Something like that. She says it can show up a number of different ways but is always some sort of physical or mental . . . deficiency. I'm the lucky bastard who got one of each."

Sterling gasps. "Your infertility?" I nod and she squeezes my hand in hers, reminding me that she's not let go since we left the chapel. "And what's the second?"

"Um." Now I hesitate. It's harder to say this one out loud. Possibly because I haven't yet. And once I do, there's no turning back.

The memory of Mrs. King's feral eyes crouches in my mind, waiting to leap and carry me away with them.

"Um," I start again. "I think I might be going mad."

Behind us, the crowd is drawing closer as the post-church mingle begins to break up. But neither of us moves.

Sterling says, "Tell me what happens," and I do. I tell her about Mad Mary's voice in my head, how the song pulls me away from myself, and how time passes without my notice. And though I try to tell it like it's just another story, by the end, I've squeezed the blood out of both of our hands.

"I think I'm about to freak out," I admit.

Her mouth is pinched tight with worry. She doesn't have to say it, but she's scared, too.

Just then, a claw pinches my other arm and I swivel to find Old Lady Clary has sneaked up on us while we spoke. Beneath the wide brim of her fancy blue hat, her clouded eyes bore into mine.

"I don't know what you did to that swamp to make it so feisty, Candace Pickens, but whatever it was, enough is enough." And here she leans in so close and says, "You're the Shine Child. *Fix it*."

Then she releases me and shuffles away to her shiny red truck and guileless husband.

Sterling is the first to speak. "I really wish that just once she would be useful."

"Why start now?" I ask.

That actually wins a dry laugh from Sterling. "I have my interview with Mr. King in a half hour, but if you want, I'll come over after. If you want company?"

I shake my head. "I'm okay. Promise."

"Call me if that changes," she commands.

"I double promise."

We part and I go straight home to change into jeans and a T-shirt. In my haste, I knock the brochures from Mom to the floor. They scatter across the carpet, a rainbow of creased female brows. I collect them and open the one that ends up on top.

It starts off with language so sympathetic and patronizing it should win awards. I skim down to where it lists possible treatments, ready for anything from excessive prayer to electroshock therapy. But the first thing it lists is merely birth control. Sometimes all it takes to jump-start the system is to introduce low doses of the right hormones.

Setting the stack on my desk, I decide I can give my mother that much. It may not change anything, but the swamp doesn't get to dictate my life and it certainly doesn't hurt me to try. For her. I fold that brochure open and with a Sharpie, I circle the bullet point on birth control. Next to it, I write: *Okay, let's try this.* I stick it to the fridge with a magnet, then settle in for an afternoon of homework.

MOM IS SO EXCITED ABOUT putting me on birth control, she pulls me out of school on Monday. We spend the day in Alexandria going through all the motions necessary to secure me a one-year prescription of pills. All things considered, smoothing this corner of my thoroughly mussed life was a piece of cake.

When I return, Sterling enforces Monday-night study nights at her house and she, Abigail, and I gather in her room with a stack of Tabasco-and-cheddar grilled-cheese sandwiches.

I tread lightly around Abigail and she does the same with me, but Sterling breaks the ice with, "I know neither of you wants to do this right now, but we're going to talk. We've been friends for too long not to talk."

Abigail turns her placid gaze to Sterling and I have to admire the way Sterling doesn't wither beneath its weight.

"Candy did a stupid thing. Two stupid things, and the odds are good she'll do another stupid thing in the future, but you love her, I know you do. And Candy, you did a stupid thing. You don't like to be stupid, but that doesn't mean you're somehow immune from being stupid. So, deal with it. Both of you. Deal with it together."

Abigail's music struts around us while she and I try not to fidget. I know it's my move. I just don't know that it'll do any good.

"Ab— Beale," I say, remembering the violence with which she denied me the intimacy of her first name. "Sterling is right. I was stupid. And not only stupid but selfish. I wasn't thinking about you when I did either of my stupid things, but I used you and that's not what friends do. I'm so sorry."

Abigail looks from me to the floor. Her hand rests on the cross-shaped pendant at her neck. A habit I used to assume was unconscious, but now I wonder if she does it intentionally.

It's a long moment before her hand falls away and she looks up.

"You hurt me," she says, and before I can accept that, she

continues. "And you should know you hurt me because I love you so damn much."

Her eyes begin to shine with tears. I feel my own eyes respond, and they must be connected to my heart because my chest squeezes.

"I love you, too," I say, cursing my soft voice.

"I know," she says as a tear slips down her cheek. "And I forgive you, but I'm also asking you to be better."

I nod. "I can do that," I say. "I'm pretty amazing."

She laughs and we fall together for a hug. Sterling joins, wrapping her tiny arms around both of our backs until we're too uncomfortable to stay put.

My relief is so real, so palpable, I could eat it like a slice of cake.

Sterling beams and sits up on her knees to say, "I have good news. Mr. King made good on his promise."

She whips out the contract my parents so casually executed against my wishes and drops it into my lap. In the face of everything that's happened, it seems like such a small thing. Even if it's a small thing I'm glad to have.

"Thank you," I say.

Sterling nods and adds, "Mr. King also wanted me to tell you that he hopes you take this as a gesture of good will and honor what Gage told you the other night."

*Stay away.* Gage's voice is urgent in my mind. Urgent and pleading.

"I need to tell y'all what happened the night Nova and I tricked Stokes." I pause, offering an apologetic glance to Abigail. She nods me forward, showing no sign of the lingering hurt she must still feel inside. This is the difficult part about moving on, but it will only get better if we keep moving, so I tell them everything that happened that night, starting with exactly how Nova tricked Stokes into an untrue confession, dwelling perhaps too long on my encounter with Mrs. King and subsequent dismissal by Gage, and ending with fleeing in my car.

"This isn't good," Sterling concludes.

"It sounds like you're in danger," Abigail adds.

"Yeah, but from what?" I ask. "The only person who's been willing to talk through this whole thing is Nova, and she's as reliable as a tornado."

We sit quietly for a moment, the only sound Abigail's recent musical obsession piping through her portable speakers. Through Sterling's window, the swamp has gone from the impenetrable black of summer to the razored paleness of autumn. Beneath the dark sky, it's revealing all its bones.

That's the only reason we see the beams of yellow light sweeping back and forth. They move slowly, edging in from the direction of the Lillard House.

"They're still looking for the tree," Sterling grumbles.

"And how is that possible?" Abigail asks. "It's always been so easy for you to find the tree, and by all accounts, they know what they're doing with Shine, so why haven't they found it yet?"

The question is so obvious that the three of us are momentarily stunned into silence.

Then something else catches my eye.

Sterling gasps, Abigail leans in, and I know they've spotted her, too.

At the edge of the fence, Mad Mary Sweet stands in her filthy white dress. Her hands grip the planks and her eyes fix on mine.

"I see her," I breathe, leaning in, gripping the window, never, never blinking.

"But not the Shine around her?" Sterling asks, tentative, a hint of fear in her voice.

"It treats her the way it treats you," Abigail adds, more solid than either of us. "It moves away from her wherever she moves."

Mad Mary begins to climb. Her movements are stilted, her hair swings like vines, and she begins to mutter a single word over and over and over.

"Bones, bones, bones," she grates in her unearthly voice. "Bones, bones, bones," as she sets her feet in Sterling's backyard and begins to walk toward the house.

"What on earth does she want from you?" Abigail asks, now horrified and leaning away from the haint in the backyard.

The word grows louder, filling the room around us like smoke. "Bones, bones, bones, my bones, bones, bones," she says.

She reaches the edge of the screened-in porch and begins to climb using the notches Sterling and Phin made as kids. Her hands slap against the wood, as little by little she raises her tortured body to reach the porch roof.

"Candy?" Sterling's voice quivers. Her hand grips my elbow, pleading.

Mad Mary says, "Bones, bones, bones."

My skin shivers. I see how pale her skin is. Beneath the streaks of mud and blood she's as pale gray as a rain cloud.

Mad Mary says, "Bones, bones, my bones," and crawls steadily toward us. Toward me.

I lean against the window frame. I know I'm safe, my touch will dispel her, but there is a solid core of fear holding me stiff. "Annemarie Craven," I say.

She pauses. She blinks her milky eyes and purses her cracked lips.

"I know you're my kin. That's why I can see you, isn't it? I know you died in the swamp. I—I know what we are."

Her voice grates again. "Bones."

And I nod as understanding hits me all at once. "I'll find them. I promise."

She reaches out one hand. It's a terrible sight, all split

nails and scraped knuckles, but I reach for it and at my touch, she's gone.

"Sweet Pete," Sterling breathes.

"How do you know what she wants?" Abigail asks, sliding the window closed and turning up the music.

"She's the only one of my kind—the cursed kind—who wasn't buried in the family plot. I think she probably just wants to go home and if I can give her what she wants, she'll quit bothering me."

Farther out in the swamp, the flashlights begin to turn away from the location of the everblooming cherry tree.

"It doesn't want to be found," I mutter.

"No, *you* don't want it found," Sterling answers just as quietly. "Trade-off, remember? It heals you, you keep it safe. It's a balance."

Something swells in me then, a sensation of expanding, and I literally feel my mind being blown. I've felt apart from my town, from my family, from my two best friends in the entire world all because I was looking at everything too closely. I assumed that my position had to mirror theirs, that because my experience of life and magic was different, it meant I was all alone.

The reality is that my differences are what connect me to everything around me. I am Sticks; I am the Shine Child; I am Candace Craven Pickens.

"They're not going to stop looking," I say, watching the beams of light snuff out.

"You know the best way to figure out what they want with the tree?" Abigail asks.

Our eyes meet. I suspect she knows that all I needed to hear was that question to know the answer. It's the obvious Candy Pickens move. The only problem with it is that I've recently shut the door I need to make it work.

"What am I missing?" Sterling demands. I love the girl, but she doesn't have a scheming bone in her body.

"I have to give them what they want," I say. "I have to take her there. I have to take Nova to the everblooming cherry tree."

# PART THREE

*She died one night as she wandered alone,*
*Nestled 'twixt the roots of a tree that shone,*
*And there she did lie,*
*With eyes on the sky,*
*Waiting for kin to take her home.*

TUESDAY MORNING, THE SCHOOL LIBRARY is closed for ghosts. Freshman debater Nina Harrison was in the stacks when she encountered two men in suits with an ax, a saw, and lascivious grins. She freaked, grabbed the closest thing, which happened to be a fire extinguisher, and hosed the whole place down. As a result, classes are even more cramped than usual.

Sterling, Abigail, and I decided there's no reason to delay. As soon as the final bell rings, I corner Nova in the hallway.

"I know you're still looking for the tree," I say.

She doesn't mask the surprise on her face, but she proceeds cautiously. "Yes, we are."

Now I lay my cards on the table. "I'll take you to it if you tell me why it's so important to you."

She considers for a moment, tapping her fingers on the edge of her books. "Okay, I'll tell you on the way to the tree. Just you and me. No one else."

I've got two friends who won't be pleased with that, but what choice do we have? "Deal. Tonight, seven p.m., behind Saucier's house."

Nova raises an eyebrow and I explain, "I can only get to the tree from there. Any other direction and I'm just as useless as you."

She nods. "Great. See you then."

Then she turns on her heel and as she walks away, I remind myself that this was the plan and there's no reason to be nervous. The swamp, as it turns out, is my friend.

We gather at six thirty p.m. I've dressed for the work ahead: long-sleeved T-shirt, jeans, rubber boots, switchblade. Sterling, Heath, and Abigail are all similarly dressed in boots and clothing they don't care much about.

"I still don't like this," Heath says for the tenth time. "Maybe we should go ahead of you. I don't like the thought of you being alone with her out there."

"Aw, Heath," I say, patting his cheek. "I'm touched, but if you guys are in the swamp, there's a chance she'll use you against me."

"You're assuming she's better than we are, than Sterling is, with Shine," he protests.

"She might be," I concede. "But the point is she can't do a damn thing to me and I'm ten times stronger than she is. All we're doing is walking to the tree and back. If all goes well, I'll return much the wiser and she'll never be able to find the tree again. And just in case she tries something . . . ?"

Abigail lifts my phone. "We text Red and Leo and gather a crowd as soon as you're gone."

Sterling shifts nervously. "My parents are gonna love this."

"Blame it on me," I offer.

Nova chooses that moment to strut around the side of the house. Like me, she's dressed in work clothes, and she has a small backpack slung across one shoulder.

"The whole party's here," she says, cheerful. "And you'll stay here or the deal's off."

"We got the memo," Abigail says with a surprisingly hard edge.

"Great." Nova beams. "We won't be long."

The three of them don't move but look at me with matching expressions of dissatisfaction. Well, Sterling and Heath match. Abigail looks at me boldly, as though courage is a thing she can pass with a gaze.

And maybe it is, because I feel confident as I turn to Nova and say, "Follow me."

I pass through the gate Sterling forced her parents to

install and assume Nova follows. I don't demand anything from her until we're in the thick of the swamp.

"Okay, I'm doing my part. Now you do yours. I want answers," I say, choosing a muddier path than necessary.

"A deal's a deal," she sings. "My mother's been sick for a long time. Almost my whole life," she says matter-of-factly. "But now she's dying."

"I'm sorry," I say immediately.

"We've been looking for a Shining tree for years. It's the only way to heal her."

The swamp feels empty. Every step is a torrent of sound, announcing us to whatever is brazen enough to live here. And in that emptiness, a taunting voice begins to spin in my mind, *Take a stone, take a flower, flower, flower, these will last only an hour.*

No, not now. I shake my head.

"Why is it the only way to heal her? Why not take her to a hospital?"

"Because she's like you. A Blind Bone."

Mrs. King. A Blind Bone. A Shine Child.

With a start, I recall the painting of her standing before a cherry tree very like ours, and her grating voice as she clawed at me: "Bones, bones, bones." She must have known that we were the same and wanted me to know, too.

Nova nudges my shoulder. "Unless we've arrived, you need to keep moving."

I do as she says but make another demand. "What can the tree do for her?"

"I think it can save her," she says, her voice tormented and hopeful. "I hope it can, at least."

"Nova, why didn't you just say so?" I turn to face her and see the pain I heard in her voice written plainly across her face. "Why wouldn't I help you to save your mother?"

And why would Gage be so vehement in his plea that I stay away?

Nova blinks against the tears forming in her eyes. "Because I'm not even sure it will work."

She steps forward again and we continue to plod through the chilly mud and layers of fallen cypress needles. After another minute, the aggressive pink of the cherry tree comes into view and my vision swirls between its branches.

*Take a bone or take some strife, these will last for all my life.*

With an exclamation of joy, Nova pushes past me and I stumble. Swamp water splashes up my legs.

"This is a thing of beauty!" Nova holds her hands out as though beholding a god. "I knew I'd find it. Oh, I just knew it. You're a true friend, Candace Pickens."

"Are we friends?" I ask. "I think we're something else."

"Oh, no, we're friends," she assures me. She moves with more speed than I'd have given her credit for and wrenches my arm behind my back. "And as my friend, you're going to save my mother's life."

"Oh?" My arm twists painfully. The voice in my mind sings, *She's mad, mad, mad.* I struggle to keep my balance. "How? What are you doing?"

"I'm glad you asked. Don't worry," she soothes against my cheek. "I'm not going to ask you to die."

*Die,*

*die,*

*die.*

She hauls me forward. Each of my steps is directed by the pain at my wrist and elbow. I try to convince myself to take the injury. Ride the pain and take her down with my left cross. But fire lances through my shoulder and my moment of bravado flees.

My head spins. My knees hit the ground.

Nova releases my hand. Pain flutters away like butter-flies, but I don't recover fast enough. Something crashes against my head and I see stars in the pale bark of a cypress tree.

Not enough to knock me out, but enough to stun and in that moment, she takes my hand in hers and presses it between the protruding roots of the tree at my back. Before me, I see the pink, pink, pink of the cherry tree.

*Help me*, I think. But I know it won't. I've been *bad, bad, bad.*

"I just need a piece." Nova's voice again. "I—I regret this, Candy, I really do. If there were any other way, I'd take it, but it has to be bone or it won't work."

Before I have a chance to parse her words my hand explodes in pain.

Bones crunch. Skin splits. Nova grunts, sawing her blade through my skin, through my bone, through my body. Red spills down my skin and into the roots of the cypress tree. My mind goes with it, spinning and crashing through the earth until all I know is the hum of silence, the cruel cold of pain.

I blink.

I'm on my side with my hand tucked against me. Nova stands over me with something between her fingers. The night sky cradles her hair until she is the sky. Her eyes are distant, dark stars on the verge of supernova, her red lips a colorful nebula. The pieces of her face are a constellation with a horrible story pulling them together.

I blink.

I'm seated with my back against the tree. Sweat slicks my forehead. I'm hot and sick. Standing will be a challenge. It's a good thing there's rope holding me up, tight to the cypress tree so I can't fall over again. The cherry tree seems very far away, isolated and small by the edge of the pond. My hand smarts, but Nova is wrapping it. She's twisting a bit of my shirt around the shortened stub where my pinky used to sit. She's doing it because she cares.

"I'm sorry," she says. "But these are the rules. The Shine

Child needs a tree. I'm sorry it had to be yours."

*She's mad, mad, mad, mad, mad, mad.*

No stars shine between the pink bulbs of the cherry tree. All the sky is a riot of blossoms with no sense to draw them together. My mind sifts into them until all my thoughts are pink.

Nova crouches next to me. My finger lies on the mud and all I can think is that it's been too long since I changed my nail polish. The bright orange is chipped in all the wrong ways.

She collects it and carefully drops it into a sandwich Baggie from her pocket.

"There," Nova says, standing.

My mind whirls like a tornado. There are words I need to say. *What "there"? Let me go. You cut off my finger!* They're all there, but all I manage is, "Why?"

She crouches near my face. "I told you, to save my mother. And because without this," she shakes the blood-smeared Baggie in the air, "she'll die. And I'll do *anything* to keep that from happening."

I grapple with what she's saying. Try to find the argument that will bring her to sanity. I say, "I would have helped you, Nova."

But she laughs and I have the sinking sensation of having missed something vital.

"You are. The laws of the Wasting Shine are simple,

remember? There must always be a balance in the world, a living force to keep the Shine in check—that's you. In order to interact with Shine, you must risk your mind. And, my favorite, in order to bind yourself to Shine, you must eat it." She lifts my disembodied finger. "My mother is dying because her tree was killed, buried beneath a soulless sub-division, so I'm going to give her yours. All I need to do is reset the system."

"Reset the system?"

"Break the bond between you and the tree," she states as though it's all so obvious.

My heart throbs in my hand, in the back of my throat, in my gut. My mind sings, *She's mad, mad, mad.*

"How do you know it will work?"

She crouches to stick her pointed nose in my face. "I don't, but I have to try and who knows, maybe you'll survive just fine and be free of Sticks like you've always wanted."

For a brief moment I see the future as she paints it—one in which I don't have to worry about Shine or madness. I feel tears begin to slide down my cheeks.

Nova sighs. "I don't think it's very likely, either. And I know you won't believe me, but I really am sorry." She pauses with an unreadable expression on her face. Distaste. But for me or what she's done to me, I don't know. "I hope you survive."

"So don't do it," I say.

"My mother doesn't deserve to die any more than you do," she says, apologetic. "If I don't do this, I'm killing her. How am I supposed to *kill* my own mother?"

She's telling herself a story to make this all okay. Maybe Mary's own madness started like that, as a story she used to soften the horrors of life. I say, "Please, don't, Nova."

She stands and pulls scads of Spanish moss from the surrounding trees, which she then drapes on the boughs of the cherry tree. Then she moves from one to the other, whispering a word that changes the color of the world: *fire*.

As flames lick across the pink blossoms, Nova returns to me and kneels once more by my side.

"When the tree is burned, you'll be severed from it and my mom can take your place."

"But you're killing the tree!" I try, one final attempt to show her the error of her ways.

Her smile turns sad. Genuinely sad. "My dad has done a lot of research on sites like these. The amazing thing about the one in Seal Harbor was how resilient it was. He discovered that it burned once long ago and a new tree grew exactly in its place. I think they're like the Shine Child. When one dies, another is born. And there's only one way to find out."

Terror dawns like a fever. She means to leave me here,

bleeding, and easy pickings for whatever predator smells my blood first.

"Nova," I call to her retreating form. "Leaving me here is the same as slitting my throat!"

Silence follows. The kind of silence that pulls everything else into sharp relief—the rope cutting my waist, the throb in my hand, the panic pinching the back of my throat.

After several agonizing minutes, her voice calls soft from somewhere in the brush.

"No," she says. "It's different."

And then I know she's gone.

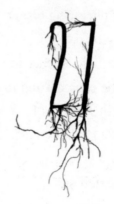

I HAVE DREAMS THAT AREN'T dreams.

They reach up from the ground and siphon through my ears and take root in the gray matter they find there.

I float in a murky pool of swamp water with the moon full overhead. My hair—what's left of it—is silky against my skin. My breath is shallow. On purpose so I can stay on top of the water. I do not want to sink. If I sink, they will see. They will pull me out and smack my face for trying to die. They will be rude for hours and I will sit in my wet shift and dig my toes into the mud.

As long as I float and only flutter my hands to stay as still as possible, they will not mind. The water in my ears transports me to a place where there are no men with shears and needles and demands. I build it around myself starting with very tall walls. Taller than the sprawling trees. Up and up and up until there's only a square of sky between them. My sky. It will be mine. I'll name each star and sweep them into my pocket before the sun rises.

One of the men calls to me. Though I cannot hear my name through the water, I can tell by the pitch of his voice. In their mouths, my name is a spear and they attack me with it whenever it pleases them.

"Mary," they say, and it tells me who I am. I hate it.

I am dragged from the pool like the rag I am. They will take something else, I think. A toe or a tooth. Having pieces of me—of my bones—makes them powerful, makes them immune to the Shine they use for dreadful purposes. They know what I am, what my bones can do, and they'll take them until I have no more to give. I am my bones, beneath them is only madness.

He sings while he steals, "You're mad, mad, mad Mary, my sweet."

I fall into my mind.

I open my eyes.

The swamp air feels over-warm against my skin.

"Candy!"

How have I never noticed how bright the stars become on a moonless night?

"Candy!"

"Nova?" I look for her. It's not her voice, but I know it's her. She smells like smoke.

"No. Candace, look at me." His voice is demanding but also tremulous.

I let the constellation of his face come together. Wide watercolor eyes crowding a nose, broad cheeks, strong jaw, bald head. Riley. "Nope."

"Candace, fuck."

"Okay, maybe."

My ropes begin to loosen. Blood rushes into my tingling limbs, bringing fresh pain with it. I shudder.

Riley pulls me against him and then up. Never in my life did I expect to find myself in Riley Wawheece's arms, but at the moment I don't mind. The pain in my hand hasn't gone, but it's a dull, almost familiar throb now. I rest my head on Riley's shoulder. He's strong and sure as he plods through the swamp. Even in my slippery mind I trust him to know where he's going. Except he doesn't know where we need to go.

"Riley, wait," I say, pulling my thoughts into focus. "Stop."

He obeys, but I feel the tension shuddering through his body. "You need a doctor."

He's not wrong. He just isn't right. "Put me down. How did you find me? Where are Sterling and Abigail?"

Reluctantly, he allows my feet to hit the soggy floor. "I was on the way to Sterling's—I got a text about a party—and saw the smoke. And then I saw her."

When I turn, I see Mad Mary. She stands several feet away from us with her feet resting lightly on top of the sludge in which we sink. The tendrils of her shredded skirt float around her as though in water. Her eyes sit firmly on me. She doesn't speak, but her lips spread in a slow, unnerving smile.

"She stood in the middle of the road and when I stopped, she, well, she made it clear I should follow. I never made it to Sterling's."

Behind us, the tree burns over the pond. Somewhere before us, Nova is returning without me. I trust Sterling and Abigail and Heath and whoever else is there to stop her, but they don't know what she's done or what she plans to do. I need to be in two places at once. I need to extinguish the tree and stop Nova, and since I have no ability to quench a fire on my own, I choose the latter.

"We have to hurry," I say, moving in the direction of the Saucier's blue house.

Riley doesn't stop me. He keeps pace beside me and asks, "You gonna tell me what's happening here?"

"Later. I'll tell you everything later. For now, please run."

It's a strange blessing that Riley Wawheece does exactly as I say. We run as quickly as the swamp allows, splashing and slipping furiously on our way to the Saucier backyard.

My hand throbs, but not as much as it should. My body is healing itself faster than usual perhaps because this wound is so much worse than anything I've suffered before. I take that to mean the tree isn't dead yet, but still mine.

*Mine, mine, mine, this deadly Shine, Shine, Shine.*

I sense her. Mad Mary. She runs along beside me. Her song spins in my mind, but it doesn't disorient me. Instead, her song heightens my senses. Her goals are mine: someone has taken our bones and we want them back.

The ground grows more solid and I know we're close. I will stop Nova King. I will stop her and save my life. I will stop her and save my tree. I will stop her and save my town.

Before us, light explodes and screams rise from the gathering in Sterling's backyard. It takes a moment for me to understand what's happened. Fire licks along the swamp fence. Flames, immediately full and angry, race along the planks in either direction. Soon, my swamp will be ringed in fire, as my tree is bathed in it.

If not for the gate, I'd be trapped, but there's a gap between the flames and through it I see Nova where she stands in the yard, hemmed in by the crowd. Sterling, Abigail, and Heath confront her, their faces streaked in fire and shadow. Sterling lifts her hands and with a pushing motion shouts, "Stop!"

Nova struggles, but her feet are rooted where she stands.

"This isn't a game," Nova shouts in return. "I *will* hurt you."

My heart races, my hand throbs, and beside me, Mad Mary groans, "Bones, bones, bones, my bones, bones, bones!"

I aim for Nova and I run. Mary runs with me, and before us the crowd blooms with terror and breaks.

People scream and peel away, racing for the front yard and the street beyond. Others stand frozen in shock, their eyes wide. Still others brace for impact, Leo and Red among them.

And in a moment of clarity, I know they see an army of ghosts. Me and Riley and Mad Mary and every ghost the swamp holds. They are Mary's ghosts and she's used them to gain my attention in pursuit of her bones. Now she uses them in pursuit of mine.

Nova growls, "Free!" And breaks the spell Sterling used to fix her in place.

Before I reach her, there is Gage, rushing toward us, chewing up the distance with furious paces.

"Gage!" Nova shouts, moving to his side in triumph. "I have it! We can save Mom!" She pulls the reddened plastic sack from her pocket.

Gage flinches away and looks to me in a panic. "Oh God," he says. "Nova."

"Bones, bones, bones." Mary's voice carries with unearthly volume.

"Give me back what's mine!" I shout.

"You won't leave here until you do," Abigail threatens. Sterling and Heath stand firm at her side and behind them, Red and Leo and a handful of others join ranks, confused and curious.

Then, a crack like thunder snaps over the swamp. It hits my chest like a hammer. I double over, gasping and burning and dry as though I were a river that was suddenly drained.

Screams.

Mine.

And Mary's.

And Sterling's.

Our tree has died.

RILEY'S HANDS REST ON MY back. The pain in my chest radiates through my body. The tree has died. My tree has died. The Wasting Shine has died. I never felt its presence, but I feel its absence and it burns like the cold, cold, cold of space. I will lose myself to it. Not now, but in time. As Mrs. King has.

"What have you done?!" Sterling shouts.

It's a struggle to raise my head, to focus my eyes on Nova standing between Sterling and me. Sterling, who grips Heath and Abigail but hasn't fallen as I have.

Nova turns her eyes on me and speaks. "It's gone, isn't it? That was the tree. Gage, we have to go. This is our chance!

All Mom needs to do is swallow a piece of Candy's bone and when the tree roots again, she'll be fine!"

Horrified, Gage backs away from her. "No, Nova. You can't do this. You can't just trade her life for Candy's. You *know* that. And you know Candy will die."

But Nova is wild with desperation. "Candy never even knew what she had! She doesn't deserve to keep it!"

"That's true," I say, and I push to my feet though every bit of my body resists. "I've been too focused on the things I didn't have. But this is my town and my life. Give it back."

I extend my unbloodied hand. Nova clutches the Baggie to her chest and backs away.

"No," she says, despairing and childlike.

"Nova," Gage pleads. "Mom would never forgive you. . . ."

"I don't care! She would be alive!"

"Nova! Gage!" The shout comes from the house and here come Mr. King and Sterling's parents and Lord knows who else.

"No," Nova mutters again and this time she shakes the Baggie until the finger—my finger—falls into the palm of her hand.

I see the crazed look in her eyes.

I lunge. She has no time to dodge and as I tackle her, the bite-size piece of me she stole falls to the ground and sinks into the grass.

After that, things happen very quickly. There's shouting and hands pulling Nova and me apart. Nova erupts in shrieks and other sounds of torment. Sterling's deputy stepfather demands answers. Riley's arms solidify around me. Red and Leo hover. There's movement and questions and a slowly dying fire on the fence.

I scan the ground, frantically looking for my finger, but Abigail appears at my shoulder and whispers, "I have it."

I wilt against Riley in relief. "Thank you."

Abigail gives my uninjured hand a squeeze and returns to the craziness swirling around us.

I don't know what happens now. Nova wasn't able to complete her spell, but the tree is gone and when that happened to Mrs. King's tree, she descended into madness. All I know is my bones are safe and I have just enough hope to keep me on my feet.

"What do you need?" Riley mumbles in my ear.

I respond without thinking. "I have everything I need."

THE NIGHT SPINS OUT FROM there. The Kings disappear and Sterling informs me that the official story is that ghosts appeared at our party and were the cause of all the subsequent mayhem—the fire, the hysteria, even my severed pinky joint were all the result of a spectral sighting. It's not so far from the truth, after all.

Adult supervision tightens around us like a vice. No one is allowed to return to the swamp. My parents arrive and accept the story as Sterling's stepdad delivers it. Red and Leo stand ready to back up everything, though they let me know in no uncertain terms that I owe them the truth and fifty bucks for "party services."

Our small crowd begins to dissipate like the smoke curling off the fence. Mom and Dad take me straight to Doc Payola's office, where Dad chooses to wait outside the exam room and Mom bravely faces the destruction of my hand. Without the tree, my finger stopped its supernatural healing, but the doc is still astonished by how bad it isn't.

He gives me something good for the pain and I sleep all through the night. I think maybe I sleep through several days because the next time I feel wholly conscious of my body and the present, it's Saturday and Mom and Dad are sitting at the kitchen table with the sun in their eyes.

"Hey, Possum, how do you feel this morning?" Dad asks, folding the newspaper and laying it on the table.

I nod. "Good. Fine. My finger itches."

Mom smiles. "Doc says that's to be expected. Part of the healing process and all that. Cheesy grits?"

Part of me still reels at the fact that they haven't questioned the tale of how I came to possess nine and a half fingers. It just goes to show how thoroughly harassed the town has been. Next to ghosts, the idea that someone might accidentally snip off the first joint of my pinky finger in the chaos of a party seemed pretty likely. And I suppose it is. Mr. Tilly has a similar injury, compliments of a circle saw, and Uncle Jack has one thumb that's twice as fat as the other thanks to a poorly aimed hammer. These things happen. Especially around here.

I sink into a seat and let my parents dote on me for a while. It feels nice. Normal. And a little voice in the far reaches of my mind says I'd better enjoy it now because there's still a chance I won't last long without the tree.

The doorbell rings and Mom hops up to answer it. She's back a moment later, calling my name with a hint of wonder. "Gage King is here to see you. I told him I'd see if you were feeling up to visitors."

I lurch to my feet and smooth my hair on the way to the door.

He waits on the front porch, hands in pockets, shoulders tight.

"Hey," he says.

"Hey," I parrot, suddenly unsure.

Most people look bigger when they wear heavier clothing. But in a sleek leather jacket and jeans, Gage looks smaller than I think he should. Maybe it's his eyes.

"I wanted to apologize," he says. "For everything. And thank you for not pressing charges against Nova."

I pull the door closed behind me. "Charges would lead to too many questions."

"Yeah," he agrees, head bobbing, eyes constantly shifting away from mine.

We fall into silence. Any way I turn, I cut myself on things I want to say and hear, each of them too awkward to ask. From the Thames' yard, the sound of a lawn mower drones.

"We thought there'd be another way," he blurts. "We knew Nova was desperate, but we never thought she'd go this far." He gestures at my bandaged hand. "We really thought—hoped—that if we found the tree, another possibility would present itself."

"But you knew I was in danger. You warned me." I feel an uncomfortable mix of sympathy and resentment toward him. It won't resolve itself one way or another, but oscillates back and forth like a pendulum.

His mouth pinches together, briefly. "Yeah," he admits. "I should have worked harder to stop all of this, I know, but we're leaving now. Tomorrow, actually. Nova needs help, and Mom, too. I think Dad's finally ready to admit that. And I just wanted to explain and apologize and say good-bye."

I try to imagine what life has been like for this boy, living under the shadow of his mother's illness. While his father searched for a cure, his sister disappeared inside her terrible hope. I can't know what all of that feels like, but I think I understand what it feels like to watch your life slip away from you.

"I'm glad you came," I say, meaning the hell out of those words.

He steps forward and catches my hand. His thumb treads lightly over my four fingers and hovers over my bandage. When he speaks again, his voice is less than stable. "I'm so sorry, Candace."

"Me, too," I say. "I'm so sorry. About everything."

He nods. Looks away. Swallows hard, and meets my eyes. It feels final before he's even spoken. "I understand if you hate me."

"I really don't."

His smile is tight and small when he says hoarsely, "Thank you."

I step forward and hug him. He tenses and after a second wraps his arms around me and presses me against him. Part of me aches to ease the pain in his future. When he leaves here, he'll face his sister's recovery and his mother's death. He'll have a mourning father to support and a growing brother to encourage. I hope he doesn't get lost in all of that. And I wish I could ensure that he won't. But all I can do is let him go.

We part after a long minute that wasn't long enough.

"Good-bye, Gage," I say.

"Good-bye, Candace."

On Sunday, Sterling, Abigail, and I meet for a trip to the grove of the everblooming cherry tree. Autumn has moved in and stripped the trees of most of their leaves and moss. We crunch through the swamp in hunting jackets, jeans, and rubber boots.

The grove happens to us by surprise. Usually, we'd know when we were near by the flashes of pink between cypress trunks. But there are no pink blossoms left, just an empty gray sky. Ashes blacken the soil in a circle where the tree used to stand. Chunks of charred wood create a small pile in the very center. The air here still smells vaguely of fire.

There's nothing to say, really. We're here because we

needed to see it again, to remind ourselves that this story is over and uniquely ours.

Sterling and Abigail kneel by the ashes. I kneel with them and together we begin carving out the blackened husk of a stump with our spades. We work quietly, tossing chunks into the pond as we explore. They're as tense as I am about what we might find. I try to keep my mind off of the tree and focus on finding Mary's bones. If my time is limited, I'll use it to make good on my promise to her.

She hasn't been in my mind since the tree died. I've had no spinning bouts of madness or stretches of missed time. The only person inhabiting my brain is me and now I understand what Old Lady Clary meant when she said I could stop the ghosts. Though they started before my visit to the tree, it was bleeding over the roots that woke Mad Mary and made everything worse. Her bones are here because this is where those men killed her.

After an hour of digging around the circle of roots, my spade scrapes against the grinning shape of a skull.

"She's here," I say, and Sterling and Abigail move over to help me unearth the stained and ancient bones of Mad Mary Sweet, held close for so many years by the roots of the everblooming cherry tree.

One by one, we place her bones in a battered green duffel bag. It takes hours and by the end, my back aches and so does my bandaged hand.

But there's more work ahead of us.

"Time to go," I call, zipping the duffel closed.

"Candy!" Abigail calls. "Candy, come back here!"

Sterling and Abigail brush frantically at the very center pile of char. I join them and find the source of their excitement is an itty-bitty seedling. It's just a puny green shoot, looking perfectly stubborn against the waste surrounding it. I recognize that kind of stubborn. The everblooming cherry tree lives.

"Do you think there'll be Shine?" I ask.

Sterling and Abigail share an irritatingly familiar look.

"Candy," Sterling says, "there already is."

My heart thuds like a baby Clydesdale, all hooves and no grace. *Please, be mine*, I think. *Please, please, please.*

I reach out and with the tip of one finger touch the little sapling.

And Sterling gasps and Abigail sighs and I laugh and fall to my back.

The tree lives and so shall I.


Exhausted and still covered in the grime of the swamp, Sterling, Abigail, and I are joined by Heath and Riley for the final event of the day.

Riley arrives as commanded, ready to work, but he skulks to where we wait behind Nanny's house.

I greet him with a smile and a shovel.

"Who're we burying today?" he asks.

"Two people," I answer. "How do you feel about surprises?"

His eyes shift side to side. His face is as much a rockslide as ever, big eyes crowding his nose, wide lips pushing at broad cheeks. All of his pieces are made to deter, but once you make it past that, I've discovered they have the opposite effect.

"I'm not usually a fan," he says, gruff, determined to frown.

But I've seen the boy beneath that frown.

I say, "I hope this is one of the exceptions," and I grip the front of his shirt and pull his mouth to mine.

Riley becomes a stone. For just a second, I'm afraid I've misjudged him and this will end in embarrassment. But it's fleeting. Riley returns the kiss with delicacy. Not what I expected, but if he was what I expected, we wouldn't be here right now. And I like the way he surprises me.

"Ahem," Abigail says, interrupting something so perfect I could just die. "We have a funeral to get to."

Riley doesn't let me go right away. He holds my head steady and I note with satisfaction that his scowl has melted away.

"Please, surprise me more often," he whispers before releasing me.

"I will," I promise.

I shoulder the bag of Mad Mary and we make quick work of the hike through Nanny's woods. Without the cover of summer brush, my family graveyard looks like a toothy grin at the top of a hill. We slip inside the low wrought-iron gates and pick a spot in a corner behind all the oldest graves. And then we dig. Again.

It goes more quickly with the likes of Heath and Riley and actual shovels instead of spades. As the sun cuts a low path through the sky, we cut a hole, four-by-two, into the ground. When it's done, I lay the bag in the bottom and step back.

"Shouldn't we say something?" Sterling asks. "Feels weird just to bury her."

I clear my throat, all too aware that I'm surrounded by the whole lineage of cursed Cravens. They live again every year when my family gathers in the graveyard and listens to the tale, weaving them into our lives regardless of where they came from. Next year, Mary will be here, too.

"We lay to rest Mad—I mean, Annemarie Craven, who died at the young age of fifteen. I don't know much about her except that she was loved by her mother and also by me. Rest in peace, Mary."

"Amen," says Abigail.

The others reach for their shovels, but I say, "One more thing."

From my pocket, I pull a plastic Baggie with a twist of

355

toilet paper inside. It's not fancy, but I don't need fancy. I just need closure.

"Is that . . . ," Heath begins to ask but fails.

"Your finger," Riley states, and nods. "Nice."

"There's something wrong with you two," Sterling says.

"I think it's fitting." Abigail takes my side.

I toss the little piece of me into the open grave. It lands on Mary's duffel.

"We lay to rest my pinky," I say. "You did your job well and I loved you, too. Rest in peace, pinky joint."

"Amen," Abigail repeats.

And now we pick up our shovels and work until the hole is filled and the sun is down. No ghosts appear between the stones—not that I would see them if they did. Tonight, it's just me and my friends beneath the tall pines.

After everything, I've circled right around to where I started: the barren, sightless creature who negates Shine with a touch. Except I know so much more than I did a few months ago. The things I lack don't define me; I define them.

And I'm completely okay with that.

# ACKNOWLEDGMENTS

Returning to Sticks, Louisiana, for Candy's story was a true gift, and I'm thankful to so many for helping me get here.

My agent, Sarah Davies, who made this possible in the first place.

My entire HarperTeen team: my editors, Karen Chaplin and Jessica MacLeish, for challenging me to rise to the level of your own amazing insights; Bethany Reis and Crystal Velasquez for copyediting like sharpshooters; Kate Engbring for yet another perfect cover design; and all the people who I don't know to name, but played a part in getting this book onto shelves and into hands.

I am endlessly indebted to the people who agreed to read and critique this book at various stages along the way—Sonia Gensler, Tessa Gratton, Julie Murphy, Amanda Sellet, and Kimberly Welchons—without whom the writing process would be much less joyful.

My writing community—Maggie Stiefvater, for essential music at essential moments; the ladies of the Hanging Garden—Annie Cardi, Elle Cosimano, Bethany Hagen, Rosamund Hodge, E. K. Johnston, Amber Lough, and Julie Murphy (again!)—who gave me a creative space that wasn't a swamp; Josie Angelini, Anna Carey, Tara Hudson, and Amy Plum, for wereboars and wine; and to the ladies of GFA, who listen and love and laugh.

My boss, Joane Nagel, to whom this book is dedicated and who has been a mentor, a champion, and a friend to me for many years, my thanks to you will be passing on all I've learned from you to girls who dare to reach for more.

I've been very lucky to have a day job I love and am grateful to the people of IPSR at the University of Kansas for making that happen.

My family. How do I thank you? For support and dinner and having the kinds of relations I can mine for stories that don't sound true, but are. And especially for my mother, who reads my first book once a month and reminds me that she loves it.

To Tess, who has been here every step of the way, challenging and encouraging in equal measure. Thank you isn't enough, but it holds the space well.

And finally, to everyone who read *Beware the Wild* and came back for more—thank you!